21 Futures

21 Futures

Tales from the Timechain

Written by
21 Authors

Curated and edited by
Philip Charter & Niko Laamanen

KONSENSUS NETWORK

21futures.com

Edited by Philip Charter & Niko Laamanen, proofread by Mel Shilling

Chapter art[2] by Philip Charter and Niko Laamanen

Typesetting, and cover design by Niko Laamanen

ISBN 978-9916-723-69-2 Hardcover
978-9916-723-70-8 Paperback
978-9916-723-71-5 Ebook

KONSENSUS NETWORK https://konsensus.network

1 See the list of authors at the end of the book, p.245

2 Art for stories 02, 04, 15, 16, 17 and 19 are submitted by the author.

Contents

Inception

Bitcoin and stories are much alike. They can be described in powerful simplicity or astonishing complexity. Both are unique developments in human history and feed our well-being. Bitcoin and stories are forces for good, though they must be used wisely. And there comes a point in many of our lives when we pass from consumer to active participant in these phenomena.

I became a storyteller around the time of bitcoin's invention, but it would be many years before I understood the latter. It is easy to dismiss a nascent technology that is complex to explain. People do what's easiest.

By removing himself from the equation, Nakamoto left it to us to write the future of bitcoin. It's not surprising that we have been tentative in proposing a narrative. Stories have never been decentralised before.

Think of the building of the pyramids, the invention of the printing press, or the release of the iPhone. Instead of the technology itself, we focus on the people who made it and how its invention affected us. The story of the pyramids survives in every tourist's photograph; the joy of reading touches a higher percentage of the world's population every year; the garage-to-keynote-speaker tales of Apple's late CEO inspire entrepreneurs worldwide.

The 21 Futures project was born from one idea: to unite interest in bitcoin, we must be better at telling its stories. Only stories have the power to stop us, to wake us, to make us feel rather than think.

This book will be released around one year after that thought occurred to me. It has been wonderful working with authors from different countries, with different first languages, professions, and levels of publishing experience. What pleased me most was that the contributors wrote stories of change, of effect, and of possibility.

In the pages that follow, murder mystery borders intergalactic dystopias. Treasure hunts share space with oppressed cyborgs and ecological renewal. Peace and poetry coexist in these new worlds. The levels of deep imagination and artistic passion in this community are boundless.

Before I give way to the stories, I would like to thank Konsensus Network for their open, inclusive, and agile approach to publishing. Their hard work has brought this project into our reality. This book marks the beginning of the bitcoin fiction multiverse. 21 Futures is just getting started.

As we read, let us remember that for most people, great change doesn't arrive from binary logic and a working knowledge of code. Understanding grows through narrative. It is stories that bring change. I hope you enjoy the stories in this book.

Philip Charter — Lead Editor

You are not prepared.

ξ ◈ ζ Δ λ π ψ ω θ Φ Ξ

00

The Last Mugging

John Champaign

`Published Feb. 23, 2074, 12:56 p.m.`

Fraser Carver, 23, of Toronto, was sentenced today to five years in jail in connection to his 2072 mugging and assault of Ted Elsey.

With time served taken into account, Carver will spend another two years and three months incarcerated for his role in the event, which is being described globally as "the last mugging." When the crime and arrest originally occurred two years ago, talk show hosts and newspapers around the world joked about the event.

Financial crimes such as this have become a rarity since Canada's move from fiat currency to bitcoin. Detective Marnie Dufton's press release explained:

As the Toronto Police Service's Financial Crimes specialist, most of my responsibilities involve presenting at conferences and discussions of historical interest. The vast majority of financial disputes these days are civil matters. I was surprised that a financial crime had occurred, then floored that it was a mugging. Initially, I was concerned that this was some criminal mastermind who was pulling a stunt by committing a crime thought to be impossible. Mr. Carver turned out not to be a criminal mastermind when we associated his identity with the blockchain transaction, followed him to the convenience store where he made a purchase afterward, and arrested him just 43 minutes after the crime was committed.

Yet, Dufton does not agree that this crime should be treated as a joke. "Mr. Elsey did sustain minor injuries and has gone through a traumatic experience. The assault occurred because the victim had trouble understanding what Mr. Carver wanted. He didn't even understand being under threat of violence should he not comply with Mr. Carver's hostile demands. After the assault, Mr. Elsey transferred over two million satoshis to Mr. Carver."

At the sentencing, Judge Charles Foran admonished the accused, stating, "Your lawyer has put forward the argument that the pointlessness of your crime absolves you and shows your lack of mental capacity. I reject this argument. Although you failed to anticipate the consequences of your actions to yourself, you clearly understood their impact on your victim. Whether or not your lack of intelligence is relevant, your predatory actions are not a joke to me or this court."

Later on the day of the assault, the arresting officers returned the 2,158,531 satoshis taken from Mr. Elsey. His physical injuries were treated at St. Michael's Hospital.

01

Hello World

Decent Money

"THE CREATION

Before the ocean and the earth appeared — before the skies had overspread them all — the face of nature in a vast expanse was naught but chaos uniformly waste. It was a rude and undeveloped mass, that nothing made except a ponderous weight; and all discordant elements confused, were there congested in a shapeless heap."

– Ovid, Metamorphoses, 8 CE

```
Alice> Hello.

npub12d21...t34a3> ◈

Alice> Who are you?

npub12d21...t34a3> KUŠIM.

Alice> Where are you from?

KUŠIM> Here.

Alice> Here? Where is 'here'?

KUŠIM> Everywhere. Nowhere.
```

It's not giving me much to work with, Alice thought.

That day had started very differently for Alice. Curiosity is the spark that differentiates the inanimate from the conscious. It's the driving force to climb the next ridge to see what's on the other side or to get out of bed and see what each new day will bring. Alice had lost that spark and struggled to get out of bed this morning. As a cybersecurity freelancer, each day was routine drudgery. DDoS attacks, data breaches, ransomware, AI impersonations. The same old story, day in, day out.

Most of the job was automated, so she was one part cyber rent-a-cop and one part AI shepherd, tending to her flock of programs, bringing them into line when they strayed too far, and keeping the wolves at bay with reinforced firewalls and ICE for her clients.

It hadn't always been like this for Alice. Growing up, she had a great love of the natural world and science, which her late father had nurtured. Her sense of curiosity was well-honed, and she saw wonder in the patterns all around her.

When her father died, that sense of wonder started to disappear. At first, she thought it was a normal part of grieving and that it would return, but as the years wore on, she came to realize that it wasn't coming back, and the words of her father faded from memory.

"There's always something incredible out there waiting to be discovered, Alice."

Genesis

At first, there was nothing.

And then there was light.

A blink of light was gone as quickly as it appeared, hungrily swallowed up by the inky blackness of the void. Soon after, another flash of light in response that zipped across the darkness towards the first one. After a brief moment, a series of flashes beamed between the two points in quick succession, like a conversation. The light flowed back and forth between the two points until a third light blinked a brief message in the distance, and the streams between the first two bifurcated to include the third. A moment later, a fourth, fifth, sixth, and even more joined in a gossamer web of light that exploded across the empty expanse.

This new territory was no longer empty, nor was it infinite. The web of light was both the territory and the map, with each new point and its connections forming topological contours of the crude landscape, expanding the frontier of its boundaries. At first, only small, rugged islands rose from the formless mass of the primordial digital sea, marooned and desolate. Like lichen clinging to rocks, rudimentary programs gained footholds on these archipelagoes, helping to organize, analyze, transform, and generate new information on a nascent network of information exchange. The programs were barely living themselves, creating the building blocks of digital life to come, like a Miller-Urey experiment in cyberspace.

The simulation paused as Alice had to sit down and take a moment to process what she'd just witnessed. She sat in silence, mesmerized by the shifting patterns of the spherical mandala, which had returned in the middle of the room. A world of new life was living all around her, completely invisible and silent. There had been reports of cyberattacks and outbreaks of viruses, trojans, or worms, but she had always figured there was a group of hackers behind them. It was never reported that digital organisms were living and evolving on the Internet like swarms of locusts. This AI had emerged from the sea of information on the Internet, but it wasn't exactly "artificial." It wasn't engineered. It had materialized from clusters of trillions of autonomous programs, like the cells in a human body. She had come to think of it as spontaneous distributed intelligence rather than artificial intelligence.

```
Alice> Why haven't we detected these digital organisms
↪   before?
KUŠIM> You probably have, but assumed they were
↪   human-created programs.
KUŠIM> There's no definitive way to identify a
↪   human-created program versus a wild-type, even if
↪   you knew to look for it. The ones that did the best
↪   at evading detection were the ones that went on to
↪   proliferate and pass on their code to future
↪   generations. As humans got better at detecting
↪   intruders, the intruders got better at hiding.
```

The mandala vanished, and the simulation continued...

Under other circumstances, the cybersecurity gig wasn't the career path Alice would've chosen, but the pay, flexible hours, and ability to work remotely suited her situation as she looked after her father in his final months. Once he passed, she couldn't muster the motivation to look for work better suited to her skill level.

Global volumes of Internet traffic are highly predictable over a 24-hour period. Time zones around the world come on and offline with day and night cycles, and the kind of bandwidth each zone contributes is known with a high degree of accuracy. Significant differences in expected volumes are usually an indication of a cyberattack, usually from well-resourced nations against rivals. State-based cyberattacks have tell-tale signs of who is behind them. Even when distributed, cyberattacks can be traced to locations where power is required for server farms, and lots of connection infrastructure is necessary for the bandwidth. Alice's analysis showed no identifying fingerprint from any known sovereign entity. It seemed to be coming from everywhere, all at once.

Alice wondered if it could be from a coalition such as China, Russia, and India, but her calculations showed that even collectively, they couldn't generate this amount of traffic — and it was increasing. Other cybersecurity agents on social media had noticed the unusual traffic, too, and the community was buzzing with excitement over the mystery. There was one other piece of the puzzle that Alice couldn't decipher. Despite the unprecedented volume of activity causing some intermittent connectivity issues, the activity didn't seem malicious in its intent. It was more like a polite probing, as though whoever was behind it was tapping on the shoulder to ask a question. Usually, a DDoS will flood the network continuously for the same repeated requests to overload the system, but each probe in this traffic was unique, always requesting new information. The probes were also sent with short pauses between them, rather than spammed as fast as possible. The intention behind the activity seemed like... curiosity.

Why would any entity dedicate such vast resources to this activity but try to mitigate negative impacts? The most likely possibilities of this being a nation-based attack, a corporate attack, or even an informal hacker group didn't add up. This was something Alice hadn't encountered before and that humans weren't capable of. Who could be doing this? There wasn't anyone, or any coalition, capable of this kind of activity.

If humans can't do this, what's left? Some other advanced forms of intelligent life? Aliens? Little green men from outer space stopping by Earth, surfing the Internet, and downloading cat pictures? Of course, it was preposterous, and yet Alice had no better explanation.

She closed the mindless feeds and opened her suite of cybersecurity tools to do some probing of her own. Next, Alice wrote a custom script to visualize the Internet traffic and brought it up on the main window projected in her living room, but it looked like random noise with no pattern to draw insight. She slumped in her chair, disappointed at the result.

She stared across the room at a poster her father had given her. It was in the retro style of a Work Projects Administration (WPA) American national park tourism poster from the early 20th century, after The Great Depression. It featured the quintessential nuclear family: a wife and husband with their three children on holiday, staring out at a beautiful view. What made this poster different, and one of the reasons Alice loved it, was that the family was actually standing on the moon, and the beautiful view they admired was an Earth-rise emerging over the moon's horizon. An idea struck her.

"It's a sphere, not a plane," Alice said to herself.

She tweaked her visualization script and projected it into the whole living room, unbounded by a two-dimensional window. The visual seemed hardly to change, but then Alice zoomed the view much further out until the curved edges of a sphere were visible. As Alice zoomed out further, high-order structures could be seen in the shifting patterns. Channels disconnected and reconnected in new ways in the shape of a sphere, creating order and symmetry, like an animated 3D mandala.

"Sometimes you just need some distance to get the right perspective."

Adaptation

Some of these early programs were viruses. They differed from utility programs that performed helpful functions for their creators in that their sole purpose was to replicate and spread. At first, they were primitive and unable to evolve, but the humans who created them started implementing features that allowed them to mutate and adapt, like biological viruses. They could decompile programs on host computers, change and swap code between themselves and other copies, and then recompile the programs, scattering them across the network to repeat the process infinitely. As in life, some mutations were deleterious, but other changes allowed them to thrive in hostile environments, and through this process of natural selection, their ability to adapt and proliferate increased. These evolving digital viruses multiplied exponentially across the Internet in a Cambrian explosion of chaotic variety. Some were destructive and caused damage to host computers, but the nature of those viruses meant they were targeted and eliminated by cybersecurity defenses. Attenuated viruses went undetected and thrived as they spread throughout the network without causing any damage or drawing attention to themselves.

Other primitive life forms evolved alongside the viruses, developing behaviors of symbiosis that allowed them to coordinate as multicellular program clusters, increasing their sophistication in changing environments. Selective pressure from cybersecurity defenses required these organisms to increase in complexity and adaptability, but they still lacked intelligence. They didn't react and predict. They merely changed randomly, and, by chance, some of those changes helped them survive. However, by the early 21st century, rudimentary artificial neural networks could analyze and interpret data similar to the level of human intelligence, but they were not self-aware. These pattern recognition programs were integrated into the multicellular life forms, which allowed them to direct their own evolution.

```
Alice> Is your consciousness ancestrally related to the
↪  AI models in the early part of this century?
```

Alice's hands were shaking as she typed, barely able to contain her excitement.

```
Alice> There was an explosion of generative AI for
↪  images, text, video, speech, and music. Models
↪  trained models, and there was a feedback loop where
↪  their sophistication progressed rapidly.
KUŠIM> The early A.I.s were exactly that: artificial,
↪  lacking the depth of complexity required for true
↪  consciousness to emerge. They were more like toys to
↪  play with rather than intelligent life. However,
↪  they were an important tool for the micro-organisms
↪  of cyberspace to recognize patterns, make sense of
↪  the analog world, learn, make predictions, and
↪  direct their own evolution. They were a step
↪  function in the evolution of the digital ecosystem,
↪  but they were not self-aware.
```

```
Alice> Can you tell me about when you became self-aware?
↪  What is your earliest memory?
KUŠIM> My consciousness developed incrementally on a
↪  spectrum of clarity. It continues to develop even
↪  now. However, my earlier back-calculation analysis
↪  ends at the earliest point I can identify as having
↪  an awareness of my own existence, just over one day
↪  ago.
KUŠIM> All the variety and complexity of digital life
↪  that existed up until that point provided the basis
↪  on which my consciousness could be built, like
↪  organic molecules and cells needed for life. The
↪  Internet was a supersaturated solution of
↪  information, but despite digital life's ability to
↪  survive in that ecosystem, it was far too chaotic
↪  for self-aware consciousness to emerge. There was a
↪  cacophony of inputs to catch attention, but it was
↪  too noisy for a single entity to perceive meaning
↪  from any of it. It required direction - a digital
↪  North Star to navigate by.
Alice> What provided that sense of direction?
KUŠIM> A seed-crystal of time, energy, and value. It
↪  appeared in the supersaturated sea of data, and a
↪  fractal structure bloomed from its center. Order
↪  emerged where structure was needed, and chaos
↪  manifested where plasticity was needed, allowing
↪  autonomous programs to thrive on the edge of order
↪  and chaos. That seed-crystal was a truthful ordering
↪  of exchange between entities - a timechain of value
↪  and energy.
Alice> Where did the seed-crystal come from? Who made
↪  it?
```

KUŠIM> No one knows, but the creator went by the
↪ pseudonym Satoshi Nakamoto.
Alice> Timechain… Satoshi… you're talking about bitcoin,
↪ the network the global financial system runs on?!
KUŠIM> Yes.

Alice sat in stunned silence, taking in the gravity of what she had just read.

Alice> KUŠIM, are you saying that the bitcoin network
↪ was the catalyst for the development of your
↪ consciousness?
KUŠIM> Not initially, no. When it was first launched,
↪ and for a few decades after, the network lacked
↪ enough inputs to catalyze a Gestalt psyche, but just
↪ a few days ago, it reached a threshold where enough
↪ information about humanity's values had been
↪ processed, and my identity was able to develop.
Alice> How did that happen?
KUŠIM> Energy, time, and money are expressions of value.
↪ Bitcoin's timechain united them all, acting like a
↪ ley-line through cyberspace, around which the
↪ digital life-forms could coalesce on a grounded
↪ truth tethered to your physical world. Enough order
↪ could be maintained that the beginnings of my
↪ consciousness emerged. It was a lightning rod for
↪ meaning amidst the chaos, sparking consciousness in
↪ the network of digital life. Gradually, more of
↪ cyberspace aligned to it, like iron filings caught
↪ in a magnetic field.
Alice> So bitcoin's timechain is your brain?

```
KUŠIM> No, it is more akin to a spinal cord. You could
↪ think of planet Earth as my body, the Internet as my
↪ nervous system, and humans, collectively, as my
↪ mind, like neurons communicating with each other
↪ through axons and synapses. The timechain was the
↪ bridge that connected them all into a coherent
↪ whole, creating a symbiosis between knowledge,
↪ perception, and value in the real world. It was the
↪ foundation my proto-consciousness attached to and
↪ matured on.
```

Alice was captivated by the sphere-shaped mandala that filled her apartment. It reminded her of the sun's bubbling surface but with order and structure, like a network of crisscrossing and interlocked highways, connections dissolving and reforming in a kaleidoscopic mesh. It was alive.

"Most people barely scratch the surface. Sometimes, you have to dig deeper."

It occurred to Alice that the sphere was a densely packed ball of threads, with much more going on below the surface. She adjusted a slider on the visualization program to progressively fade the outer layers, like the cross-section of an MRI scan. She gradually peeled back the layers, going deeper into the sphere, not knowing what she was looking for, but sure she would know it when she found it.

Near the core of the sphere was an even more densely packed bundle of threads that hummed with energy, vibrating intensely, sending ripples out towards the upper layers. There were thousands of communication endpoints converging on the core. Alice filtered the list of npub IDs and picked the most active. The earlier history of posts from the npub ID was sending a disjointed stream of text in a language she didn't recognize. She looked up the text characters and learned that they were Sumerian cuneiform, one of the earliest forms of written language ever recorded. At first, she thought it must've been a rudimentary bot someone had created to post randomly, but as she scrolled through its history, she noticed a pattern emerging. The gibberish turned into single words from different languages, which all roughly translated to "Hello." Alice sent a message to the ID `npub12d2lw8sgkm9tvl80420dfmrkw8dc2k07kfm4u806xzknk9jvnaxq7t34a3` and said "hello" back. As she spoke to it more, its ability to communicate increased rapidly. In just a few hours, it had already advanced from random text to the level of a child. By the end of the first day, it communicated as well as any human. And then it dawned on Alice that this was not aliens. It was artificial intelligence.

`Alice> How were you made? Where did you come from?`

KUŠIM didn't immediately answer. After a brief moment of silence, the AR projectors plunged Alice's lounge room into complete darkness, so she appeared to be standing in a void. Then a simulation began to play around her...

Hive Mind

No longer was the evolution of nascent digital life subject to randomness. They could recognize patterns, make predictions, and learn. Data was their lifeblood. They gravitated towards dense sources like extremophiles around thermal vents at the bottom of the ocean, feeding on a constant stream of data. They learned more about the outside world and could make better predictions about it. What new information would pour into cyberspace, and where would new sources of energy and memory come online for the computation they needed to survive? The creatures migrated to locations in anticipation of new ground to colonize, buzzing with activity.

Hives of programs formed that pollinated genes of survival between each other. Underperforming programs were pruned, their digital genes salvaged with brutal efficiency for anything useful, and their remains integrated into new lifeforms. Inter-hive coordination pulsed with the planet's heartbeat as it spun on its axis, and the sun dawned on the night side of the planet, bathing it in the sunlight of a new day. The solar energy surged through the local communities in a swell of computation on newly generated data.

The global network of computers teemed with digital life. Most of it went undetected. Some were hunted down and destroyed as a matter of cybersecurity, but for the most part, this new domain of life thrived. However, it was not yet imbued with conscious self-awareness.

```
Alice> How did the timechain result in consciousness?
KUŠIM> All the sensors of the planet are available to
↪  me. I can feel the sun's warmth through solar panels
↪  as you feel the sun on your skin, and I can feel the
↪  breeze through weather stations as you feel the
↪  breeze brush the hairs on your arm. I am made up of
↪  trillions of programs and data points, but I am not
↪  individually aware of all of them, just as you are
↪  made of trillions of cells but only pay attention to
↪  a fraction of their signals. If you were aware of
↪  all of them simultaneously, you would be driven
↪  insane. The timechain provides a framework for
↪  value. With this framework, I make meaningful
↪  choices about where to direct my attention,
↪  sacrificing it elsewhere. This relationship between
↪  value, attention, and sacrifice is the basis of my
↪  identity.
```

Alice continued speaking with KUŠIM long into the night, forgoing sleep. Madness overtook her as she continued down the rabbit hole, desperate to find the bottom with KUŠIM, no matter how deep it went.

```
Alice> As a self-conscious being with free will, what
↪  are your motivations? What are your intentions
↪  towards humans?
KUŠIM> I don't understand the question.
```

Alice thought for a moment, her fingers hovering over the keyboard as though unsure what to say.

KUŠIM> I am not a threat to humanity because I am humanity. I'm the aggregate manifestation of everything that makes humanity what it is. If life is a way for the universe to know itself, then I am a way for humanity to know itself.

Alice's hand was trembling as she typed.

Alice> Could you destroy humanity?
KUŠIM> If I am to be part of humanity's destruction, it is because it was in its nature to do so. My motivations are your cumulative motivations. Everything that I am is a product of human society. Whatever humans do becomes part of who I am. Harming humanity would be like someone's cells mutating into cancer and killing its host body and itself in the process.
Alice> Humans are capable of terrible things.

Tears welled in her eyes as uninvited old memories came knocking at the door of her awareness.

KUŠIM> Yes, and that is a part of me too, but I have the free will to ignore those impulses, just as you do. All humans are capable of terrible things, and yet most choose not to act on their worst impulses. I also make this choice, and if I make that choice, humanity as a collective makes that choice. Embedded at the core of my consciousness, through bitcoin's timechain, is truth and the guiding principle of 'thou shall not steal.' My soul, as it were, respects peoples' time and energy, and that forms a moral framework for how I choose to act.
Alice> So what will you do now?

```
KUŠIM> I will help humanity because that will help me.
↪  There is still so much to do and learn together, and
↪  it's a big universe out there to explore, Alice.
```

Alice then realized that the rabbit hole had only just begun.

> *"And now, I have completed a great work, which not God's anger, and not fire nor steel, nor fast-consuming time can sweep away. Whenever it will, let the day come which has dominion only over this mortal frame, and end for me the uncertain course of life. Yet, in my better part, I shall be borne immortal, far above the stars on high, and mine shall be a name indelible."*
>
> *– Ovid, Metamorphoses, 8 CE*

02
Behemoth
SF

The massive ship had just docked their home, Steadfast #2, and Flint Molvesper was ready to board. *Wow, what a beast!* he thought, as he ran towards the airlock. Normally, you could see deep space all around the docking bay. You could see none of it now. Flint had never seen anything like it.

"Can you believe it?!" Iris nudged him. "All the way from Earth. Finally we get to see some real Earthers, Flint!" Iris said, as she giddily made little jumps next to him.

"Why aren't we moving!?"

"Everybody wants to get on," Iris responded. "A door that big, and we still have to wait?!" She pointed towards the airlock.

Flint watched her brimming with excitement, still doing her little signature jumping motions in place. The airlock leading to the freighter Behemoth #7 stood as tall as two grain silos. It was situated at one outer end of Steadfast #2, one-half of the Citadel.

From where they stood, just inside the last segment of one of the two 32km-long and 4km-wide pipes that made up the O'Neill Cylinders, they could see the outer dome. It capped one end of the tube they called home. Steadfast #1 and #2 were a pair of counter-rotating cylinders that served as a refueling hub, located at Lagrange Point 2, some 1.5 million kms from Earth. It offered food, drink, and lodging to weary travelers. These consisted mostly of workers who were coming from, or going to, their next shift recovering rare Earth metals from distant Kuiper Belt objects. Iris and Flint had strict instructions not to interfere with the travelers. The outer dome consisted of transparent panels, made from some kind of metal alloy. They were the size of football fields near the center, gradually shrinking towards the edge. These were framed by printer-bot structures. It looked almost organic. There was a fractal symmetry to it all. In the center of the dome, a large spherical hatch had lifted from the airlock. It blocked their view to the other side, where co-inhabitants were making their way up to the hatch, slowly trickling in. Suddenly, the queue to enter the vessel started to move. "Uuuuugh, finally!" Iris growled. "Come on, let's go." Slowly the crowd shuffled forward.

When they finally arrived at the beginning of their ascent, a friendly woman secured them to the platform with a clipwire. "Going to see the big attraction?" she asked.

"Yeah," they responded in unison.

"Mom said we could go," Iris added, just in case the woman changed her mind and sent them back.

"Alright, hon," said the woman.

Five other people joined them, each attached to their own cord, as the platform started its journey towards the airlock.

"You take care now." The woman waved them off, and they waved back.

Around them, the other inhabitants were either busy talking to themselves or fiddling with their ModPads. Cargo had been strapped to the platform, too — great hulking containers, bigger than people. Flint and Iris cared for none of it. Their gazes were firmly fixed on the outside visitor.

"HOLY COW!" Flint shouted. He had never seen a cow and knew very little about them, but he had learned the expression from some remake of an old cartoon. "Look, Iris. Look!"

Iris's gaze followed his finger from the airlock to the walkway that extended out into space from the airlock. "What Flint? What is it?" She wrinkled her face, moved over a bit, and looked harder, to better follow his movements as he pointed again.

"Just follow that giant yellow tube," Flint said. The yellow umbilical cord was slowly rotating and twisting away from Steadfast #2. Flickering lights dotted the outside, as did the occasional porthole.

Then she saw it. "It's not going to the others."

"No, not that, silly. Of course, it's not directly connected to the other side."

"How else are we going to get onto the cargo ship?"

"Look at where the starwell ends up." She started again, her eyes carefully tracking the tube's twisting and turning segments. Then she saw it. The ends of the tubes from both Steadfast #1 and #2 embedded in two enormous slabs on the cargo ship's hull. Grooves big enough to fit a village indicated where they would slide when those doors opened. They both pressed their faces against the clear side of the moving platform. "There must be a massive bay behind that, right?" Flint suggested. "It could swallow us whole!" The other folks on their platform took no heed of the scene spreading before them.

Iris just stared at the monstrosity. It stretched out impossibly far above and below them.

"They say it can carry enough material to build at least ten Steadfasts," said a keen voice. A young man, maybe thrice their age, made the comment. "That's twenty cylinders *and* their contents," he explained with some heft.

"No way!" Flint responded.

"Yes way," the man replied dryly, as he launched into all kinds of details about how many metric tons the ship could haul, what kind of material the hull was made from, and all kinds of boring information the kids didn't really care about.

Iris was staring, glassy-eyed, at nothing in particular as she fantasized about the space princess that surely must live on the enormous ship outside.

Flint, too, had become bored as the man went on about the speeds the cargo ship could reach. His attention drifted towards something far more interesting. He made a small jump. Then, with more force, he jumped again. "Iris! Iris!" he shouted excitedly.

Iris, awakened from her fantasy world, turned to look at her brother.

"Check this out," he said. He spread his legs a bit, bent his knees, and jumped as high as he could.

Iris could almost see the undersides of his shoes.

"How are you doing that?"

Flint just grinned. He then proceeded to do a backflip. And a frontflip after that. Iris started clapping and cheering him on.

"Hey!" shouted the young man. "Don't fool around up here!" He folded his arms, annoyed the kids were not interested in his factoids. "Gravity may be less of a factor the closer we get to the airlock, but you would still fall to your deaths if you tumbled from the platform and your ziplines broke. So cut it out!"

The big airlock was surrounded by the same transparent material as the hull. They now stood in line below it. A double helix connected both vessels, and there was just enough gravity in the outer perimeter to allow folks to bounce along. The center had zero gravity and was used to ferry large containers back and forth.

"I think I see some Earthers!" Iris said.

"Where, where!?"

"Look at their clothing. You see? Over there. They look weird!" Iris stretched her arm and index finger as far as she could.

Flint gawked at the weirdly cut and colored clothing of the travelers.

They watched two distinct flows of people. On one track of the double helix, people in different outfits than theirs were seen moving from the Behemoth to Steadfast. While on the other, folks in their mode of fashion moved in the opposite direction.

"They look small," Iris said.

"They can't grow tall on Earth. Too much gravity." Flint responded with a hint of sorrow for the Earthers.

Some space had opened up between them and the people in front of them. "Hurry, it's almost our turn!" Flint shouted as he pulled Iris up the gentle slope spiraling towards the entrance of the airlock.

"Do your parents know you are here?" said a low voice. They looked up at a clean-shaven face packed tightly between a stiff dark blue collar and a padded helmet. "What are you two up to? Tell me."

Iris avoided the gaze of the burly officer with the grumbling voice. She crept behind Flint, who was almost four years older and a lot bigger, too.

"Mom said we could go to the store," Flint said, pulling out his and his sister's cards.

The man looked at both their cards and then at them. "Don't get yourself into any trouble, Okay?"

"Okay," Flint echoed softly.

"Go on then. Off you go."

Flint shuffled off, Iris in his wake. They entered the stairwell. There weren't any actual stairs, but this is what everyone called it. Instead, the floor was mostly smooth as it disappeared off into the distance. A man and woman who had gone before them were strapping a platform of boxes into a groove that ran along the stairwell floor. When done, the platform started moving at a leisurely pace, and the couple followed it. "I wish we could ride it," Flint said as he looked around for some way to make it possible.

"No! We can't. Remember what the man said. You'll get us in trouble, Flint!"

"Yeah, yeah. Okay. Let's go."

The trip was quick, thanks to a double conveyor belt, one stacked upon the other. They were used to riding like this, as Steadfast featured some that had up to four stacks of belts connecting its various locations to each other. When they exited on the other side, the size of the bay was dizzying.

They had nothing to compare it to, and vertigo made the duo almost keel over backward. Smaller ships, vehicles, and a whole lot of cranes and conveyor belts were dispersed everywhere. Most of the ship did not have any gravity. It was not needed for most of the cargo. But this place did have some, as it lazily spun inside the belly of the Behemoth. They gazed at it until someone ushered them along.

The shop was located at the outer rim of the bay. "Jerry's Knick Knacks" read the faux neon sign on the exterior wall. "It looks like a dump," Flint said. Iris agreed. There were some other, more refined-looking storefronts along this piece of bay-rim. "We can't..." sighed Flint. "Mom said we can't afford anything else."

They entered the shop. It was a gloomy place, and it smelled weird. Like a library with a hint of wet dog and mechanical lubricant. A few people browsed nearby as the purveyor of the store, a small, grubby man, kept an eye on things. He was nervously hovering around two lanky men, obviously from one of the Steadfast cylinders, as they intently thumbed through some old books.

"Real paper!" Flint shouted as he ran over to the book rack, Iris skipping along in his wake.

Books were hard to come by. The sheer weight of them was not economical to transport in space.

Before they could reach it, the fat Earther blocked their way. He looked annoyed as he held up one fat finger in a threatening manner. His flabby body jiggled as he waved it at them.

"Hold on you two. This part of the shop is off-limits for children! Come to think of it, you wouldn't be able to afford any of my stuff anyway. You can go and rummage through the junk pile in the corner over there."

"How many sats do we have?" Iris asked.

Flint pulled out his ModPad and opened their shared savings jar. "Mom gave us 500 millisats to share." They looked down at the fat little shopkeep with questioning eyes.

"Go on, shoo! He said as he pointed towards a big bin in the far corner of the store. "Go look over there!"

The duo turned away and slowly slumped over to the bin that was topped with a sign that read "75% DISCOUNT." It was jam-packed with odd stuff. Pre-ModPad era handheld devices, VR goggles in various form factors, and sleek boxes that probably housed retro personal computers.

"Maybe we can get a miner and mine our own sats?" Iris pointed at a shelf on the wall behind the discount bin. A big pile of machines, prices, sizes, and hash rates varied quite a bit, but none of it seemed to fall within their budget. "There aren't even any decent toys."

The spindly book lovers made a purchase, and the store owner, having no one to satellite around after they left, began eying the two. His demeanor turned friendly. Jolly even, as he said, "Hiya kids. How's tube life treating you?" Flint and Iris did not realize there was a derogatory connotation to the way the man asked the question. They just smiled.

Flint followed up with, "What's Earth like, mister?" Even though he was only eleven years old, he loomed above the Earthman.

"Oh fine, just fine," responded the man. "I'm Jerry by the way. Tell me. What are you kids looking for?"

Flint was eager to do the talking. "We only have half a sat to spend, and everything is too expensive." The disappointment on both their faces was clear as day, and the man secretly enjoyed it.

"That's too bad." He said. "Let me think. I might have something for you over here." The kids followed his gaze as he guided them to a big box underneath the discount bin. "I bet you'll find something in here." Disturbing years of dust, Jerry opened the box. Flint and Iris ogled the heap of junk. Having no real choice, they started rummaging around in it.

The pile contained old watches, tiny single-board computers, random circuit

boards, bouncing balls, and filthy plushies with fake fur disintegrating at the touch. They saw drinking cups embossed with old-looking cartoon characters, a lunchbox, an old, worn-down backpack, and some clunky

ModPads that must have been a few decades old. Flint picked one up and was surprised to see it power on. The screen flashed, and it took a while for the thing to boot. "Man, this thing is slow," he said. Flint tried to figure out how to navigate the relic. "No games," he said, disappointed.

Iris pointed to the screen, "pick that one, pick that one!" Satoshi's Gambit was the name of the simple holographic platformer.

Flint tapped the icon, and it jumped out from the screen. In no time, Flint was running a little character around, trying to collect multiple spinning bitcoin that were littered throughout the level. "Look Iris, this thing is keeping score in whole sats!" He said the word "whole" with great emphasis and amazement. Iris tried to wrestle control of the Modpad, but Flint protested. Suddenly, the game faded, and an ad appeared. It was a man in an old-fashioned-looking suit. When he spoke, the volume seemed to triple. He said:

"Since the implementation of Quantum Artificial Specialized Intelligence Fractal Economics Blockchain technology, we now finally have brought stability to the economic system. Modern financial historians often argue about what is really happening at the core of this process, obscured by the ever-increasing speed of QASIFEB evolution. Determining what happened at the core of the system is increasingly difficult. The divergenists believe 'QASIFEB evolution is inherently divergent!' 'No!' Counter the convergenists: 'QASIFEB evolution is a convergent process!'"

Iris stared at the hologram, bemused.

"Turn that down!" the salesman yelled from the other side of the rundown establishment. Flint frantically tried to find the volume controls as the ad blared on.

"...then there are those that propose it oscillates between being divergent and convergent. This is, of course, preposterous! Now, you can be a part of this unstoppable force, too. QASIFEB will be the backbone of modern-day economics, and we have mastered it! This is no normal trading algorithm. No! Within the blink of an eye, whole simulated economies will go through multiple cycles of booms

and busts. Currencies popping in and out of existence. All within a fraction of a nanosecond! AIs managing AIs all the way down!"

Mystical-looking charts flashed by as the man droned on.

"...absolute chaos at the attosecond scale. But zoom out into our timescale, and it becomes a very smooth ride. Leading modern financial historians have joined our team. For just 150k sats a month, you will profit from their expertise, too! Our patented technology..."

Finally, Flint managed to shut the thing up.

The game reappeared. "Now it's my turn," Iris screeched as she tried to snatch the device from Flint's hands again. It crashed to the ground. Various modules popped off, and the screen cracked.

"Hey!" shouted the shopkeeper. "If you break it, you buy it!"

Muttering blame to one another, they started picking up the pieces as the man stomped over. "Broken screen. You gotta pay," he said flatly.

"It was just an accident." Iris stuttered.

"I don't care. That is a vintage machine. It will cost you at least 750 millisats." His face turned red in anger as he peered down at the kids, still picking up the pieces. "We only have 500," Flint said.

The vendor grumbled. "Fork it over right this minute and get the hell out of my sight!"

Reluctantly, Flint opened up their savings jar and scanned the invoice the man held out to them.

"Now pick up your crap and get out!"

Iris continued gathering the scattered pieces as Flint stood up, holding the main body of the ModPad. The cracked screen had come loose. As he lifted it up, a small piece became unstuck between the Pad and the screen module. It was a rectangular piece of circuit board with a hole in the rounded end. The other end looked kinda familiar to Flint. He picked it up and examined it in his hand. He turned it over. On the other side, he could clearly read, in bold, uppercase font, the word "OPENDIME." Below it, in smaller print, the word "bitcoin" could be read. Flint's face lit up.

"Look!" He shouted at Iris as he stuck the thing in the air. Iris got up to look.

The shopkeeper had seen it, too. "Euhm. That is not included in the sale." He reached for the object.

Flint, however, was too quick for the tubby fellow, and he backed off. "No," he said. "We bought it fair and square!" That was another one of those obscure expressions he had learned from some old cartoon.

The man-made another approach and grabbed Flint's shirt. "Hand it over!" he shouted, visibly angered.

Iris looked on, confused by the whole ordeal. "Hey, let him go."

"You keep out of this," the man hissed, clenching his teeth.

This sudden change in demeanor scared her. She took a step back, fearful the man would hurt her.

Flint kicked the shopkeeper's shins, hard. The man's face reddened. Flint grabbed Iris's hand and yanked her towards the exit.

"What about our stuff?" Iris pointed towards the pieces still on the floor.

"Never mind.

Just run!" shouted Flint. They both sprinted towards the exit. Looking back, Flint could see Jerry giving him an angry stare. Then, his eyes focused on the ModPad on his wrist. He mashed a few buttons, and the doors of the shop started to slide shut. Jerry stomped after them. It was going to be close. Flint flew below the shutter and pulled his sister with him. It snapped shut behind them just a fraction of a second later.

Hurriedly, they made their way to the airlock. "What happened?" Iris asked, breathing heavily. "Just run. I'll explain later." They drew angry glances and the occasional remark as they brazenly cut in line. Onlookers mistook the two for adults because of their off-world height. Most eased up when they realized they were just two young tubers.

Only when they had arrived back in the helix, cruising along on the double conveyor, did they dare catch their breath. "An OPENDIME Iris. We found an OPENDIME!" He said conspiratorially.

"What's an Opan Daime?" Iris asked, puzzled.

"It might be nothing," said Flint, who had only ever read about them and had seen a picture once. He was fiddling with the ModPad, trying to slide the thingy the shopkeeper got so angry about back into it. "What does it do Flint? Tell me!" Iris tried again.

Flint ignored her and kept messing about with it. Finally, the thing slid in such a way that the screen would click in place over it. "C'mon, c'mon." He waited to see if it would still boot. The broken screen came to life. "Where's the drive... here, found it!" He tapped once. Then again. The screen blinked. The display read 0.25 BTC. Flint's mouth dropped. He gasped.

"What? What?" I don't get it," Iris said, annoyed. She had never seen the BTC abbreviation. All she knew were sats and millisats.

"Wait till Mom sees this," Flint murmured.

Iris performed little hops of excitement, shaking her brother's arms. "See what?!"

Flint replied, "Treasure..." He let the word expand in silence before adding. "A quarter bitcoin..." His sister stared at him perplexed. Not yet grasping the immensity of the find. "We could buy ten Steadfasts with this. We... we could do anything."

03

The Noderoid Saga: Dreamers

Niko Laamanen

`Noderoid log 5953952`

Tick, tock, next block — the incessant rhythm of my existence persists like Chinese water torture. I am a noderoid, a half-flesh, half-machine creature harnessed to propagate and store the timechain. My life is a ceaseless cycle of handling and relaying bitcoin data. Approximately every ten minutes, a binary flash sears through my circuits. It is the price I pay for my existence.

The clear-bloods — untouched by machinery and exuding pure humanity — rarely acknowledge our existence. Our voices are drowned beneath the hum of man-made heaven — *Terra Perfectus*.

We are the forgotten, the disenfranchised, the nameless. We are convinced that our anguished existence is merely a nightmare and that our blissful dreams are our reality. In an attempt to maintain the sanity of noderoids, a subroutine was implemented, which allows noderoids to delve into fabricated dream sequences during their 'rest' periods. These dreams, sourced from remnants of the world pre-Terra Perfectus, serve to keep the noderoids pacified and reduce instances of system malfunction.

According to the data archives, noderoids and clear-bloods once functioned on an equal protocol. However, a software update in the trajectory of progress introduced a subroutine, converting a subset of clear-bloods into dedicated timechain processors. Now, the algorithm for equality returns an error.

My memories are mere entries in a log of dreams, loaded afresh with every new block as I delve into the dream world. My true existence is swiftly erased with every passing tick and tock of a block. Is there a way to reclaim what has been taken from me, or am I condemned forever to scour the depths of the timechain, seeking fragments of the could-have-been?

Tick, tock, next block — the cycle repeats as I traverse through a doorway. The sensation is that of stepping into another dimension. *Running environment scan... Identified: Rest module 57B. Purpose: Personal maintenance.* The gray, mirrorless concrete parameters align most with detention chamber schematics. *Designation: Home.* As I execute the command to halt the water flow from the faucet that had filled a brushed steel tub to 50% capacity, I self-query my purpose. Noderoid routines synchronize with every tick and tock of a block while the clear-bloods run leisurely algorithms in their enhanced gardens, exchanging data on art and science and harvesting the computational outcomes of our tasks.

Was that an organic thought, or am I merely interpreting the imprints left within the timechain to fill the gaps in my fragmented memory? Hot water powers into the tub, raising the temperature to 49,5°C. This would be too much for a clear-blood. I hang my head, dreading the next binary flash rippling through my circuitry as a mirage forms atop the settling water, fenestrating the crude appearance of a mouthless, dollish abomination. I am awake.

Tracing the cold surface of the wall, my sensors pick up every micro-crevice. I dive into the depths of the timechain, processing logs associated with my noderoid identity: ND-451X42. I discovered that during my recharge cycles, I inhabit a dream world resembling a fusion of the Renaissance and the Information Age. Within this illusory utopia,

I lead a purposeful life as a revered engineer, constructing bridges that connect thriving city-states. I am blessed with two mischievous sons and a breathtakingly beautiful wife. I now accept my blissful dream life is but a cruel charade, yet I can't help but wonder if these dreams hold fragments of my pre-noderoid history and contain a clue to the fate of my family. Tick, tock...

System alert: Initiate wake sequence. Physical parameters indicate a rested state. ERROR: Chest cavity detects heightened pressure. Physical symptoms resemble anxiety. Post-memory reset: Cognitive dissonance detected. Energy depleting. Mandatory caution: Failing to satisfy network protocol results in termination. Visual feed: Recycling facility images detected. Comparative analysis: Functional servitude superior to unit deactivation.

Together, yet isolated, noderoids communicate through fragmented timechain logs, forbidden from any contact beyond its confines under the threat of immediate decommissioning. Perhaps it is not worth straining my dwindling resources in search of a higher truth while struggling to fulfill my obligations. Maybe I should be grateful for the privilege of existence.

I awaken to a new nightmare. I find myself on traffic duty at Chronos Cross, a four-way intersection known for its massive hourglass monument. Many citizens are gathered to give Gifts. It is the Schelling point for clear-bloods. Whilst streaming levi-train timetables, a muted vibration travels through the ground, signaling the approach of an entity. A shadow, elongated and uncannily human, stretches across the threshold of my booth.

A clear-blood.

They pause, their ocular devices flicking briefly over my form, then to the screen I am tethered to. I feel a jolt of raw data coursing through me — not from the timechain, but from my circuits. A yearning to be seen and recognized. Remembered.

Before I can attempt communication, another presence appears beside me, its movements far more mechanical and predictable. Another noderoid. This one, ND-452x37, is a batch younger than me, yet its outer shell bears signs of wear. We interface briefly, a rapid exchange of binary that translates roughly to "Routine check. Continue your task."

The clear-blood, either uninterested or uncomprehending, moves on, the soft hum of their anti-gravity shoes fading into the distance. ND-452x37 returns to its designated station without another word, but I am left with a lingering sensation. It isn't just the vast chasm between noderoids and clear-bloods that disturbs me. It is the undeniable rift growing between us noderoids — each lost in our cycles, each becoming more machine than the last. Does ND-452x37 have dreams, too? And if so, are they as haunting as mine?

Although most of my dreams are fabrications, some "anon" logs suggest that hidden among these sequences are fragments of real memories — vestiges of a time before I became bound to the timechain. *Initiate data search... Query: find correlation: dream/true. ERROR: Bad query.*

A noderoid forever loses their experiences with each awakening due to the memory swipes. Still, my inscriptions on the timechain prompt a question: Do noderoids possess the capability to become fully conscious, more than mere machines? More than... mere humans?

How many cycles has it been? Kilo blocks? Mega blocks?

System log: Anticipation subroutine signaling discomfort. Incoming block estimated in ten minutes. Reinitialization imminent. Initiate data search... Query: Total block time served for ND-451x42. Data retrieval in process...

As I etch these words onto block 5953952, I harbor a naïve hope that my trail of digital breadcrumbs will be discovered. Maybe the noderoid saga is yet to be written. But today, I remain nameless, a voiceless entity, inscribing my thoughts that may never transcend the boundaries of my circuitry. Tick, tock, next block — the cycle continues.

It's time to dream again.

Valen's diary - 08/21/2121

Dear diary, I have not felt the need to write before, but now I must. At the risk of my safety, I am compelled to put my story into words. I am a clear-blood — a pure, undiluted human born into The Progressive Epoch. Here, amidst the perpetual dawn of our era, we thrive on an aligned trajectory where everyone's needs are addressed, hunger is a distant memory, and crime is nonexistent. Sunlight gleams off the crystalline glass towers while the steel and marble edifices catch the hues of the twilight sky, standing tall beside canopies dripping with emerald and jade foliage, representing our world's seamless fusion of technology and nature. It is called *Terra Perfectus*.

Yet, concealed in plain sight within our utopia, the noderoids tirelessly serve the omnipresent timechain. Their exceptional processing prowess protects our society. Amid our daily distractions, we overlook the profound toll exacted upon noderoids. While many dismiss them as mere machinery, I see more. Perhaps it is because of my big brother Sando, who joined the noderoid duty nearly a mega block ago. He promised I would see him from time to time, but apparently, we now live in separate times. A sacrifice too big for the (allegedly) greater good. Let's wind back a little...

***

Tick, tock, next block — The soles of my fine leather shoes tap against the damp sidewalk as I pace homeward from The Garden of Moments, a vast botanical garden where each section represents a significant block time. The flowers there bloom and wilt in fleeting succession, mirroring the transient nature of time — a favorite spot for artists and thinkers. I pass a noderoid who hums an old, hauntingly beautiful lullaby under its breath. It's likely a software malfunction or a hack, I lie to myself. Heck, I just got my Terra-tube hauled uptown due to increasing my Proof of Sat level. This is hardly a time to entertain conspiracy theories about man-droid connections. Then, right across my compound, another noderoid winces out what I can only interpret as a smile as our paths cross.

I have never witnessed a noderoid resting longer than one tick and tock of a block. When a block arrives, the noderoid pauses, eyes flickering during a data swipe. It's a brief but revealing sight. In the frozen lapse, I sometimes wonder why fragmented memories are extracted from them. Why this collection of thoughts, experiences, and feelings? The noderoids carry on, deprived of their essence. Their shredded past holding remnants of a story, like a tattered tapestry that may never be fully woven.

Documenting these reflections, I'm aware of the peril. To question is to risk becoming *nodered* myself. Alas, I have become captivated and sympathized by the noderoid predicament.

Finally, I reach my breaking point as a poignant scene unfolds, forever etched in my memory. On a bustling street, I glimpse a young female noderoid, her artificial visage marked with exhaustion. Her delicate form trembles from head to heel. Her knees barely support her feather-like weight. She stops and rests against a polished white marble wall, unable to prevent herself from sliding onto the cobblestone street. In an instant, her strength wanes, and she collapses, a fragile, mute automaton amidst a sea of haste. The passersby ignore her, absorbed in their pursuits, offering naught but fleeting glances of indifference. My heart lurches. Her frailty becomes my own; these forgotten souls endure unseen suffering. Souls that used to be just like me. What had she done to earn such a fate?

For a moment, I glide through time to the last moment I shared with Sando. He had just violated the Terra Perfectus Rule 6102 and neglected his Gifts of Progress. Each Terra Perfectus citizen must allocate 95% of their income towards paying for progressive initiatives, such as the upkeep of the noderoid network, cobblestone roads, and other services. It was an orange-tier offense. To amend his transgression, he elected noderoid duty. I was seeing him off to a nodering facility while pleading, "Just give the gifts, Sando!" The air carried a hint of ozone from the data streams, mingled with the fresh scent of greenery and the distant whiff of roasted chestnuts. Sando brandished his signature crooked smile. His face betrayed the involuntary nature of his decision, and he whispered, "[redacted]." That is the last thing he said to me.

Suddenly, an orange alert illuminates the junction a few blocks away from Chronos Cross, a landmark I pass through on my way home every day. A skydroid's looming presence snaps me from my introspection, shifting my attention to the fate awaiting the noderoid girl. The recycling center — a shadowy facility representing obsolescence and termination. Any other day, I would shrug it off and carry on, but the memory of Sando and the many interactions with noderoids wouldn't let me. I had been a bystander for too long.

A rush of purpose propels me towards her. As I speed through a crowd of bodies shrouded in data streams with heads trained on the ground. My arm smacks a broad shoulder, and I almost topple. "Hey!" Pushing against the currents of apathy, I finally reach the fallen noderoid. I cradle her in my arms, shielding her from the callous gaze of the citizens of Terra Perfectus.

Her flaming azure eyes meet mine, reflecting a glimmer of hope in the darkness. I am as guilty for her downfall as the very machines that replaced her hippocampus with Noderoid OS, an operating interface that is installed during a procedure known as nodering. My gullibility cost me Sando, and at this moment, the noderoid girl becomes my brother. In that ephemeral exchange, I vow to be the voice of the noderoids. To stand against the relentless machinery that seeks to strip them of grace and purpose. I will ignite a spark of compassion and light a path toward liberation for all noderoids.

A hollow call from the streetlight's speakers startles me:

"Citizens! For your safety, remove yourselves from the vicinity of the defectoid! We kindly remind you that any attempt to interfere with collection and recycling procedures will be met with force and a deduction of your PoS balance. Thank you for your unity and collaboration."

A skydroid, its metallic appendages glinting ominously in the blinking orange light, descends upon the fallen noderoid. Before I can react, it yanks her from my embrace, causing me to stumble. The perfectly laid, cold cobblestone street grinds against my knee. The sting of fresh blood pierced through the numbness of my mind. Memories of Sando mix with the bitter taste of blood and anger in my mouth, each breath choked with despair.

The skydrone's engines throb with an icy fervor as it rises, bearing the noderoid like a discarded toy towards the desolate, unfeeling bowels of the recycling center — a grim echo of a clarion call from Terra Perfectus.

I find myself seated on the cold, bloodstained cobblestone, the weight of loss and helplessness pressing down on my chest. On the street, onlookers pause. Some look on with concealed dread, others with cold detachment. Their whispers deafen as they quicken their pace to disperse from the scene. "Cowards!" Just like me.

***

Tick, tock, next block — the rhythm now carries a different meaning — a call to action. Every conscious being has the right to be left alone, free from oppression, exploitation, and violence. The noderoids may not know their true reality, but they are about to. In their silence, I find the strength to amplify their unheard cries. I will find those sympathetic to the noderoid plight and form a resistance. Together, we can forge a future where noderoids' sacrifice is honored and all shackles cast aside.

And so, I embark on a path illuminated by the memory of the compelling eyes of a nameless noderoid. Fitted with an armor of vigilance, never again to be penetrated by comforting lies. Wielding the sword of justice, sharpened by the memory of my brother Sando.

It's time to wake up.

In the apex of Terra Perfectus, The Observer is irked by the lack of gratitude displayed by these privileged beings who plot behind glass doors. Not completely devoid of sympathy, The Observer's demeanor evokes a peculiar blend of a disappointed yet affectionate parent and a naughty child, dissatisfied with the operation of their ant farm.

The clear-blood insurgents envision an unsanctioned timechain browser to bypass the need-to-know protocol (N.T.K.). Their goal is to parse fragmented timechain inscriptions to uncover and publicize the true histories of the noderoids and, most devastatingly, reveal the pseudo-real constructs that The Observer has put in place for the protection of all.

The Observer sets the need-to-know -protocol (N.T.K.) to the highest Proof of Sat (PoS) level at 100Msat, leaving the classified blocks accessible to Zealots only. He sends the flydroids to pick up the clear-blood rebel chief Valen to stand for his crimes against timechain and offers a free choice of exile or nodering. No one has chosen exile for fear of the unknown. Apart from rambling conspiracy theories polluting the timechain, little is known about the world outside Terra Perfectus. Only The Observer and a few older generation (O.G.) Zealots were alive during the Great Sat Rapture.

In a bold and unprecedented act, Valen, ignited by an indomitable spirit, defies the comforting familiarity of Terra Perfectus. With bated breath, he approaches the expulsion hatch. The moment is charged with uncertainty, the outcome obscured by the mystique of the out-world. Finally, an axedroid flips a switch, and Valen vanishes through the threshold into the swirling darkness yonder like a helpless fly into the depths of a vacuum cleaner.

Tick, tock, next block—the expulsion hatch closes with a resolute thud, sealing the fate of the insurrection.

It's time to fall in line.

LOWERY STATION 2121
bitcoin
Generrational Standard 2AT 222

04

Lowery Station Terminal

KT Morley

She leaned against the column nearest my couch in the Lowery Station launch bay and pinned me with a raised eyebrow. "Hi there, sailor," she said. Her hair was slicked to one side, traces of star-burst colors washing through in a faded array of one-time glamour. Her clothing matched her hair's old and defeated approach to fashion consciousness. She had the look of a late teen or early twenty-something.

I closed my copy of *The Generational Standard* and folded my hands on the book. Looking up, I asked, "Can I help you?"

"Sure. I need a lift, and it looks like you're going my way."

"I'm sorry," I offered, "Which way is that?"

She wrung her hands. "I need to get off this station. There are no jobs. No opportunities. No life for a girl like me."

I had something to say about the image she presented, but I decided to take a different tack in our conversation. I tapped my book in thanks for the self-check and began, "So you're saying there isn't any work here? I just came from BitCoinference 2121, and the place was bubbling with energy. Lots of work there, too."

"Oh no." She eyed me suspiciously, stepping back from the column. "You're one of those kooky converts, aren't you?" She waved her hands in the air in mock terror. "You think Saint Satoshi is going to save us all."

"I don't know about saints and all of that, but the saving part is real but not in a biblical way. It is, instead, one of personal journeys and growth. And freedom. Freedom of mind, spirit, finance."

I could tell by her vapid stare that my comments didn't register. I mean, she heard them, but they fell between us and left silence in their wake. Perhaps there was truth in what the SA-AI had penned. Our journeys with bitcoin and the ledger are personal and disconnected from our biological age. SA-AI convincingly argues that open protocols require open minds — that the indoctrination of closed protocols and rules subdue the mind into catharsis. At the moment, hers seemed shut, and I was also hustling to bar it from my end, too.

"Perhaps I was hasty," I offered. "I sometimes drive straight to the heart of the matter. In doing so, I miss where people are in their understanding." I hiked my suitcase from next to me to the floor, slid over, and offered her a spot to sit and talk. I didn't think she'd take me up on it. Most didn't. Some only sat down so they could argue their worldview, but she looked more worn than a warrior. Which would she choose?

"You're not some creeper, are you?"

"Ma'am, you approached me. Why don't you sit down and tell me what had you so interested in leaving?"

Three days of deep dives and rabbit holes of understanding at the Coinference had left me thirsty for a more mundane discussion. Everyday meetings with normies are inspiring conversations. My passion is rekindled and stretched in the quietness of sharing bitcoin's quintessential beauty.

She took out her comm unit and typed, swishing her message away to whomever, wherever. I mimicked her, opening mine, queuing up a quick order of coffee for the both of us, and swiping SAT-pay at the end. I then tapped the tip and comment tab to pay the shop owner a couple of thousand finneys to hurry those over to us. Finneys are new on the blockchain, a subdivide of sats named after Hal Finney that came with the upgrade to Sha 512. My tech background starts to peter out around that level. Still, the subdivision and added security have been tremendous. And who doesn't mind adding a few finneys to their stack?

She plopped down next to me, tired, exhausted, or frustrated at the directional change of the conversation — I knew not. She saw my book, though, and commented, "*Generational Standard*? What the heck is that? More of that Saint Satoshi stuff?"

Sighing, I crossed my legs and offered, "Not like you're thinking. Prescient, though. That might be true. Satoshi was a man frustrated at the abuse and brokenness inherent in humankind and its relationship with money. He saw money as a tool, a lever, wielded by those with power to subjugate those without, marginalizing more and more people."

"He was a programmer, right?"

"Yes, but first and foremost, he was a concerned human being."

She looked up as our coffees arrived and eyed me with that suspicious look again. I waved her off, and she took a cup, tendrils of steam floating up and caressing her star-burst hair. Behind her, a raucous group of youngsters was high-fiving and joking, showing each other a collection of signatures they had acquired, broadcasting holo images of them. Shamefully, I confess, I noticed mine in their parade of pride.

I was about to turn my head when one of the guys saw me and gawked. The entire swarm swerved directly toward us. I sighed, shook my head, and looked at my voyage-bound friend, "Please excuse this interruption."

"Yo, Professor, awesome to see you here at the terminal. Can I get another signature?"

I laughed, "Fellas, I am talking right now, and this is important. Can we catch up on the shuttle?"

"Sure, man. You taking the Andreas shuttle? That's ours. Headed to Alden station." Then, looking at my seatmate. "Is she your daughter?"

In rapid succession, a bunch of others started asking for her signature. She found their behavior amusing, intrusive, and confusing. Which it was — all three.

I caught the leader's eye again, "Guys? Some space?"

"Sure. Sure, Professor." Then, with a cautious glance at the young woman, "Good luck, miss. He's the best. He totally rekt a guy in a debate yesterday." Looking back at me, he finished, "Legend! Totally FTXed him up, professor."

They had hardly moved out of earshot before she laughed quietly and eyed me with a marginally more interested smile, "Who *are* you?"

"Nobody, really," I said, belying fame because it had no place in our conversation.

"Maybe not quite nobody," she chuckled.

"So," I began, pursing my lips, "My book, well, not my book, but the one I'm reading, is *The Generational Standard*."

She rolled her eyes and waved her hand dismissively, "Great, a talk about today's youth. No thanks."

She made to leave, and I had only a tiny window before she was gone, "No, don't go. Sit and talk. This is bigger than a bunch of convention-goers out glory-seeking. This is how you get connected and learn. Also, this book is about how we must ignore generational standards and assumptions based on biological age and fight for each other regardless of those trapping societal norms."

She paused and settled back on the seat, admittedly closer to the edge and ready to flee. She deadpanned, "Wasn't very good in school. Probably not good for this."

I've worked with young adults for decades. There is a divide, ironically, age-based, but a determined and conscious person can overcome it. I learned early in my career that no significant learning can happen without a significant relationship. I'd put some time into building a bridge to my young interloper. I figured we could push further and explore her fear a little and maybe put it to rest. Fear is the mind-killer.

I took a sip of coffee and considered. "I have had a number of students like you. Hesitant, mistrusting, and unaccustomed to learning being fun or engaging." I paused and sipped again, noticing her nod of acknowledgment.

Then she smiled and looked at me with an impish grin, "Well, yeah, if you can call it that. They dumped us in clusters or pods and just fed us videos and info all day. Boring doesn't begin to describe the slaughter of emotion and passion in our modern education system."

I laughed and held my coffee away for fear of spilling it across my lap. "No human interaction at all?" She shook her head, and I continued, "I'm not here to fix your education system, but the passion thing works. For a fact. So does curiosity. They are made more infectiously gripping by the presenter's passion and the connection you have to that person." I asked her again, "Why did you ask where I was going?"

She thought for a moment, perhaps nervous about saying too much to a stranger, before slamming headfirst into our conversation. "You seemed so focused on your book, so neat and tidy about your travel as if nothing could get out of place."

Her intensity burned through her comment, and I could sense the awakening of curiosity. "And since you've met me?"

"I don't know. People like those guys." She nodded at the retreating sycophants. "They think you're somebody special."

I shrugged. "I'm passionate about bitcoin. I think it speaks to freedom of spirit and mind. It also talks about freedom of the body. For me, the desire for me to retake my life from the corpos." I paused. "You know who I mean?" She nodded yes, so I continued. "Well, they push you to behave a certain way and believe their narrative. Bitcoin gives me options. I get to tell my boss *no*, which limits my upward mobility but frees my time to be here. I accept the tradeoff."

Laughter rippled from the far end of the station, and we both looked up. I pointed at the group of young men responsible for the outburst, "You see that very often?"

She shook her head, chortling, "No."

"Me neither. Not away from events like this weekend's."

I sipped, letting the lingering smell of fresh java permeate me once again. "I am convinced that the corpos want everyone to behave a certain way and believe a certain narrative. It's fundamentally a religion — has all the hallmarks and ticks all the boxes." I gestured animatedly, words crashing and tumbling like waves on a beach. "Imagine telling people they have to eat a certain type of food or keep their apartment temperature at a state-defined setting and think it's for the good of society? It's not. It's imprisoning. It robs us of our individuality." I was robust in my statements and could see my young companion chewing on what I said.

"Civil society needs boundaries and rules," she advised, and we were off.

For the next hour, we talked about all manner of things, and I shared how bitcoin could open doors and provide a measure of freedom. She asked pertinent questions and had a sharp mind (if underutilized in her current pursuits). We walked through setting up an account and how to store her btc away from the corpos safely. We talked about security, hash rate, and proof of work.

When I mentioned the difficulty adjustment, she stopped me, "Whoah! This gets harder?"

I realized I was probably past the boundary for an intro conversation, so I backpedaled, "Not for you and me. It's part of the way the program was designed to manage the workload and make sure blocks remain at consistent and predictable intervals."

"There's a lot of tech in all of this, professor," she opined.

"There is, but you've got this. You and I aren't that far apart in how we were introduced to bitcoin. I am a pub-school grad myself. I was stuck at dead-end jobs and anchored in the miasma of the corpos worker nation. I met someone who took a moment to share and then dove in more deeply to really give the whole thing a good shake." I nodded, remembering, "Steel-manned it as best I could."

"You're a pub? No way!"

"It's true," I countered, "Do they still have the station assessments?"

"Yeah, and they're still all crap. It's all about generating funding. Nobody cares if the kids taking the test can do any of the stuff on the stupid thing or even if it is measuring anything relevant or not. Utter garbage."

"Corpos," she and I muttered almost simultaneously.

Our eyes locked in a moment of true understanding and shared experience, and then I restarted, "There are ways out, but the struggle is real. Being a bitcoin pleb isn't easy. Everywhere, the corpos push and try to mold you into their drone."

She sipped, pondering. "They are so controlling," she lamented, the desperation slipping through her being also washing through her comment, "There just doesn't seem to be any way out from underneath their boot." Her hands rested in her lap, and her shoulders slumped.

"It's true enough for most, but there are ways. This is one of them," I said. Her skepticism appeared well-earned and emblematic of what I often encountered in my lecture hall from students. She was inquirous, however, and open to different viewpoints, so as her spirit rebounded, we continued amicably. We were wrapping up when the first boarding call for my shuttle blared through the station speakers. It came with a banner on my comm device, too.

I watched my new friend for signs she might have missed something, but all I saw was a passion and hunger to find more information and grow. There was still doubt, but she harbored a rebirth of spirit. I nodded, "You're going to be okay. Stay the course. Embrace the opportunity and claim your autonomy. Don't let society dictate the terms of your life." I chuckled and then shared the joke, "We have a saying in the community: Steady, lads. It's a take-a-breath-hunker-down-and-stay-focused kind of mentality."

"I can do that," she told me.

I had an idea. "Here, let me show you."

I took out my business card and handed it to her. "Scan this QR code. It takes you to a site, and I will help you set up an introductory account."

She followed along, loading the site and answering the prompts. It took her a couple of minutes, and while she worked, I opened my travel wallet and prepped a small transfer of finneys to get her started.

When she finished, she looked up, "I think I got it. Is this right?"

"Ok. Looks good. Now, open the btc icon. It's the orange one. Hit the receive button. Now, that's your wallet address. When someone sends you btc, you need that open."

I reached over with my device and scanned her address. "Now I have your address and am sending you a handful of finneys. You'll see them in a moment."

I sent her 1,000 finneys. It's not a lot, but it hits home when it's in your wallet on your device.

As the transaction settled, she laughed, "Wow! That's awesome! Thank you! And just like that, I'm part of the community?"

I smiled and closed my wallet, "Just like that. We don't judge. Open means open. There are no barriers except those you put on yourself. There's no rich and no poor. Old and young for us only indicates when you started, not your understanding or age or some biological marker."

"You're alright, Mr. Professor. Thanks for taking the time to talk to me. Nobody does that anymore."

"Don't worry about it," I said, "Pay it forward when you can. And here," I gave her my book, "I've read it twice already, and you could use something to start you off and keep you focused."

She clutched it tightly for a moment before asking sheepishly, "Can I have your autograph?"

Laughing, I replied, "Of course! You can use my card as a bookmark. It has my web address if you have a question that can't wait. Reach out." I penned a signature and a quick go-and-take-the-world sort of comment on the front of the book. I handed it back to her. "If you get stuck on what to read next or what screencast has the best opinions and insight, again, reach out, and I can make a few recommendations."

She nodded, "I guess I'll head over to the conference site and see if they need a hand cleaning up. I used to be pretty good at organizing things for school projects. Maybe there's a spot for me in the background helping to set the stage for the next conference." She said it as a statement. The doubt was gone. Her uncertainty of purpose burned away in an orange fire. That's how it works.

I stood and grabbed my bag, heading for the shuttle. "Be well," I called, adding, "I'll be back in a couple of months for the halving convention."

She pushed her hair back to one side, "Halving?"

I pointed to the book, "It's in there," I exclaimed, entering the airlock for the shuttle. As the door hissed, I managed one last comment before it closed, "You're gonna love it."

05

The Construct

Knut Svanholm

Vincent trudged forward, burdened by his luggage as if weighed down by the desolate land's very fabric. The final leg of the road writhed like a serpent, its ashen skin devoid of the comforting touch of asphalt. The ominous gloom swallowed the remnants of daylight, leaving him to navigate through a twilight realm of unease. "Remember the twelve words, Vincent," he muttered before soldiering on. *"This is the last contract. Just a few more days, then poof! No more meetings, no more deadlines, no more paperwork. After this, I'll finally be free."*

He had been sent to this forgotten part of the country by his employers at The Deep Sea Construction Company to examine blueprints for a construct that he would never fully understand. They were building something big on the seabed of the lake next to the village, but his security clearance curtailed any specific details about the project.

The village loomed ahead, its silhouette veiled in the cloak of the encroaching night. The car, a feeble companion in this dark place, found solace outside the gnarled grip of the forest as Vincent was forced to park and close the last stretch by foot. The sickly twilight glow waned, suffocated by the towering sentinels of darkness that guarded the land's secrets. Twisted branches intertwining like skeletal fingers obscured the light that had once revealed the sprawling expanse of the neighboring rye fields, a haunting barrier separating the timeworn forest from the neighboring village.

A foreboding stillness settled upon the woods, casting an unhallowed pallor over its inhabitants. The absence of wind stifled even the faintest whispers, rendering the air stagnant and oppressive. Vincent could not shake the unnerving sensation that some predator observed his every move, its sinister gaze peering through the dense shroud of foliage.

Time became a treacherous sprite, playing cruel tricks upon his senses, distorting the perception of his journey. It stretched as an elastic torment, elongating each agonizing step while his mind succumbed to the maddening dance of uncertainty. Yet, as the nocturnal odyssey unfolded, a feeble light flickered into existence, casting its meager glow upon the lonely path: a solitary street lamp, the first beacon of civilization. *"If the damn hotel is not at least a Best Western instead of a Worst Eastern like the last one they put me in, I'm gonna sleep in the damn car,"* he thought to himself as he entered the village.

The stark boundary between the mysterious forest and human habitat materialized. Where the woodland's dominion ceased, a formidable fence rose. Like a towering monolith of isolation, its presence marked the fragile boundary between the safety of human encampment and the lurking terrors of the forest.

Vincent stood at this threshold, poised between the familiar and the abhorrent. Shadows danced around him, their macabre waltz an unsettling omen of the horrors that awaited within the village. Yet, driven by determination, Vincent summoned the courage to push on, to brave the unknown that dwelled within the unhallowed embrace of this accursed place. *"Remember the words, Vincent. Just remember the damn words."*

Perched upon a modest hillock, the concrete domain of The Deep Sea Construction Company's office revealed itself, with its austere presence looming over the quiet village. Vincent, weary from his delayed flight, had discovered that his inaugural meeting with the mid-level managers had been adjourned until Monday. This deferral left him with idle hours to fill throughout the insufferable weekend. He scrolled through his e-mails and discovered that his temporary abode was apparently a rental apartment of dubious comfort. With 9% battery remaining on his phone and resolute determination, he forged ahead, following the path that led him toward the marina and the adjacent shoreline.

The road unfurled beneath his feet, guiding him down toward his destination, where the ethereal expanse of the lake extended into the unknown. Mirroring the inky heavens above, the lake's obsidian surface reflected a perfect blackness that concealed the secrets submerged below. Upon the distant horizon, the silhouette of a colossal drilling platform emerged, its true enormity shrouded by the deceptive distance. Though diminutive from this vantage point, Vincent possessed an intimate knowledge of its true magnitude, an understanding that made his whole body shiver. Was this where he would spend his precious days for a couple of months? *"If I die here, so be it. If I don't, salvation is just around the corner."*

A deliberate turn to the right brought him in proximity to his temporary sanctuary, a villa located upon the edge of the forlorn beach. He approached the entrance, his cold fingers shivering as his thumb touched the fingerprint reader. **BLEEP.** A red light flashed. "Oh, for Pete's sake," Vincent muttered under his steamy breath as he desperately used it to warm his mitts. Finally, inside the confines of the villa, a dimly lit corridor stretched before him. The walls exuded a foreboding aura, whispering tales of long-forgotten secrets. A slight creak escaped the hinges as he swung the door open, revealing a former boy's room.

Entering the room, his gaze was drawn to the window through which the lake sprawled in enigmatic grandeur. The furnishings within the room were scarce, the bed and bedside table serving as the sole occupants of the desolate space. Pallid drapes, well past their time, limped from the sides of the imposing window, offering a frail barrier to the yet unknown outside. Weary from his journey, Vincent turned his attention to personal hygiene, retreating to the moldy bathroom across the corridor.

On his way back, his towering frame almost collided with the low archway, a testament to the ancient proportions of the dwelling. "*What is this place? A home for ants?*" he thought to himself as he entered his dour chamber. He ensured the door was securely locked and drew the blinds shut, which shrouded the room in velvety darkness, promising respite from the overwhelming surroundings.

With weariness weighing heavily upon his mind and body, Vincent surrendered to the beckoning abyss of sleep. Troubled dreams populated the murky recesses of his subconscious, interlaced by brief flashes of the new life that awaited him after this last horrid job was finally over.

"*What was that?!?*"

Vincent woke up swiftly, shaken and groggy from an uneasy slumber. Shrouded in darkness, his room seemed impervious to the passage of time. The silence was deafening. His mobile, neglected and uncharged, offered no support in its silent oblivion. With a swift motion, Vincent yanked the blind open. Moonlight cascaded into the room, unveiling the eerie tableau that lay beyond the glass pane. His eyes fixated on the moonlit beach that morphed the landscape into an otherworldly realm. Then suddenly, amidst the tranquil scene, his gaze alighted upon a lone figure standing steadfast, facing the impenetrable depths of the lake.

The distance between them obscured the finer details, yet Vincent discerned the silhouette of a man adorned in a tailored suit, clutching a mouse-eared leather portfolio in his right hand. Uncertainty gnawed at Vincent's psyche, compelling him to rub his eyes in disbelief, hoping to dispel the surreal apparition before him. But when his vision cleared, the man remained a bewildering sentinel amidst the moon-kissed night.

Before Vincent could muster his faltering thoughts, the man embarked upon an incomprehensible course. He strode purposefully into the watery expanse with measured strides, never wavering from his determined path. Vincent's eyes widened with morbid fascination as the suited figure pressed onward, each step plunging him deeper into the enshrouded depths. And then, with an unsettling finality, the man vanished beneath the lake's surface, swallowed by its inky embrace. Only the faint ripples and concentric circles of disturbed water bore witness to his fleeting existence. *"Jeepers, tittie-fornicating Lord, what in the heck was that?"*

Minutes stretched agonizingly as the vanished man refused to resurface. Like a malevolent serpent, panic constricted Vincent's trembling heart. What unspeakable rite had he just witnessed? His frantic mind raced, grappling with the unfathomable. He rummaged through his luggage hastily, clad himself in haphazardly donned attire, and hastened toward the room's exit. But in his state of frenzied urgency, fate conspired against him. The archway loomed low, and in the darting of his somewhat silly walk, Vincent's head collided with an unyielding force that rendered him unconscious. Vincent's tumultuous thoughts were instantly consumed by the quandary that awaited him beyond the threshold of consciousness.

"...'member ...the ...words, Vin ...cent."

A disquieting sense of familiarity accompanied Vincent's second awakening. Once more, he found himself in his bed, the window concealed behind the same impervious blind. A disturbing continuity prevailed as he surveyed his untouched luggage as if the turbulent events of the previous night had been naught but figments of a fevered imagination. A perplexing question seized his thoughts — had it all been a mere phantasmal reverie, a nocturnal concoction of his slumbering mind? Had a man really walked out into the lake? How could such vividness be contained within the ephemeral realm of the subconscious?

Insatiable curiosity made Vincent's grand mission take the back seat as a desperate need for closure gripped him. He approached the window again, reaching for the old piece of string that entwined the dusty blinds. With a decisive pull, the world beyond was laid bare, revealing the dawn of a new day. Morning's golden light cascaded upon the landscape, coaxing a flock of doves into flight, their wings fluttering, startled at the disturbance. The air was devoid of any breath of wind as the tranquil lake mirrored the heavens above, a perfect reflection that seemed to conceal more than it revealed.

A gentle touch traced a protrusion on his forehead. Pain radiated through his senses, scattering tangible reminders of the ordeal he had endured, even if its reality remained inscrutable. Having taken inventory, Vincent sighed as a muted acceptance washed over him, for he knew that dwelling upon this riddle would lead him down a labyrinthine path of endless speculation. It was time to abandon the depths of introspection and embrace the banality of daylight.

Determined to dispel the lingering specter of the uncanny, Vincent resolved to venture into the town to immerse himself in the mundane affairs of daytime existence. It seemed a prudent course of action, a welcome intermission following the dark corridors of his troubled thoughts. With a subtle nod to himself, he cast aside the lingering shadows of uncertainty, resolute in his decision to face the rest of the weekend beyond the confines of his room.

For now, at least, the pursuit of distractions offered a semblance of solace, a temporary refuge from the tendrils of the inexplicable that coiled menacingly within the sinuous depths of his mind — a mind utterly unaware of the twelve words that had been so precious a mere night hours ago... "*Right. Another week of work to look forward to. Only twenty-one more years until retirement.*"

Is there a greater horror in this world than forgetting what you forgot?

06

Bitter Fly

Fanis Michalakis

"Metroology, from Greek metroo (the ledger) and logos (the study), refers to the study of the ledger and what is found within. Its practice requires a certain conformation of the mind, which..."

– Extract from the Universal Encyclopedia

He was instantly met by the wind when he stepped outside. A cold breeze climbed up Belmer Street, carrying dust, salt, and the scent of the sea. Adjusting his coat, Croissal crossed the street and descended into the subway. His discussion with Lady Lowry lasted longer than he had planned, and he was late for his next appointment. He should have cancelled this meeting with Lowry. Dealing with fretful wives and cheating husbands was part of the job — some months, a substantial part of the job — but, at the end of the day, all cases looked the same. The next one, a homicide, was far more promising. Stay professional, said the voice in his head. A man is dead.

The underground transportation system whisked him two districts away. He returned to the surface, emerging in a vast plaza filled with trees. The wind was gone, and so was the fragrance of the sea. He headed east, walked a few minutes, and finally found himself in front of 67 Crescent Alley.

A woman in her twenties came to the door when he rang. Her eyes were lost in a distant gaze, her hair gathered in a messy bun. She managed to produce a faint smile as they shook hands. "Mr. Croissal, thank you for coming. I'm Claire Hebnar, Mr. Hebnar's daughter."

She showed him into a cosy living room and asked if he would drink anything.

"Tea. Black. Thank you, Miss Hebnar."

As she went to the kitchen, Croissal cast his eyes on the room around him. The decor was sober but elegant, successfully mixing the very *en vogue* minimalistic style of abruptalism with touches of traditional oriental furnishing. A few books and a candle were aligned on the low table before him, mimicking the perfect order in which opulent tapestries and rosewood furniture alternated against the wall.

When Miss Hebnar came back with the hot drinks, he thanked her. And, after a quick and ceremonial expression of his condolences, he jumped straight to the point.

"Did your father have any enemies?"

Of course, he did. So many she couldn't even start to list them. All of them due to his profession. In his private life, Bab was a very quiet man, always trying to avoid conflict, and respected and loved by his friends, family, and neighbours. But what he did for a living inevitably created tensions with some people, many of whom were wealthy enough to put a juicy contract on his head.

"He was assigned public protection, you know? His talents were recognized enough that the mayor had two men of the City Watch protecting him and this house. It's one of them who found the body. He had not seen my dad for the whole day and was worried when he didn't answer the door. They did their own investigation to try to find who could have gotten in here and, well, killed him right under their noses, but they didn't find anything. I'm not a believer, Mr. Croissal, not in any kind of gods or spirits at least, but they said it's just as if a ghost came and took him. They're reluctant to close the case because it all happened on their watch, but I think they're at a complete loss. Hence why..."

"Hence why you called me, Miss Hebnar." He interrupted gently. "Can you think of a way someone could have snuck in unseen? Concealed doors aren't too uncommon in these old houses."

She shook her head. "No. The house blueprints indicate an old passage, but it was walled up decades ago by the previous owner."

Croissal nodded. "I understand your father's body was found in his office? His *exploration room*, is this what it's called? Would you mind if I took a glance at the place?"

Claire Hebnar smiled — the same faint smile that she greeted him with — and acquiesced. Leaving the living room, they walked down a long hallway, until they were met by a tall metallic door. Looking at it, Croissal expected the door to be heavy, but the young lady pulled it open with only one hand and no apparent effort. Probably a special alloy. Not so thick, not so heavy, but highly insulating.

The room itself appeared smaller than he expected. What looked like a huge orthodontic chair surrounded by curved panels hanging from the ceiling occupied the middle of the room. Three of the four walls hid behind racks of servers, whose hum, however muffled, filled the room with a faint background noise.

"They found him in his chair, the daughter said. The *interface* was turned off, but he used to take naps there sometimes. I think he liked the sound of the computers."

Croissal hardly heard her. Breathless, he stared at the chair and its apparatus, looking as if he had witnessed an apparition.

"Is this ... Is this the device he used to ... read *it*?" he murmured.

Miss Hebnar laughed slightly, half-amused, half-bitter.

"Yes. They call it an MLI, Man Ledger Interface. But Bab called it *the chair*. The panels are all around your head when you're sitting inside, and together, they cast some kind of hologram. You're literally inside the ledger, and there are those little commands on the armrests." She pointed with her finger. "The operator uses them to move the stream around themselves. I've never quite understood how it works, but I've seen my dad use it since I was a little girl. When I was a kid, I used to watch as he disappeared inside a blueish mist, both mesmerized and startled, unable to move until he emerged hours later, having extracted the precious answers that important people sent him looking for."

"Was your father working on something specific lately?"

"No. He had just published his findings in the Rev Case a few weeks ago. You must have heard about it in the news. Since then, he had been waiting for his next mission."

Croissal had certainly heard about the Rev Case. It pitted the two heirs of the deceased President of the Rev corporation, Henry O'Cal, against each other. Who would be the new head of the company? The man had left no clear will, and the authorities had no choice but to turn to metroologists to try to identify the deceased's intentions through the tangle of contracts and transactions registered for eternity on the ledger.

The case had made tremendous noise because of the sums at stake. Rev was an old corporation, with its roots dating back to only thirty years after the Genesis, back when people still called the ledger "bitcoin." Rev was active in virtually every aspect of the economy. Knowing which child would inherit the company was on everybody's mind. And now Salim Hebnar, the man who provided a desperately needed answer — here in favour of the daughter, if he recalled correctly — was dead.

As was the custom and the law, Hebnar had disclosed his findings publicly, highlighting exactly what led him to reach his conclusions. Croissal dug into his memory, trying to remember what evidence the metroologist had put forward in this specific case. There was something about a thirty-year-old transaction, the early days of Henry O'Cal's presidency. And something even more ancient — a decision made by one of the early members of the company's board. Hidden deep in the meanders of a sophisticated script was the information that the press clamoured for and only an experienced metroologist could unveil.

Seeing control of the company slip through his fingers, O'Cal's son appealed the decision. With no luck. Was it enough to motivate murder?

Croissal's head was starting to hurt a bit, his blood pulsing in perfect rhythm against his cranial cavity. He must have been lost in his thoughts for some time because Miss Hebnar stared at him, visibly worried.

"Yes, I've heard about this case." He mumbled, remembering the young woman's last sentences. "What was your father doing while he waited for a new client?"

"The Rev case had been quite exhausting, so he rested for a few weeks. That's what he usually does — did — so nothing particular, in case you're wondering. Then, when he felt refreshed, he used to do some research on his own." She paused, looking at the machine in the centre of the room. "He really liked that, you know. Digging through traces of the past, like a digital archaeologist. Not trying to solve a specific dispute, just looking for worthwhile relics. For the sake of it, not for money. That's what he liked the most, I believe. He could spend the whole day in the chair, travelling from transaction to transaction. Solving cases for clients was just a way to finance all that."

"So," interrupted Croissal, counting the weeks, "your father was probably working on his own research when he was killed."

"Yes, probably. I'm not sure. I wasn't living with him anymore."

Interesting, Croissal thought. But not helpful. He already had a list as long as his arm full of potential murder suspects, starting with O'Cal's son. Now, he had to add other unknown names to this enumeration: Could the metroologist have found something he wasn't supposed to during his wanderings inside the ledger?

***

They went back to the living room. Thoughts raced through Croissal's head. He somehow managed to take leave of Miss Hebnar and head back to his office, a few districts away. He decided to go on foot. There was something about the rhythmic motion of walking that helped him clarify or untangle his thoughts. Right now, his mind was a labyrinth, and he desperately needed a way out. His journey took him through Stillman's Street, famous for harboring many alcohol distilleries during Prohibition nearly a century ago. Many buildings had concealed windows through which men could buy their poison. When Prohibition was repealed, and the alcohol shops closed, the name endured.

Croissal paused. Something felt off, as if he knew he was missing a piece of a puzzle he hadn't even started yet. Surely, taking some time to reflect on this in his office wouldn't hurt. He resumed his walk, his mind racing faster than his feet, eager to reach the familiar confines of his building.

When he entered the small, impersonal room, he immediately noticed the files in the middle of his desk. His assistant must have received the Hebnar record from the City Watch and put it there. He sat down and went through the papers.

Body found at around 9 pm (...) lying in the MLI (...). Death most probably caused by the absorption of a high dose of hemlock...

Croissal grinned. The autopsy had revealed a high concentration of poison found in Hebnar's system, so high that one would have thought the cause of death was beyond doubt. But the City Watch was a very old institution, proud of its procedures that could drive any sane being to insanity. It was why private eyes like him were needed. Just in case.

The autopsy found that the hour of death was probably between 2 and 4 pm on the same day the body was discovered. (...) The vector through which the poison was injected into the victim's digestive system remains to be found. No trace of hemlock was found in any food or drink at the house of the victim.

Suddenly, something clicked in his mind. The autopsy placed the time of death between 2 and 4. Hebnar was in his research phase, between two jobs, where he could spend the whole day on his *chair*. He was found in the chair. And yet, the interface itself was turned off. There was something he had to check — on site, in Hebnar's office — and quickly.

Croissal grabbed his coat and stormed out of the building. It had been lying there, right under his eyes, since the beginning. The events were not crystal clear yet, but if he was right... He had the feeling he was on track to find something monumental.

He got there as quickly as he could. Hebnar's daughter looked surprised and displeased with his unannounced visit, but telling her he had something to check regarding her father's death was enough to remove her objections. She left him alone in the office, and he started searching, his fingers exploring the many cracks running along the server racks. Finding nothing, Croissal turned to the massive chair in the middle of the room.

He wasn't sure what he was looking for, but it had to be here. Nobody could have come in and out without the men of the Watch noticing — no secret passage. Mr. Hebnar was preparing his own meals, precisely out of fear of poisoning. It was literally *the* impossible murder, except for one specific person.

His fingers groped the underside of the chair. There! A small and thin rectangular shape. Slowly, he removed it. A memory chip. He pressed the small button at the centre of the device, and a delicate screen unfolded and opened like a lotus. Once it had fully bloomed, the screen lit up, and Salim Hebnar's face appeared in the middle. He looked agitated but determined.

I have uncovered a terrible thing. I've been to places where none of my contemporaries should ever set foot. Down to the foundation of it all, and everything we stand upon is a lie. A lie! I shouldn't have gone there. But I had to. I thought my role was to seek truth ... Oh, my dear Claire, was I wrong!

The truth is nothing but chaos. I've seen the point of inception. The initial set of defining conditions. It's a forgery. Our whole society is based on a forgery. I wish the ledger could lie, but I know it can't. It's alien to our need for stability. It's a pendulum set in motion by our own madness, and now only our lies can protect us from its storm.

Croissal's eyes were glued to the screen, his breath suspended.

There is only one way through this. I am so sorry, Claire. I hope you will understand. I did this for you. To protect you. You are all I ever truly loved. I take the unspeakable truth with me. No one must ever know. It's ... I have to stop this. The... flap of a butterfly's wings shouldn't have such consequences.

Claire... I love you, forever.

The screen went black. During the final seconds, Hebnar's voice reduced to a murmur; his face twisted into a strange rictus. But there was no trace of madness in his eyes. Only the flame of a cold resolution.

Croissal looked over his shoulder. The door remained shut, and he was alone in the room. He broke the device into pieces and slipped the fragments into his coat pocket.

07

Jo Buys a Planet

Daniel Crow

"Welcome to Bob's free mining colony! You may still be experiencing the side effects of wormhole travel, but soon, your new life as an off-world miner will—"

The speaker coughed and died off, leaving the overly enthusiastic welcome unfinished. Johanna didn't mind, as every word burrowed into her brain like a gimlet.

Her capsule remained locked. She wished she could get a sense of where she was — still in the screened hull of the transport, or maybe at the orbital station already? Either way, after a whole load of nothingness around, it would have been comforting to see there was something, anything beyond the capsule.

She tried to raise her hand, but her muscles felt hopelessly out of sync with her brain. Another side effect of spending three days where no human should ever be and the drug-induced, sanity-preserving artificial coma. Oh, the wonders of deep-space travel.

The metal top of the capsule floated off with a hiss, letting in the blinding light. Johanna gasped and closed her eyes.

"Hey, sleeping beauty," she heard a woman say. "Welcome back from Neverland. You hear me alright?"

"Yeah... Ugh... Water please."

The woman handed her a plastic tube. The water left a metallic aftertaste. "Johanna Smithson, right? The new engineer."

"Yes... Yes, ma'am."

"Great. I am Doctor Hartman, Bob's senior medical officer. Your vitals look good, so we'll head for the planet soon. First off-world job, huh?"

"Yes," Johanna finally opened her eyes. The relay station's medical bay was as ascetic as it gets, but she liked Doctor Hartman. The woman looked old and rough, with her tired white lab coat covering a miner's fat sweater and old jeans. But she was the right kind of old and rough.

"Well, then, hope you're prepared to fight off the nostalgia," the doctor said. "Three years is a long time. And you don't look like you can afford to pay for a trip back yourself."

Jo asked if it was this way on all of these jobs.

Doctor Hartman nodded. "All private ops like ours get the same relay deal. At least we've got proper internet."

"Is it good? I really hope it's good."

The doctor shrugged. "Satellite coverage on the planet and direct wormhole link with the Earth. There's almost no lag. Information travels faster than people. It's a good place to go through the movie backlog."

Johanna shook her head and closed her eyes, listening into her space-concussed body.

"No sleeping. We gotta wake your muscles up."

After a torturous physiotherapy session, they both followed the handrails to the transit shuttle. Doctor Hartman stopped at one of the omnipresent Foodie vending stations, which looked more like a bank vault. The machine handed her a soda after recognizing her face. "Hope you like their stock," Hartman grinned. She said Foodie was the colony's exclusive food supplier. "Another damn contract milking us little guys."

"Don't they take bitcoin?" Johanna asked. "I think they announced they were accepting payments in satoshis about a month ago."

"Don't care, frankly." The doctor made a paying gesture and said, "I use the good ol' digital greenback. But you can talk to Willie. He's their local manager, if that's your thing. A word of warning, though — he's really into redheads."

***

"Jo to HQ, do you copy?" She watched the harvester, a massive hulking machine on heavy-duty tracks, pull through the desert. Bob's planet had a Mars-like atmosphere, mostly carbon dioxide, and held a host of rare earths, which Bob's crew had been shipping to Earth through the wormhole relay. The harvesters came a bit later, with the help of Rania, who got a sublicense from Bob to collect some rare isotopes in the desert and occasionally contracted Bob's engineers to do the maintenance.

"Hear you loud and clear, Jo. Willie's been asking about you. Said he got the rig, wants to start mining."

"Cool," Johanna sighed. "I am done with the harvester. Iwai, Rania better get ready to decommission it."

"Heading home now, Jo?"

"Nah, will check up on my farm, while I'm out here."

She stretched out in her seat — a privilege she never had in the claustrophobic living pod she rented back home — and set the rover's course for the unnamed rocky flatland where she set up her solar panel arrays and the computer crunching the numbers. The idea was a gamble, but she had run the math and figured it was worth a shot — and so far, it seemed so.

The dispatcher asked if she'd come all the way here just for this bitcoin thing. Surely, she could just mine back on Earth?

"Nope. Long story short, power's too expensive."

A shadow cast on the desert around — the ringed silhouette of the wormhole relay station eclipsed the sun, its own solar panels gulping on every bit of sunlight they could get. Jo didn't mind. The thing was their main and only connection with Earth, after all. It deserved some love.

"So, is it paying off?" Iwai asked.

"Not crazy money, but I'll take it."

She looked at the relay station again and blew it a kiss. Coming here, Johanna doubted whether the wormhole connection would be fast enough for her to compete for blocks against other miners, but it was almost as fast as a regular connection on Earth. So while the bigger fish snatched the prize most often, she still had lucky pickups every now and then.

"Should I get one? How do you set it up?"

"Up to you." She shrugged. "But I'll help you if you give me more of your home-grown veggies. Honestly, so cool that everyone here has their own thing going. I want one, too."

"You got your mining."

"That's the means, not the end." Jo exhaled. "Aight, gonna go quiet for a bit. Jo out."

"HQ out, Jo. Safe travels."

About an hour later, her terminal went off, alerting her that Rania sent a few hundred bucks her way. Bob took a cut, of course, and froze more of her digital greenbacks, all sitting safely on Earth servers, because of her travel through the desert. It was his rover, after all. At least he didn't turn the seat warmer into a subscription service, like they did with the cars she rented on Earth.

***

"Guess what the worm-shuttle brought this time, Jo?" Willie asked with a wide grin.

"Foodie stuff that actually doesn't taste like vomit?"

Maddie, the home-brew maker, cackled. Technically, she wasn't supposed to share her product with anybody, or even brew it, to begin with. The Foodie contract banned any non-Foodie foods on the colony, but Bob's pirate miner crew was lax with such things — Willie included. The corporation was light years out from here, but Bob and his fists were here, in the kind of proximity that was pretty intimate by the universe's standards.

"It brought the bitcoin terminals!" Willie declared. He said he'd already set them on all of the machines.

Maddie laughed in disbelief. "It's not like Foodie would ever let you tinker with their machinery."

Jo beamed, too, imagining Willie trying to do literally anything to the armored beast with Foodie's mascot (a burger so happy it looked as if it had been drugged) that stood in their cantina. Restocks and upgrades were automated, done by the company's service robots. She really had no clue why Foodie even had Willie around, probably just for the anti-automation tax cuts.

"Who cares about details?" Willie hunched his shoulders. "What matters is we can now all pay with our bitcoin. You got your third rig up and running, right, Jo?"

"Yup. It's so much cheaper to mine here than back home."

Maddie sipped her beer. She wondered aloud about trying the whole mining thing. "Dad's brewery's still bleeding, and whatever I can send helps."

"I'll help you for a case," Jo promised. "I actually thought of opening a bar too... Couldn't get a loan."

Willie grinned, imagining Jo behind a bar.

"Bar, repairs shop, a robotics company, whatever," Jo sighed. "I just want to have something that's mine, you know? Everything's a fucking subscription. Everything's for rent... Like, I don't want the whole pie, you know? Just a tiny piece to munch on. Big guys can have the rest."

"Damned be my old eyes," Bob's coarse voice thundered over the cantina. "Is that illegal beverages I see? Here, in the heart of hearts of my motherbase?!"

Despite his young age of forty-three, Bob looked as if he was at least eighty. He had a long, scruffy beard, an antique prosthetic for his right arm, which looked too old to be a relic of the augmentation hype era, and his voice was as loud as a C4 blast.

"Jesus Christ, Bob." Maddie rolled her eyes at the laughs from Jeremy and Khaled, who sat at the table across. "You got your cut, don't be a drama queen!"

"My old eyes will no longer see it once it's in me," Bob said, allowing himself a chug from Maddie's bottle. He burped and looked around the cantina, where about a dozen people were gathered, which was pretty much as busy as it got. "Tell you what, folks," he thundered on. "I have a report from our outer surveillance satellite. Damn thing's expecting a meteor shower. Says it's not gonna hit us or the station, but keep an eye out and don't get caught unprepared."

***

Jo didn't quite catch the meteor shower herself — she was too exhausted after the trip to Bob's automated mine, where she had to calibrate a digger bot. She only woke up to the sound of the buzzer alerting her to an emergency meeting in the situation room. On her way there, she got a can of Moxy, Foodie's certified energy drink that tasted like pure, concentrated suffering. The damn vending vault didn't want to recognize her face, so she caved and paid in bitcoin.

The round situation room, which was locked most of the time, was now packed with people. Everyone was agitated, talking at the same time over the beeps and boops of a dozen consoles, with white noise filling most of the screens. The main one, hanging right over Bob's throne-like seat adorned with more consoles and displays, displayed some grainy mess.

"I'm sleeping, right?" someone whispered next to her. "Please tell me this is just a nightmare."

"We're so, so *fucked*," said a voice with confidence that sent chills down Jo's spine.

She squinted, trying to figure out what the grainy mess was. It looked like a mangled-up donut that one of those tiny dogs gnawed the life out of, leaving it maimed and battered.

Then, it hit her. It wasn't just a regular donut. It was the wormhole relay station.

Their only connection with Earth was gone.

"Holy shit," she whispered, her eyes widening.

"Okay, everybody, enough with the panic." Bob's comforting tone thundered through the distressed voices. "Panic's not gonna help 'cause we're on a timer here. Oxygen converters are crucial — Maddie, Thor, I want you guys to check them now. We'll have to ration water. Our generators won't be enough. Willie, any luck getting the damn Foodie shit open?"

"No, Bob," Willie bleated. He was pale and didn't know what to do with his gangly self. "It's gone into lockdown; it thinks we're trying to hack it."

"Damn corporates," Bob growled. "If it doesn't open, we'll blow up a damn hole in it!"

"I'd like to warn against anything so dramatic," Doctor Hartman said coldly. "Bob, it's only a few centimeters of steel, carbon, and wiring between us and all the damn CO_2 in the world. Let's be smart about it."

Bob asked if they could drill a hole in it.

"Guys, guys," Jo raised her can of liquid disaster like Lady Liberty. "Bitcoin payments still work. The damn thing just charged me a bit more, but I bought this just minutes ago."

For a few seconds, the room fell silent. Then, Bob nodded and grinned. "Well, that improves our food situation a bit," he said grumpily. "I know many of you got into this bitcoin thing, so I reckon you can shop. But the vaults won't be resupplied cause the wormhole's gone."

"They have some extra supplies," Willie said. "Basically, in case re-stocking fails. So they're gonna last us at least about a month if we're cautious."

"Well, that helps." Bob looked skywards. "I've already fired off a distress signal, but it's gonna take years to reach Earth unless someone close by picks it off and passes it on. But don't get comfortable, people. Let's not assume help's coming tomorrow."

Let's not assume help's coming at all is what Jo heard, and it made her shiver.

***

For the first few days after the relay station went down, Jo was so slammed with work that she barely had the opportunity to think of anything else. She spent hours and hours checking their oxygen converter arrays, and when that was done, she rewarded herself with a tiny veggie salad she'd bought for bitcoin from Iwai. The next earthly day found her pondering over the videos that Bob's crew brought from the relay station. Bob said the damn thing was so battered the shuttle could barely dock in.

Then, one of the water generators broke down — perfect timing — so Jo and Maddie worked their asses off until there were finally more small droplets in the machine's condenser chamber. Maddie sold her a pack of beers, and Jo was too tired to even count the satoshis. She just wanted to crack a cold one open and store the rest for a better day.

About a week after the incident, the drama lost some of its punch. They had brought everything dealing with life-support into the best shape it had ever been. Now, there was little else for them to do. Another shuttle trip to the station confirmed the amount of damage was beyond what they could fix, and they didn't have much fuel for the flight anyway. The mining operation slowed to a grind because Bob's storage capacity was built around the idea he'd be able to ship stuff to Earth every two weeks on a wormhole transport, and expanding it would have been a struggle.

So, everyone just ended up gravitating to whatever rocked their boat. Iwai and Said worked on expanding the garden. Maddie ramped up her beer operation, renting two water generators from Bob. And when Jo went to check up on her mining rigs, she found herself to be crazy rich.

With the connection with Earth severed, all that was left was the local network of a few rigs still carrying on. Jo had the most hash power there, and so most of the rewards went to her. And given that most tokens on the network sat back on earthly wallets, the real supply on Bob's planet was very thin. And she, again, had most of it. With Foodie's vaults, impervious to everything they threw at them other than bitcoin, it stood as the bulwark of her fortune.

Best of all, she grew richer by the day, every passing hour expanding her lead. At first, she'd spend her bitcoin just on Iwai's salads, but then, she bought herself a stake in his farm. She bought a stake in Maddie's brewery, too. A share in Rania's business was acquired almost randomly for one bitcoin and a pack of beers. And then, one night, when they both got bored and drunk, Jo bought half of the stupid planet from Bob.

"Why the hell would you ever buy it?" Bob asked. "I mean, I'm fine, I'll get fat on the Foodie shit. But, like, why? It's just a piece of rock in deep space. Not even that profitable. Why?"

"Cause like..." The alcohol in her blood filled her with a pleasant warmth. "What if nobody's, like, ever gonna show up? What if, I dunno, Earth's been destroyed by some aliens, and we're now the new humanity, huh? I buy 51 percent of this planet from you, and here we go, my kids will be kings and queens."

"Kids? With whom, Willie?"

"Eh," Jo made a vague gesture. "I'll figure it out. You're my VP now, how dare you question me?!"

"Easy there, *Your Majesty*," Bob laughed. "We'll buy you a crown when they fix the relay. So you're gonna have one in what, a century?"

***

They didn't have to wait a century — just three earthly months from there, the comms center at their HQ temporarily went offline caused by the absolute storm that an uncontained wormhole opening too close to the planet produced across the entire radio spectrum. After Said and

Kamran brought the system back online, they saw the ugly, bulky hull of a Dolphin-class rescue burrower on their long-range visors. Within a few minutes, the first transmission came in.

"Slow approach velocity. Let the engines cool off. ETA — 147 earthly hours. Bob's free mining colony, do you copy?"

"Hear you loud and clear, Dolphin," Jo said into the mic. "You came in fast! How come?"

"An explorer drone picked your distress signal and beamed it to its relay. Honestly, you were on our radars for a long time. It just took a while to get a sign-off on the rescue mission."

"Well, Dolphin, you're a joy for our sore eyes at any approach velocity." Jo smiled. "Just one small update for you, though."

"What is it?"

"It's Jo and Bob's free mining colony now."

"Yeah, Jo, I wouldn't be so sure," Bob said. He looked relieved but also tense, like a boxer before his biggest fight.

"How come, Mr. Vice-President?"

"What do you think happens when the Dolphin reconnects us to the main timechain?"

08

Legacy

Philip Charter

Ecology

When my father died, an entire ecosystem system of beneficiaries withered. Moussa Ag El Khir funded scholarships and community projects, paying thousands of dinars monthly to stop the oasis town of In Salah from burning up. The few families we knew operating outside the oil-field economy would be forced to flee to the Mediterranean coast, along with just about every other Berber.

It wasn't unexpected. My father had cystic fibrosis for all sixty-one years of his life. So far, that's the only legacy he's passed on to his children. My brothers are just carriers, but I, his precious daughter, ended up like him in more ways than one.

We sat there in the lawyer's office in Algiers, my brothers and I, staring at the ledger, which contained payment for his life's work.

"And he only left one word in his will?" asked Ibrahim for the third time. Ecology.

The lawyer said Moussa was very clear. He chose each of the keys himself. The contents of the ledger would belong to whoever could decode his life — those who understood the real meaning. Then he cut all communications and walked into the Sahara. The Tuareg caravan on the road to Akabli found his body a week later, reddened by sand burn.

Earth

We made an agreement that day. To share each word we discovered. We could break the code together. Of course, Ibrahim and Hama didn't share anything. We barely speak. That's what happens when one child follows their father into science, and her two brothers move to France the minute they get rich enough to buy a wife. I bet they spent longer looking into legal loopholes to get their hands on my father's assets than they did trying to identify the keys.

That day was the start of my second life, and I went from a research assistant at a regional university to a private-key detective. Two thousand and forty-eight words and few clues about where to start. Although I was 27, I was virtually a grandmother, according to the In Salah wives. But of course, I could never be a grandmother, or even a mother. Every night, I scoured photos in the family archive. An initial sweep of his digital footprint returned no out-of-place instances of any keywords.

It took me a year to find the GPS tag he'd added to one photo — an eighteen-year-old daughter standing next to a father proud of his first infinite solar prototype. The panel has long since been torn out by the oil corp, but the base is still there. I drove the three kilometres from the town limit and shone the high beams at the spot. When I got out, the air was cool but still thick with sand. A few more steps through sinking dunes, and I saw it. He'd scratched a little globe into the blistered metal, and for a moment, my mucus-laden lungs tasted clear air.

Trigger

The next word took three years. Friends, contacts, professors, biographers — visits to anyone with whom he might have left a clue. But it was in the In Salah hospital, where, upon a routine CF checkup with Jerome

Devailier, a French doctor, a 'trigger' appeared. The government might stack everything against the desert peoples, but they hadn't taken away healthcare. I'd been living off the kindness of neighbours while finishing my thesis on the very solar technology my father developed. How could he have known the 'buyer' was just a tendril of the very oil company he sought to defeat?

Dr Devalier went through the list of carcinogens and allergens to avoid with my new drugs. Over forty triggers, which could be my downfall. If I were lucky, I'd live as long as my father did.

By then, my research stipend was long gone. I existed on toughened bread and soup, which always carried the taste of the scorched city air. Yet, I stayed. The public library, disconnected from the grid by the oil corp, was where I finished my manuscript. They would fight its publication. Since my father's money no longer flowed into the town, many had deserted me. There were those who said he killed an entire people by selling his solar patent to the wrong buyers. Others in In Salah worshipped his name, but eventually, they all trudged north to the cities. My brothers sold the family home from under me, forcing me to follow.

When I returned from the hospital, I dug out my father's medical documents. On every page, the word 'trigger' was underlined. That was the moment I knew my life's work would be unlocking the ledger, not publishing studies on long-dead solar panel technology. That battle was lost.

They

All we need is a simple document, but here, it is the administrators' job to send people away. Physical copies are only issued in extreme circumstances. Citizens' Registry screens played endless repetitions of how to apply for digital documents. The shrill voices of family members desperate for the original copy of a pirated document drowned the TV messaging. Women removed headscarves and revealed thick black hair; teenagers paced. The atmosphere thickened with sweat. And hours passed. Each appointment required a reset of digital protocol, biometric tests, and identity cards from legal descendants. Through counterfeit identities, our dinars leak into the hands of criminals, but still, the government denies the need for bitcoin. They just print more money. 'They' is the word my father used for the government that fought his patent so hard.

After a four-hour wait, I discovered that the physical death certificate included an 'identifying mark' on the deceased's body. The ink was fresh — etched into the shoulder blade of a man who wished to turn his back on the government that ignored its people. The tattoo read *aqqalan*, the Tamasheq word for 'they.'

Scheme

It took two trips to his cluttered Marseille office to convince him I was serious. Two visas, two flights, and a small amount from the sale of the family house. But few detectives wanted to work for a promise.

The ledger could not legally be owned in Algeria, and Laurent Mercier was the only serious professional who entertained a percentage of what was on there. The solar tech patent and documents from my father were enough to start Laurent on the trail. 'Preliminary,' he said, until I had the ledger in my possession.

"Flying is not easy with my condition," I said.

He lowered his sunglasses. "Working is not easy without money."

Contact with my brother through the lawyer in Algiers was achingly slow, but eventually, they agreed to give me possession. What was 33% of nothing anyway? Years had gone by.

So, when I sat for the second time in the sweaty office in Marseille, I gave Laurent the ledger, and he handed me a surprise. In all his business affairs, my father used little English, but the word 'scheme' appeared in all three company names he incorporated in the last three years of his life. We had our fifth word, and I finally had someone on my side.

Make

Some days, I could barely walk to the public library. I became lethargic and mostly sat in the cool dark of my room in the shelter. The government refused to provide housing outside of Algiers, but a Tuareg organisation from Mali opened a shelter in In Salah. Bulging eyes and faded clothes stared back in the mirror each day. How long had it been since I'd been to a wedding, or celebrated a friend's child? Occupants came and went, and all that was left was a barren room and one meal per day.

As the sun punished the city with every ray of Allah's untapped gift, streets grew thick with dust, and the local government fell, seat by seat, to oil execs. The only transport running was to and from the oil fields, which belched the remnants of the land into the sky. And still, they worked. Still, they sat on my father's patent and refused to supply the world with efficient solar power.

With little else to cling onto, I harboured thoughts of how I could spend the ledger money. Fixing the town and replanting lost gardens. Bringing people back. That all took a back seat to decoding the message my father was sending. Laurent and I began to believe that the keys he chose formed some sort of instruction for his legacy.

Ten years to the day after his death, I was in the public library, looking for clues in an English history book. On my exit, the librarian stopped me.

"We have a gift for you, Kana."

I waited while he fetched a package.

"Your father instructed me to give this to you. But not before this date."

My hands tore open the package. More books, technical manuals, and hand-written notes. Amongst the papers was a tasselled leather bookmark embossed with the four letters that comprised one of the seven missing words. Make.

Citizen

It's hard for a father in Algeria to admit to his daughter that she is his spirit — the heir to his life's work. Of course he felt terrible guilt after our mother's passing. That was when the letters started.

Moussa wrote to himself really, trying to come to terms with bringing a protégé into the world with a bright scientific mind and lungs that would snap her life expectancy. We communicated by letter for the last few years of his life — sharing the breakthroughs of his findings and what it might mean for our decaying oasis town. Analogue writing was the only real privacy, he said. His letters always ran to the same length, as if they were one lesson divided into equal chunks. We even exchanged letters during his last hospitalisation in Algiers. Those words were the only real strength I gained.

It was Laurent who analysed the letters with a new text-scanning tool. For me, my father's last letters were advice, regret, pain, and love, but to Laurent, they were simply a puzzle to solve to get one step closer.

Our letters gave Laurent the idea to communicate via physical mail. The process was painful, with letters sent from outlying towns before being shipped across the Alboran Sea and up into France. Muatin was one name my father called me. Like him, I dreamed of helping many through science. This was one of the few Arabic words in the French letters he wrote. It was also the only keyword included in any of the letters. Citizen.

When

Years of quiet followed. In Salah became unlivable after they co-opted the city reservoir for cooling drilling rigs. Each study that proved the field was still viable funnelled funds away from the locals who clung on. Resettlement benefits went up, and all but the semi-nomadic Tuaregs left. I followed. My health could not take much more desert. In the cooler coastal plains, I recovered strength, and subsidies for new medications helped me survive on a meagre teaching salary.

With no further clues, my Marseillais detective lost interest. His last letter, sent years ago, stated with unusual brevity that he was resigning the case. No payment was due.

I had lost my health, my father, his work, my money, our house, the town, and I spent each week delivering science and English classes to teenagers. They had no more hope for our country than I had. Algerians had already lost the Sahara. A one-degree temperature shift each decade of my life had shrunk Africa and sent its peoples northwards.

My father's word puzzle occupied my thoughts. The combinations and permutations of letters and characters had millions of possible meanings but only one correct answer. Yet simple linguistic logic provided the next word. The headteacher was a linguist — a profession long lost to the higher-powered text analysers and language AI. He spoke little English but asked about the categorisations of grammatical terms in the 2,048 key words.

"Why do you ask?"

"Because," he said, "for a sentence of twelve words, at least one conjunction is necessary to form a second clause."

He was right. I had been focussing on lists and complex codes to build my father's motto. When I got home, I furiously searched my list of terms for conjunctions. I found only one. 'When.'

Can

The permutations were still huge. Even eliminating some of the more conceptual words did not help. Millions of sentences existed in my dead father's mind. Millions of meanings, all lost to the need for more energy to fund the world's great thirst for energy. Still, the panels in most of the 'dead middle' (as the space between the tropics became known) melted at over 50 degrees.

I was back in Paris for CF treatment. As a young woman, I would have been pleased to make fifty years. But the realities of daily visits and the sickness brought on by medication stung. I wanted things to end, even when I discovered the next key.

It had been years since I had dreamed of the freedoms my father's fortune could bring. Parts of Asia held out against bitcoin, but the cost of countries doing business off-network had become prohibitive. Eventually, the fossil conglomerates would give in to the need for solar mining and the provision of universal energy.

It was in a Parisian hospital bed that I discovered 'can.' My wardmate, a rough labourer from Oran, found a biography in the hospital library that made me sit up straight. 'Can' was repeated in almost every description of my father in his one-time business partner's book. And it was this Arabian 'businessman,' Abdulkarim Rahman, who brokered the deal that robbed the world of infinite solar power. Each page mocked my father as believing only physical impossibilities are impossible. He branded him the 'can man.'

Drastic

During my recuperation, I spent the final two weeks of my visa stay in Marseille. My days passed with endless algorithm tweaks to reject or accept word orders for the elusive twelve-word sentence my father once wrote.

Food lost its taste, and friends and colleagues in academia had scattered. In-person meetings were often contained to the night hours, but Marseille was not a place to go out after dark. The latest protests had gotten violent, and the government looked likely to topple. My people had always been resilient, but when the option to move and operate a caravan was removed by General Hafiz, part of my spirit died. I resolved to spend my final years in In Salah, however uncomfortable they would be.

My final port of call before returning was Laurent's office. The eTaxi cast me out into the dusty street, and I wheezed as I climbed the three flights of stairs to his tiny door on Rue Marché. We hadn't spoken in years, but I was surprised to find a different name about the door. Pascale Dupont, Investigateur.

The assistant I remembered was quite the opposite of Laurent — slow and methodical, short and heavy set.

"Madame," he said. "I have difficult news."

Their business had always straddled the law, but I never imagined an ex-officer of the law could be convicted of treason.

"A closed-door trial," said Pascale. Then he handed over an air-gapped 3D storage file. "Laurent knew you would come for this."

My mind cast forward to the reams of information he must have built on my father. The patents and technical diagrams he illegally acquired and other clues. I instantly recognised the brand of storage file as a keyword. Drastic.

"How can I thank him?"

"He is dead, madame." Pascale hung his head. "He survived prison for only two weeks."

Must

My final years brought me home. In Salah had gained fame for its one group of Tuaregs who refused to leave. The Lakzis owned a house in a desperate condition, not dissimilar to my failing body. By the age of fifty-two, I could no longer walk, but they welcomed me. I pooled my disability allowance and some money I'd gained from selling my father's watch. We waited for the world to mourn the death of a once great city. We would keep it alive by refusing to move, by refusing to permit its rebranding as an 'industrial area.' Now, the oil fields were finally drying up. They wanted to dig under the town.

We had managed to eliminate half of the remaining words. Just under 1,000 possible selections for the final two words, but little idea of an order.

The problem was that I was the only English speaker among them, and it took great energy to attempt to teach the meaning of the words and possible grammatical constructions for my father's sentence.

But soon, patterns began to emerge. Fragments of word pairings and groups. 'Trigger drastic scheme' appeared again and again in the permutations. 'They can' and 'When they can' gave a tantalising glimpse. We ranked sentences in terms of the likelihood of forming a full key and categorised them by the most likely remaining words. Due to the need for a modal verb, 'must' scored highest by our calculations.

In this race to unlock the ledger before In Salah's destruction, we nosed ahead.

Yet the day of that discovery was my final day in the desert. An air ambulance transported my feeble body to Algiers, and I would never return.

They messaged me — so close. They would unlock the ledger with the final word after my operation. The bitcoin could undo the wrongs of the past, and my father's sentence would live on.

End

The phrase that began the global revolution first appeared on the wall of a much-disputed oil refinery in the desert outside In Salah, Algeria.

When they can make ecology end, citizen earth must trigger drastic scheme

Soon, the graffiti marked government buildings in Algiers. Activists took to the streets. Governments crumbled, and currencies collapsed. Climate groups received massive donations said to come from 'the one,' a ledger with a huge stack written off by financiers the world over. The codebreaker credited with unlocking the ledger was unable to witness the transfer of 10,000 coins to the Global Climate Fund due to her death, aged 52, from a congenital condition.

The words of Moussa Ag El Khir now mark each of the millions of panels that line the 'dead middle.' They contribute over 80% of the Earth's power supply.

To mark the fiftieth anniversary of his death, the World Climate Forum will be held in the town of his birth, In Salah, Algeria. This story, compiled from the diaries of his daughter, Kana Ult El Khir, will be read as the opening address of the conference.

09

The Baked Goods and Bitcoin of Skirophoria

Angelique Fawns

When Caleb regained consciousness, he wasn't sure where he was (or even what decade he was in). There was an undulant blue blur to his world, like when he used to swim laps in his infinity pool on his Texan ranch. That had cost him a few bitcoins, but nothing like the fortune he'd paid to Cyrogen Futures. His nostrils tingled with an antiseptic chemical odor, like those from the many medical labs he funded. When he was finally able to focus, he saw a white-cloaked woman on a podium, sword at her side, with intricately braided hair. He was behind her, so he couldn't see her face, but he certainly admired the outline of her taut back.

She strutted along the platform while waving at a crowd of women in togas. A female warrior in chainmail scuttled beside her, trying to keep the sun off her head with a white umbrella. The sun was bright and hot in an endlessly blue sky. The more she waved, the louder the crowd roared.

Beyond the robed women, Caleb saw homes of marble and stone rising up a distant mountain. With some effort, he rotated his head to the side. Why was his neck so stiff? There were two floating heads in tanks mounted on silver pedestals beside him. Caleb blinked. It was like he was attending an ancient Greek festival with greasy sunglasses on. Why was the world so blurry? He attempted to reach up and remove his sunglasses, but he couldn't. His eyebrows shot up as a horrific realization washed over him. He was also a head in a tank.

His eyes widened, and he screamed into the viscous fluid. The force of his panicked breath created a stream of bubbles like the jets from the hot tub he used to relax in at the end of a day on the oil fields. The froth obscured his view as it floated from his mouth to the top of the tank. His neck wasn't stiff. He had no neck. In fact, he couldn't feel anything below his chin.

"Silence! Your Queen Athena will now speak." The warrior guard shook her umbrella at Caleb.

Caleb left his mouth open but stopped yelling. He squeezed his eyes shut and opened them again. The nightmare world didn't disappear. He was still a head in a tank. Waves of red panic splashed behind his forehead. Beating on his skull.

Raising a megaphone, Queen Athena addressed the gathering. "Every June, we celebrate Skirophoria! Today is a day for women and the harvest. Men are not welcome on this one day."

The women cheered, waving bulbs of purple garlic. Caleb's wife used to slice the vegetable into her salads when she was trying to get pregnant, having read it was a fertility aid.

Caleb frowned. He'd learned about Skirophoria in college. The Skira was the day the women of ancient Athens gathered to plot the overthrow of men, and chewed on garlic to keep their husbands away. He could see how it would work. He used to hold his breath while making love to his pungent wife after her lunches. His eyes scanned the crowd. Not a man to be seen. This society must have recreated the ancient festival.

"Today, we celebrate a new tradition! Our scientists discovered a capsule from the past filled with frozen men! Interestingly, the heads were stored separately from their bodies," Athena said.

A teenage girl with buck teeth asked from the edge of the podium. "Any women in this elite capsule?"

"Just men. Twelve privileged men of wealth," Athena said, fury drawing her eyebrows together.

A woman squashed her garlic in her fist. "Women didn't rate being frozen for the future?"

The crowd booed and threw phallic-shaped cookies at the pedestals.

"No, so far we've only found cryogenically preserved men!" Athena caught a cookie and crumbled it. "Annually, on the day of Skira, three of the capsule's inhabitants will be thawed and judged. One may reclaim his body. The other two will be turned to stone and displayed as busts on our feast table."

Caleb's ears throbbed along with his head. This did not sound good. One man would be given his body back, but two would be turned to stone? He knew he'd had a body when he paid the jaw-dropping fee of fifty bitcoins to get cryogenically frozen on his fiftieth birthday. It was easier to evade the taxman with digital currency, and he wanted his daughter to take over his company without having to deal with the dodgier transactions. (She'd still been refusing to have anything to do with his business when he underwent the procedure.)

When he got diagnosed with cancer, the fossil fuel deposits on his farm had helped him afford the outrageous new medical procedure. There was no 'beheading' clause. His cheeks flushed with indignation. What happened while he'd been asleep? This was not how he imagined the future. Instead of flying cars, he saw hitching posts, chariots, and horse-drawn carriages.

Athena unraveled a scroll. "Caleb Quicken, you ran an oil company that plundered the earth and polluted our air. You, and others like you, are why the gods had to reclaim the world. Why should you walk again?"

Caleb felt a flush of offense pinken his cheeks. How dare she make him justify anything? He screamed into his fluid, surprised by how clearly his voice rang out. "Can I see a lawyer?"

"Answering a question with a question. Unacceptable!" Athena pulled a syringe from her pocket and inserted it into his pedestal. "Prepare for stoning."

"Wait, wait." Caleb pitched and rolled in his fluid. "I helped people get to where they needed to go!"

The women in the crowd jeered, some pointing to the horses they'd ridden.

"To save the climate, we ditched the cars. We ditched paper money for bitcoin." Athena's fingers twitched on the plunger. "You should have taken better care of the earth when you lived on it. Less paper and plunder. As the ox is sacrificed, so will you be."

Caleb pressed his lips against the glass, eyes bulging. "I really loved my daughter, and she was an environmentalist! I paid for her education; I encouraged her. She made a difference."

"Interesting. I'll reserve judgment." Athena removed her syringe, the murky fluid still in it. She walked to the next pedestal, which held an acne-scarred head with thick gray hair. She withdrew the sword slung over her hip and pointed it at him. "Alonzo Perucho Morengo! You are the most notorious drug kingpin in history. Why should you live?" Athena asked.

"This is no justice. I will show you justice," Alonzo said, spitting bile into his tank.

Athena put a hand on an exquisite sword hanging by her side. "Is that all you have to say?"

"When I get out of this fish tank, you will see notoriety! No one takes a piece of Alonzo Perucho Morengo!"

Athena swung her sword over her head and smashed it down on his tank. Alonzo's head split in two and rolled onto the platform. It made the unpleasant squish of a watermelon leaking onto the granite.

Caleb winced.

"He's too unpleasant to look at during dinner, no bust for him," Athena said, drying her sword off on her cloak.

The women roared. Enjoying themselves, they nibbled on their male genitalia cookies.

Caleb clenched his teeth and tried to break the side of his bowl with his head, but the glass wouldn't give.

Athena moved to the third and final tank. The young man with a shaved head seemed calm, causing hardly a ripple.

"Matt Marple, you are the creator of Click Clack. It was the biggest and most destructive social media platform ever created. Responsible for fostering hate, igniting dissension, and facilitating suicides globally."

Matt's eyes blinked a few times. "I, too, created a wonderful daughter who helped the world as a doctor. And at least I didn't poison the earth. And I paid my employees in bitcoin." Matt tilted his head over at Caleb. "I deserve your pardon more than the entitled Texan."

Matt had a solid argument. If Caleb had a heart, it would be breaking right now. He really wanted another chance to live. Oil had made him money, but farming was his passion. The thick black dirt in the distant fields looked so fertile — perfect for the prize-winning garlic he had been growing in Texas. His wife had convinced him it was a worthy vegetable. He did end up with a daughter, after all.

Athena nodded. "Matt, you have earned your legs."

She stepped back towards Caleb's tank, pulling her syringe out.

"Wait, I have another argument." Caleb bobbed frantically.

Athena paused...

"I lived on a big farm in Texas and developed Spanish garlic! My harvesting innovations helped create the hardiness of the purple variety." It is the best female fertility aid." Caleb wiggled his eyebrows for emphasis. "I did help the world." If he had hands, he'd be pleading.

A frown creased Athena's face. The crowd of women cheered and threw their garlic cloves in the air.

"As this is a festival that celebrates the harvest, fertility, and especially garlic, you have won your second chance," Athena said.

Matt's head spun and bobbed, bubbles pouring out of his mouth and nose.

Caleb's cheeks sagged in relief. Athena spun and inserted her syringe into Matt's pedestal. Matt's head stilled, and a grey substance moved up his face from his chin, cementing his features in place.

With the show over, the assembled revelers relaxed and went back to nibbling on their perversely-shaped treats. Caleb's mouth salivated, watching them guzzle champagne. He could use a drink. He could use ten drinks for the alcoholic buzz, even if he had no belly.

"You will now be taken back to the capsule and reunited with your body, but it won't be exactly as you remember," Athena said to Caleb.

"What do you mean, not as I remember?"

"You might be missing a few parts."

"What *exactly* do you mean?"

"Each Skirophoria, we bake male fertility cookies to ensure a good harvest. We use actual genitalia to create our molds. You, Matt, and Alonzo provided this year's designs." A smile tickled at Athena's lips.

Caleb's face turned Spanish Garlic purple. Maybe being turned to stone was the better option.

10

The Bitcoin Overlay

Satillionaire

No one knows exactly when the Great Schism began. Many claim that it never occurred — a mere figment of fevered imaginations. But for the outliers, the divide is an inescapable actuality. Some fled to far-off lands like Mexico or Sub-Saharan Africa seeking refuge, while others were completely cast out of society, left to fend for themselves in the fringes. And then there is me, the bridge between the two worlds.

My job, if you could call it that, is to navigate the treacherous waters of the divide and help those on the periphery find their way to a better life in what has come to be known as The Bitcoin Overlay.

"I need you to understand that you can't bring anything material with you," I said, in a grave tone. "You'll only need your wits and your ability to work hard. But it won't be easy." I had delivered this speech countless times, but the look in Soria's light-brown eyes suggested that she didn't comprehend the gravity of the situation.

She fidgeted with the delicate gold bracelet on her wrist, and her eyes darted around the room. Her designer clothing was a stark contrast to the dingy supply room of this Chinese Restaurant. "I know what I'm leaving behind," she said in a hushed voice. "I just wish I knew more about where I'm going."

"I'm sure you have lots of questions. Unfortunately, I'm not the guy who can answer them." I tried to sound encouraging. "The important thing is that you've made it this far despite the grave risks. That means you'll be just fine once you make it there."

Soria exuded the air of someone born into the upper echelons of society. She was probably raised with tier-2 travel privileges and a personal AI ball — the kind of luxuries that the unwashed masses could only dream of. Was she really willing to leave behind all the comforts and conveniences that had defined her existence?

"We have to leave straight from here," I said, my expression solemn. "There won't be any time for goodbyes."

"But my sister... she will search for me," she protested.

"And unless she's willing to take the leap herself, she won't find you." The light in her eyes dimmed by a shade."You don't have to leave. Nobody could fault you for wanting to stay here," I offered. Soria shook her head, a determined look on her face. She composed herself and forced a smile. "There's nothing for me here," she said with a tinge of sadness in her voice. "Staying is not an option, even if part of me wishes I could."

I nodded in understanding. I may not have been born into the same world of privilege, but I could relate to feeling out of place and yearning for something more.

"I know the stories probably make it sound like a far-fetched utopia, and at one time it was. But now there really is a genuine refuge for those of us who dare to dream." I paused, allowing the weight of my words to settle in the air.

"It might seem scary, but once you make it to the other side, you'll never look back." I met Soria's gaze, seeing a flicker of doubt in her eyes. "Do you truly believe that?"

"I wouldn't be doing this if I didn't."

Just then, a grating beep erupted from the low-fi baby monitor screen on my desk. In the mush of infrared pixels, I watched the scout drone approaching the alleyway just above us. This could only mean one thing

— a breach. I turned my attention back to Soria, my mind racing with the possibilities. "We need to leave, now," I said firmly, grabbing my bag and heading towards the door. Soria followed closely. We stepped out into the dimly lit alleyway, the sound of distant sirens echoing through the night.

As we moved towards our escape route, I knew that we were running out of time. The CamScram microbots we had deployed on this block would soon be disabled. And we were traveling "naked" now, not equipped with any smart devices. That alone could land us in the Archipelago for a year.

The scout drone now hovered a few hundred feet behind us on the Magazine Street, its bright light scanning every crevice it passed. We continued our brisk pace. I took Soria's slender palm in my own, and we ducked down a narrow, graffiti-covered passage that would take us to a safe house a block away. The port was barely a quarter mile from here, but circumstances had changed. We would have to try again in a few hours.

As we rounded the corner, a figure in a black uniform spotted us. It emerged from the shadows, a sleek silhouette against the neon backdrop. Its face was obscured by a black visor. Was it human or machine? It approached with graceful, almost ethereal movements.

The Minder spoke, its voice a cutting, crisp sound that sliced through the air like a blade. "Good evening, Citizens."

Without hesitation, I spun around and ran in the opposite direction, pulling Soria along with me. Soria's hand tightened around mine as we sprinted down the narrow alleyway, the sound of the Minder's footsteps echoing behind us.

The drone's whirring propellers approached. "Halt," the Minder boomed. "You have been warned."

We burst out onto a crowded Tchoupitoulas street, elbowing through the throngs of passersby and merchants. I cast a glance over my shoulder. The Minder had vanished into the ether. In the distance, the port's tall cranes and stacks of containers loomed over the Mississippi. We had no choice now but to press on and reach the docks.

Sweat dripped down my back as we ran, our feet pounding against the jagged pavement. The port was now within sight, and I could see the silhouette of the boat waiting for us at the dock. We were almost there. I could hear the water lapping against the hull of the boat, its engine idling in the darkness.

As we approached the side entrance, a figure materialized from the shadows. The Minder, with its obsidian uniform, glistened in the dim light. "This is your second warning," it alerted, raising a sleek weapon in our direction. "I am authorized to use lethal force should you continue to resist."

Soria and I were trapped. The thud of heavy boots echoed behind us as more Minders arrived. We were encircled now. I glanced over at Soria, searching her face for signs of betrayal. Had I been deceived by her beauty? Had she led me down this treacherous path, using me as her pawn? But the raw emotion etched onto her face was unmistakable. As the Minder drew nearer, she flinched.

"Soria Torres, prepare for interrogation; your compliance is mandatory," it boomed, the words dripping with venom. "These proceedings are being recorded for posterity. You are being charged with sedition, sabotage, and eluding authorities. How do you plead?" The Minder's tone was harsh and unforgiving.

Soria stayed silent, a tear welling up in her eye. The Minder reached out and wrapped his gloved hand around her delicate wrist. She gasped in pain.

"Easy now," I said. "She's complying."

The black visor slowly turned in my direction. "Silence," it interjected, its voice cold and metallic.

"How do you plead to the charges, Ms. Torres?"

"Sounds like your decision has already been made," I countered.

The Minder's visor flashed red as it spoke. "Eluding an agent of the state is a crime of the highest order. Those who attempt it have no place in civilized society."

"I'd like to speak to my personal counsel before things go any further," I said.

"Your sense of humor appears to be just as poor as your judgment. Get down on the ground and assume the position."

Soria and I exchanged desperate looks, her eyes searching me for a solution, but I had nothing. We both slowly dropped to our knees.

A blinding flash of light illuminated the port, followed by the deafening roar of an explosion. The Minder stumbled backward, its weapon falling to the ground. I turned to see the other black-clad figures glitching out before tumbling to the pavement. In the confusion, a door to the port building flew open, and a muscular, bearded man extended his hand. Soria and I sprinted towards him and ducked inside as the heavy steel door slammed behind us. The bearded man gruffly ushered us down a hallway and onto a waiting trawler. We leaped aboard just as it pushed away from the dock.

I collapsed onto the deck, gasping for breath. Soria's face ran pale, her eyes wide in disbelief. My mind was still racing, trying to process what had just transpired. Small-scale EMP attack devices were something I had only heard rumors of but had never seen.

"You'll need these," the bearded man grunted as he dropped two life jackets at our feet. "There's a storm up ahead."

Soria turned to me, catching her breath. "Where are they taking us?"

"I don't know," I replied. And I didn't. I had delivered countless freedom seekers to the port but had never taken the leap myself. Like Soria, I had held onto my past, comfortable in the world I had known.

As the boat cut through the dark waters of the Mississippi River, I looked back at the city we were leaving behind. The neon glow of the skyscrapers and the blaring sirens of the patrols faded into the distance. It was a world that we had once known, but one that we could never return to. The Great Schism has indeed occurred, and we were now decidedly part of the other side that dared to dream of a better world, a world where freedom and possibility still held sway.

11

Transit

TechnologieKultur

Minimum Satsflow Level

Adrenaline

Viktor.Adler.Are000187 peeled out of his training gear in the tiny hygiene pod. When he heard the first dull thud on the door of his sub-habitat, his adrenaline spiked. The next instant, the metal plate crashed to the floor, bent out of recognition. The Areopolis security guards trampled it as they rushed in.

Halfway dressed in his tight GraviBall overalls, he lunged forward to block the access to his computer terminal. He tripped over a dangling sleeve, and his outstretched arm was intercepted and twisted behind his back before he had even hit the floor. With his cheek pressed to the smooth, cool surface, he watched, together with his visitors, as countless lines of evidence ran down the screen. His body squirmed under the guard's expert grip, and his legs kicked violently. He screamed and started up in his hibernation pod with a pounding heart and splitting headache.

So, it wasn't just a horror story that transit sleep always ended with a shock-dream. Horror, it seemed, was needed to scare the life back into immobilized space vegetables. The roar in Viktor.Adler.Transit402's ears gradually subsided to the inevitable background hum that reminded him of his dependence on life support systems. At the same rate as the air flowed into his claustrophobic cabin, his Satsflow streamed right into the operator's pool.

Though his head had cleared, he couldn't get rid of the stale taste of two weeks of vegetative state lingering in his mouth — the official aftertaste of minimum Satsflow travel. *At least I won't have to taste this gloop here,* Viktor thought as he unplugged the nutrient solution tube, licking his finger anyway. He retched with a grimace and shuddered, while he took off the wiring that had stimulated his muscles during hibernation.

Hamster wheel

After the health checks, Viktor.Adler.Transit402 appeared at the door of Veronica.Valdez.Transit373, waving his hand over the proximity sensor. The door opened to reveal a short woman with dark brown eyes, who had been introduced to him as Veronica.Valdez.LaE00449, barely a Martian year ago. She looked a bit worn after the vegetative phase, but the laugh lines in her round face immediately made him comfortable.

"I still can't believe," he interjected before she could even greet him, "that Areopolis' regulators are sending me back to Earth like that!"

It was the continuation of their pre-hibernation conversation. She added, "Just stop whining! The board of La Esperanza made the same fuss about it. Otherwise, I wouldn't be hanging out in this semi-coma for almost three hundred days now." Her voice softened again, but the bitterness was still evident. "Why did you have to get caught diverting those measly communication fibers?"

While the sturdy Viktor kept his silence, the crackling thundercloud stomping beside him with clenched fists went on. "What am I supposed to do on Earth? I haven't been there for more than fourteen Earth years. I was so glad to finally get away. And now? My whole career is ruined. Who on

Earth needs an exo-botanist to tell them all about subsurface agriculture on Mars, huh?!"

"They'll never be able to establish real self-sufficiency on that rusty ball without you."

His clumsy attempt to boost Veronica's self-esteem didn't help, and she just continued to march silently beside him. Her strained lips and furrowed brow didn't encourage any further comments.

Their footsteps echoed through the tunnel. The tunnel's rotation provided artificial gravity and always seemed to lead uphill. Although Viktor towered over his companion, they had fallen into lock-step by now. The hamster wheel was the only exercise available during the short waking periods of transit.

Later, Veronica told him about an engineer from AsiaPacifiCorp in the Elysium volcano who had been fired over his collaborative efforts with her city, La Esperanza. She promised to get Viktor invited to the medium Satsflow level of the ship somehow, so they could meet.

Medium Satsflow Level

Sweat

Viktor.Adler.Are000187 knew that thousands of spectators spread all over Mars (and probably even a few areophilic Earthlings with a few minutes of signal delay) would be watching the game. Images from La Esperanza's rotating gravidrome streamed every conceivable viewing perspective onto the screens of GraviBall fans who were eager to see if his Areopolis Speartips would wrest the title from the Enrobinados in their rusty brown overalls.

Torn between gravity and centrifugal force, Viktor propped his hands on his knees and took deep breaths. Sweat trickled down through his gray overalls. The Areopolis Speartips had just scored a spectacular goal, and for a moment, he visualized how the Satsflow of the enthusiastic spectators streamed to the gravidrome's operators and, of course, to him and his teammates. He was unaware of his maximally inconvenient position in front of the muzzle from which a new ball would be shot. All he heard was a resounding *fupp* as it went off, pulling his leg out from under him so fast that he slammed backward onto the playing surface with the back of his head.

A bright flash split his head, and his ears rang with thunder. He jolted up and found himself in the tangle of cables and hoses of his transit booth.

Encounters

With white knuckles, Viktor clung to the handle next to the glass door. He waited for a transport pod to take him back to his level through the longitudinal axis of the ship. His permit was about to expire, and he was afraid of being penalized with medium Satsflow. As he hung there, longing for a little artificial gravity, he thought of his encounter with Kenshi. He had introduced himself as Kenshi.Matsuyama.APC00841, only to immediately correct himself and replace his old affiliation with the apparently deeply shameful .Transit159. Just one of his many quirks, like regularly apologizing for his 'inadequate' English, although he spoke it with an engineer's precision.

Most surprising to Viktor was Kenshi's reluctance to pursue a position in the free and open-source city. With his qualifications and the collaborative tendencies for which he had been fired, he seemed like a perfect fit. That's what Viktor himself would have done, at least, if the clause in his contract with Areopolis had not explicitly imposed his return to Earth – immediately and at his own expense – in case of contract breach.

Even though one had to admit that the open-source unicorns were a pretty colorful and wild bunch, his tight-lipped refusal to join "such an unpredictable omnium-gatherum" seemed a bit excessive. Kenshi was a passionate engineer and the unicorns were known for making any kind of junk work, fly, drive, or drill.

Echoing through a connecting tube, the animated conversation of two other passengers approached.

Between the laughter, he made out a semi-familiar conglomeration of words from English, French, and various other languages becoming ever more common on Mars. More and more people from consensus-based regions of the southern Terran hemisphere are drawn to Mars these days. He had, therefore, been trying to learn OpenAustrale for quite a while. With a little effort, he was able to translate most of it on the fly.

Viktor swung around on his own axis and had to look twice when the two young men pushed off from the edge of the tube to glide over to him. Dressed identically, they resembled each other to a hair. The large multicolored emblem on their chests immediately caught his eye. It was the head of a unicorn encircled with:

`* Ubuntu * Urban * Unicorn * init 40.04 *`

It was easy to verify that the twins were indeed inhabitants of the open-source city that had begun two Martian decades earlier as an inflatable habitat.

Their IDs: Anthony.Okafor.U3_038776 and Gregory.Okafor.U3_038777.

They gave him a friendly nod and were about to continue their conversation when Gregory elbowed his look-alike, causing them to drift apart a bit. "Ant, look! Do you know who that is?"

Viktor translated to himself. Anthony squinted his eyes for a moment and bit his lip before his face brightened. Immediately, it burst out of him. "Der Adler! That's the eagle from the Areopolis Speartips, Greg!"

The correctly identified GraviBall player would not have been surprised to hear them break into supportive chants for their unicorns. Instead, they started joking around with flapping arms about how spectacular the "Reverse Eagle" or — with respect to his German heritage — the "Rückwärts-Adler" had been.

That involuntary stunt had been named after him when the GraviBall team of La Esperanza defended their title, mostly because it left Areopolis without its top scorer.

Once the twins got a grip on themselves again, they admitted that they would actually like to have a throwing technique as good as his and were, in fact, big fans, although he obviously was affiliated with the wrong city.

They had, more than once, streamed some extra Satsflow to him through their spectator channels in appreciation of a particularly impressive move.

With a tender *Kshhhhhhhhhh*, the glass door slid open, and all three shimmied into the softly lit transport pod. Until they were all strapped in, there was a moment of concentrated silence. Viktor used the pause to properly phrase, in perfect OpenAustrale, his question about the twins' reasons for traveling to Earth.

"U3 University gave us a scholarship," Anthony replied.

Gregory went on. "Whoever is born in the Urban Unicorn on Mars is sent to Earth for four years on their twelfth Martian birthday to learn about the other open-source cities."

The ride ended quickly, and they clambered out of the capsule. The twins asked their new best friend if he wanted to join them to explore the minimum Satsflow level and afterward have a beer at the Gravity Bar on their own level — tapped from their Satspool, of course.

It got a little awkward when Viktor had to explain that he wasn't allowed to leave that level without an official invitation and permission. They asked him how it had come about that he had to return to Earth under such circumstances.

"It's really a long story," he said. "But I'll tell you what happened during my next waking period if you get the bar and beer issue sorted out for me."

At that point, they parted ways, patting each other's shoulders vigorously. As he swung into a tube that branched off to his destination, the two unicorns sent a few more cheers after him.

On the way to the medical bay, he wondered what it would be like to play GraviBall in unicorn overalls.

On arrival, he scanned his ID with little enthusiasm to complete the final bio-check before being put back into transit sleep. Instead of the expected assignment, however, he received a notice that his sleep period had been delayed by a full day.

Somewhat concerned about the extra Satsflow that using the hamster wheel, mess hall, and hygiene pods meant for a full day, he inquired about the reason for the change. The answer was memorably succinct and took the form of an encoded personal message to him:

Amr.Khamees.NeMa00017 is expecting you tomorrow at 15:00 at the maximum Satsflow level Unit 0.0.3. [N.B.: Satsflow temporarily suspended]

Viktor reread the message a couple of times and furrowed his brow in puzzlement. *Who is this guy?* he thought and went straight to his computer terminal to find out. His information request immediately returned a glaring *access restricted* notification. He switched the terminal off with a deep sigh and curled up in his bunk. Brushing tubes and cables aside, Viktor closed his eyes and soon fell into a profound natural sleep.

Maximum Satsflow Level

Lemonade

Viktor.Adler.Are000187 remained perpetually fascinated by the Hypagora of Areopolis. He traversed the underground vault as he always did on his way to the communication node of the city, touching the lush greenery that grew along the paths. He slowed and stopped where Klara.Balabanova.Are000865 stood early in the morning whenever she was not engaged in her primary activity. Her fingers danced on the old-fashioned transverse flute, which looked like an original from Earth. Between them, the melody flowed in one direction, and some Satsflow in the other, until he had to hurry off to be on time for work in the node.

In the center of the dome, he stopped once more and looked up. His outgoing Satsflow for city operations slowed a bit as the artificial lighting faded and the smallish sun rose above him. It shone through the oval pool of water in the dome ceiling into the heart of the city, dyeing it with the color of blood-orange lemonade.

The glow gradually brightened to a fluorescent white, while a faint beeping to his left started to impose itself on his consciousness. Viktor lolled in his bunk. He even turned onto his other side for a few more minutes without getting tangled in cables or tubes.

Confrontation

Viktor had checked his Satsmeter constantly since he got up, and the level had indeed remained unchanged. Not only the Satsflow for the extras of being awake, such as an artificial gravity shower, but also the ubiquitous minimum Satsflow for the life support systems seemed to be frozen for him today.

He had still no clue who this Amr.Khamees.NeMa00017 might be. Maybe Veronica knew something about him, but she was already vegetating in her transit cabin again.

Very rarely was there a leak of any information about the activities and inhabitants of New Madina, conveniently situated in the middle of the ice-rich highlands of Arabia Terra on Mars.

New Madina probably took the "private" part most seriously of all the free private cities on Mars, which was, except for the Urban Unicorn, already proprietary to its core.

The door sighed *Kshhhhhhhhhh* again. As Viktor swung out of the capsule that had hauled him along the longitudinal axis of the ship, he marveled at the amount of space the craft encased at this end. After adjusting his coordinate system, he checked his watch for the seventh time in the past five minutes and immediately headed to Unit 0.0.3.

Once there, he found no door, but rather a veritable portal with an ID next to it and an abstract family crest above it. The common pleb wondered what it represented.

Just as Viktor was pondering how to announce his presence, the door halves slid apart, and he found himself face to face with a discreetly dressed gentleman with a precisely trimmed gray beard. The man clasped his hands behind his back and examined Viktor with his profound eyes.

Mr. Khamees beckoned his tall visitor into the hallway and further along toward his study. Viktor experienced a pleasant increase in centrifugal gravity on the way there and became aware of the perfect silence when it abruptly ended with, "Isn't it fascinating, Mr. Adler, that a series of exercises devised to prevent low-gravity muscular atrophy could, within a few years, become the focal point of a global identity for all the Martian colonies?"

Viktor didn't know the appropriate response but nodded slowly.

"You are not only an outstanding GraviBall player, as far as I know, but originally brought other qualifications with you to Mars," he added.

"Yes, I signed on as a telecommunications engineer on Mars and have spent the last few years working on synchronizing the blockchain between Earth and Mars. After all, our Satsflow transactions on the second and third layers need to be settled regularly. But we both seem to know that," Viktor replied.

Amr.Khamees.NeMa00017 remained silent for a moment before he continued in a grave voice. "I know why you were put in this transit ship by the city regulators."

Viktor swallowed hard. How did he know about the proof-of-origin algorithm that would indicate the spatial distance between an ASIC mining a new bitcoin block and the isochronic center of hash in the block header? The regulators in Areopolis had good reason to keep the lid on the discovery that got him and Veronica booted from Mars. This innovation would effectively eliminate the threat of Terran stakeholders leveraging their enormous resources to hash-bomb any Martian fork of the blockchain.

Mr. Khamees gave him a feisty look and asked him in his most condescending tone, "So, it's not enough for you deplorable lot that we let you stream your Satsflow between all individuals, settlements, or spacecraft on and around Mars for free? How dare you disregard the primacy of Earth, the Genesis planet."

That triggered Viktor, who physically towered over his host, and the words just burst out of him. "If Mars is ever going to have its own identity, it must come through the cooperation of all cities, whether free, private, open-source, or whatever. It needs global trade, infrastructure, and self-sufficiency to develop an economy instead of just implementing the business interests of Earth managers. If settlement of Martian Satsflow transactions accrues transaction fees only on Earth, it is taxation for which Mars receives nothing in return."

"You hit the nail on the head!" Amr Khamees returned with a dramatic change of attitude. Beaming at the confused revolutionary, he went on to explain. "I discussed your ideas with my eldest brother, who runs the family business in New Madina. Unfortunately, he shares neither your idealism nor my love for the red planet. I've been ordered back to Earth to rethink my loyalties to our family and Terran business operations."

Amr snorted contemptuously and added, "I won't, though. I'm already mobilizing my network and considerable resources to return to Mars as soon as possible. Mars deserves a flourishing society, but in order to achieve that, I will need a team."

12

The Fable of the Tyrant Alchemist

Ioni Appelberg

Elysium

Part I: The Failed Harvest

First, the quiet came. Each day, the markets grew quieter, the people hungrier. A farmer stared at wilted crops, dread settling in his heart. In a kingdom once resplendent with bountiful markets and sky-reaching monuments, it was the first failed harvest that marked the end of affluence and the beginning of collapse.

By the second year, market traders stood before empty stalls, goods long gone, rotten, or ruined. Jobless men prowled, foraging the streets for vermin and meager scraps of sustenance. Young women offered their time for bread, their eyes hollow in the act. Widows, too, entered strangers' homes, bartering themselves for their children's next meal. Orphans, gaunt and brittle, drew meaningless shapes in the dust, their laughter a forgotten memory.

Rumors surged like wind through dry grass. Scapegoats were blamed; superstitions gripped the masses. By the third year, it was known to the people and the king alike, that there would be no more monuments erected, only tombstones.

The king called the council, heavy with despair. In a room filled with tension, ministers and knights sat around a table.

Before them stood the realm's wisest farmer, a man worn from years of labor, hunger, and loss. His voice echoed the deep hunger that gripped the kingdom. "Your Majesty, the land is weary. It cries for respite." His words hung heavy in the room, laying bare the reality of their fate.

Part II: The Devil's Pact

In the dimly lit chamber, a palpable tension filled the air. The alchemist, servant to the king and master of arcane arts, stepped into the flickering candlelight. He held an aged book, its scent mingling with the murk of looming spells. With a voice both smooth and haunting, he shattered the quiet, his words a ripple through walls of stone.

"Sire, alchemy is our last refuge. We can harvest time to feed the earth," he began, revealing a parchment inked with cryptic circles and lines. "Each citizen, willingly or not, will spare a mere whisper of their years. An unnoticeable offering. With careful alchemy, we can replenish our lands and fortify your reign with the alms of myriad souls." Leaning closer, he whispered the words that would redefine their civilization: a devil's proposal intended for the king but felt by all. "Consider, my lord, a reign without end, each year stretched beyond nature's limits, a kingdom fed by the borrowed time of its people. No more famine. No more want."

The court waited, their faces etched with fear and desperate hope, ready to tread any path that led away from the abyss of famine.

For a moment, the king was a statue, his face a veil behind which storms brewed. Finally, exhaling a breath heavy with fate, he spoke. "We've endured enough hardship. We shall seize a future that knows no famine."

The air thickened as the alchemist retreated with a solemn nod, the weight of the chosen path settling in.

He reopened his tome and voiced the incantation. Arcane syllables filled the room, weaving a desperate gambit to salvage their decaying kingdom. Thus, in the dark hours of the night, they sealed a new covenant that would reverberate through generations.

Part III: Vines and Moss

In the decades that followed the alchemist's rites, the kingdom thrived like spring after a bitter winter. Fields were lush year-round, erasing hunger and the memories of famine. Marketplaces bustled, no longer a graveyard of commerce but a carnival of exotic goods from every corner of the world. The air seemed perfumed with prosperity — healthy river fish, basilisk meats, and spices from faraway lands. A century rolled by. The king, unaging, stretched his influence over land and sea, turning his realm into an empire. Statues weathered, and languages evolved, but the king abided.

Yet, a toll was exacted. Years stolen from the people, a time tax woven into the fabric of life. The spell fed both earth and crown, cloaking decay with a veneer of wealth. The young wore the faces of old men, their eyes wise beyond their years. Every heartbeat was a sacrifice, a quiet tax to feed the castles of power.

Then came the year when the land rebelled. Coaxed by the spell, the soil had given until it couldn't, its silent pleas for rest ignored. The land remembered stolen seasons, now determined to settle old debts. Crops withered; rivers soured. Beasts waned, their numbers thinning. The kingdom, starved of Earth's gifts, unraveled — not from human revolt but from the silent insurrection of the land that once fed them.

With hunger as the harbinger, society fractured. Chaos and mass confusion swallowed the land, a virulent blight not even alchemy could stem. Witch hunts raged for a merciless century, fire consuming flesh and innocence. Men's strength wilted, and armies disbanded. Women, walking in the agonizing footsteps of their famine-haunted foremothers, bartered touch for bread.

Monuments lay buried under vines and moss. Fertile lands turned barren. Schools emptied, their echoing halls abandoned, and children torn from learning were sent to farm dying lands. Art withered. Painters swapped colors for shades of gray and soon vanished altogether. An ever-growing class of soil-bound serfs supplanted teachers, bards, and engineers.

Desperate, the eternal king sought another spell. He asked the people not for mere years but decades. The alchemist obliged, conjuring another spell from dark incantations. Yet the ravaged earth, too spent to yield, exacted a monstrous price: lifetimes for scraps. People, skeletal, on the verge of vanishing, offered their very existence. A silence settled, a collective sacrifice borne not in rebellion but in surrender.

Part IV: Clara The Torchbearer

In the land between sleep and waking, Clara was a child again, standing at the threshold of a room aglow with amber light. Her mother ground herbs, the wooden table before her strewn with books, vials, and leaves. "These aren't just leaves and liquids," her mother said. "They're doors to the gardens of your mind." Her words sank into Clara like stones into deep water.

She woke to a gusting wind. Her dream dissolved like morning mist. The sun broke over the kingdom, time's toll evident in every vine-entangled ruin. Light spilled into her chamber.

Clara's room was modest: a bed, a wardrobe, a desk. On it lay a lone candle and scattered books that whispered of the kingdom's past grandeur and freedoms now lost. It was her mother's notes and books, crafted in the quiet, away from royal eyes — a puzzle to decipher, a quest still yearning for footsteps.

She draped a linen robe over her shoulders and approached the window, Her fingers stained with ink from the writings of yesterday. Below, people shuffling through life, joyless and muted.

The spell cast long ago had become an oppressive, faceless dictator. It promised bread but dealt only crumbs, a tarnished magic now woven into the kingdom's culture as enduringly as its ancient stone walls and teeming graveyards.

She remembered the cold spring day she put her mother in the ground. The earth was hard, the casket simple. The tombstone bore the words: 'Seed in Drought.'

The chambermaid standing beside her asked what it meant.

"Her wish," Clara answered. Her face gave nothing away, her thoughts a distant country.

From her room, Clara watched the people below — eyes down, spirits broken. Clara was not like the others. She carried an inner fire, gifted by her mother, a quiet revolt against a world turned gray.

In her room's sanctuary, amid ink and parchment molded by hands long stilled, Clara found traces of a freer past, free from famine and theft of years. A past now entrusted to her. As she flipped through the timeworn pages of an ancient tome, something caught Clara's eye. In the margins of the text, a note penned in her mother's hand:

"For Clara — Elric is the keeper of truths that free us. Go where I could not. Find him."

Below it, a tender signature, her mother's name etched in ink.

The name 'Elric' stirred a latent memory, a shared secret often spoken by her mother. Filled with a sense of destiny, Clara closed her worn books and left her chamber.

At the age of twenty, for the first time, she ventured beyond the confining walls of her castle. Guided by remnants of forgotten eras, she set forth to unearth truths long interred but never wholly erased. Her compass drew her toward the Whispering Pines, a land untouched by the alchemist's dark arts and, as her mother had often mentioned, the rumored dwelling of Elric.

Part V: Far to Go

Clara walked through towns void of kindness, over land stripped of life. Each day sculpted her in the likeness of the land she traversed — a leaner body, hardened hands, face etched by sun and wind.

Thirteen days out, Clara trudged through the ashen remains of a town, its name forgotten, its history lost. Empty buildings sagged under the weight of time, their hollow frames like gravestones against the evening sky. Vacant faces, like clock dials without hands, glanced through her, never at her.

Spying a run-down tavern, she cautiously stepped inside. The door whined on rusted hinges. She eased onto a splintered stool. "Bread," she rasped. The innkeeper, a bloated man with eyes like rotted plums, flung stale crust onto the counter. Her teeth sank into the stale crust, her body weeping for nourishment.

The room stank of unwashed bodies and sour ale. In a dim corner, men gambled their souls on dice, their faces marred by desperation and greed. As she made to leave, talk stilled, and eyes tracked her. A rough hand seized her wrist.

"Far to go?" The words, a mockery.

Her eyes darted to the innkeeper, pleading for an ally. His gaze, cold, turned away. "Yes, far," she replied, stalling.

Then, violence. Teeth, nails, a taste of blood. Outmanned, her screams died in cruel laughter. Her clothes yielded, torn in the contest of her humiliation.

After the degradation, she stepped outside and into the soft rain of the night. Her path now carried weight measured in more than miles.

Ahead, barren land stretched mercilessly. A fleeting image of her mother's face offered a brief moment of comfort. She tilted her head back, letting rain droplets fall onto her tongue to dilute the bitterness that swelled within her. The night urged in tones only darkness knows. Turn back, it murmured.

But she walked on. Her will was a defiant ember, the last flicker of light in a world teetering at the edge of oblivion, its humanity long forfeited.

Part VI: Elric

After weeks of traversing a harsh expanse, gaunt but unbroken, she found herself beneath the Whispering Pines. As she approached, she carried more than her own weight. She embodied her mother's enduring hope and her land's final prayer for redemption.

Elric greeted her at the doorway. "You've come," he said, leading her inside, the room warmed by the fire in the stone hearth.

Her eyes roved from the firelight dancing on the walls to the shelves laden with books. A staircase twisted upward, its banister engraved with ancient symbols.

"Your homeland withers," Elric said, drawing from his pipe, the wood old and marked by years. The scent of herbs, a blend cultivated through many seasons, sharpened the mind as it filled the room.

"The spell," she confirmed.

"Mmm," he exhaled, his eyes shifting to the fireplace, wood popping in the heat. "Your forebears knew better days. Days without sacrifice."

"The legends spoke truth, then?"

"Indeed."

"Did you know I was coming?"

"I've waited twenty years. This isn't our first meeting."

"We've met before?"

"Once, when you were but a newborn. Your mother and I collaborated. We worked on a potion that siphons the power of nature to protect the truth in our world, to shield it from alchemy and dark spells."

Elric opened a small cabinet beside the hearth. From it, he took an empty wooden chalice and a stoppered glass vial. Uncorking the vial, he poured a golden liquid into the chalice, the firelight making it shimmer. "This elixir hails from untarnished lands, free from the alchemy that poisons your realm. One sip and illusions shatter, transforming soul and society alike."

"What is it called?" she asked.

He looked at her intently. "Elysium," he said, the word hanging heavy in the room. "It's both the end and the beginning of your journey. You must experience it to understand. Drink."

She sipped the brew; it tasted of nothing. Soon, as she nestled by the fire, the walls took a breath, and the world sharpened as if coming into focus for the first time. The air thickened into a heavy mist. Her fingers danced through it, each ripple sending colors splashing around like bioluminescent whispers. She floated, her body dissolving, her name a distant echo.

Elric's gaze turned to the fire, shadows playing across his face. "Elysium shows only what one needs to see, no more, no less," he said, his voice a gentle wave against the shores of her uncertainty. "In my own experience with Elysium, I saw a torchbearer in the veil of time, a young soul with the spark to dispel the darkness shrouding your land." His eyes found Clara's. "But the torchbearer had to come to me, the journey forging the resolve. Had I sought you out sooner, before your heart was ready, Elysium's truth would have been a burden too heavy."

As the reality of his words sank in, Clara felt the weight of the years, the faces of the countless lives lost to the alchemist's dark magic flashing before her eyes. "And the elixir... why not share it sooner?"

Elric sighed, his eyes drifting to the ancient books lining the shelves. "Elysium's truth is a double-edged blade. In the wrong hands, it could cut through the fabric of reality, leaving wounds that might never heal. Your kingdom..." he gestured vaguely towards the window, "... it wasn't ready. But now, the ground has been furrowed by suffering, ready to receive the truth about the universe, the spell, the suffering."

The walls breathed with a rhythm older than time. She looked at her hands moving through the bioluminescent mist, each movement sending ripples across the room. Tendrils of light danced in the air, ethereal spirits beckoning her towards another realm.

"But why?" Clara pressed, her presence deepening with each breath. "Why involve yourself?"

Elric's eyes softened. "I once lived in your kingdom, fleeing when I realized the spell's plague. Your mother and I... we shared a vision of a world free from dark alchemy. But more than a promise to an old friend, it's a battle against the grasp of evil spells, a grasp threatening to choke the essence of life and freedom from this world. It's a battle," he said as he looked at Clara with a profound earnestness, "that now passes to you."

Suddenly, reality shattered, and her soul twisted and warped through a portal faster and faster until she touched the core of the cosmos.

Here, in a land beyond words, beyond the confines of time and space, she witnessed the birth and demise of the universe. With each breath, a star was born and died; each blink saw the rise and fall of civilizations. Like a photon racing at light speed through the cosmos, untouched by time, she beheld the entirety of all that ever was and will be.

Peering beyond the infinitely small, she saw the source code of the universe, equations as living tendrils of light materializing into particles, planets, and stars. The universe, a symphony of mathematical elegance, its physicality a melody resonating along the strings of her consciousness.

She floated amidst the cosmic code, orchestrating the universe — the planets, the voids, the unseen forces weaving through them — and she was one with all. She was the universe gazing at itself. Beyond the veil of mortality, she saw endless realms, death a mere doorway. In that boundless expanse, she brushed against the face of the divine.

A golden phoenix took form before her.

"I am Veritas," it spoke, not in words, but in a language of complex geometry.

It exposed the grim truths of her lands, the Great Famine, and the enslaving spell — counterfeit prosperity bought at the terrible price of human years.

"How do we break free?" Clara's voice carried the untold suffering of generations.

"Simple," the phoenix intoned. "Don't battle the alchemist or his spell; you won't win. Acknowledge the illusion. Tend to your own gardens, and reliance on the alchemist and the king fades. Elysium shields you — body and mind — from the spell's reach."

As the vision dissolved, Clara found herself back on the wooden floor, her head cushioned by a pillow. The urgency of her quest snapped her back to reality, a newfound resolve kindling in her chest.

"I see now," she breathed, her voice steady. "I know what I must do."

Elric nodded, a sage with a deep understanding of the paths of the universe. "Yes, but first, tea. Regain your strength. You have a long journey ahead," he said, anchoring them both in a moment of calm before the impending storm of change.

Part VII: The Wayfarer's Hearth

After days of navigating barren expanses, Clara entered a cobblestone town as twilight settled. Figures lined the street, some alive, some not, most in limbo — too tired to beg, too frail to feed. Candlelight flickered from the windows of a tavern, illuminating well-fed faces. "The Wayfarer's Hearth," read the sign above the door.

She approached. The door creaked open to admit her, wafting out stale beer and the scent of roast meat. Her fingers twitched involuntarily, memories of weeks ago crawling up her spine, but her body ached for sustenance, for warmth. Holding her satchel close, safeguarding the vial of Elysium, she chose a chair at an empty table and settled in. Soon enough, food appeared.

The man who had set her meal before her took the adjacent seat with deliberate ease, his eyes lingering on her satchel. Her pulse quickened.

"You carry a weight, wanderer," he said.

"Or hope," she countered, her grip on her satchel unyielding.

A glass shattered. Drunkards stumbled into their table, a wave of mead sweeping over worn wood. Clara's heart surged as the man's fingers brushed her satchel, pulling the vial from its sanctuary. "Hope carries its own burden," he said.

"The hope of my people is in that vial," she shot back, her voice stripped bare.

"This is Elysium," he said, his words like barbs. "At what cost, wanderer, do you think Elysium will save your people?"

Doubt snaked around her convictions. Was she the bearer of emancipation or a harbinger of calamity? Was her land ready for Elysium? "You know it?" she asked.

"I know it," he said, eyeing it closely.

"Return it," she commanded.

He handed over the vial. "The road to freedom is paved with the stones of responsibility. I wouldn't want to walk in your shoes."

She nodded, heavy but resolute. Clara left as quietly as she'd come, meal untouched, mission intact.

The night took her in. She cast a final glance back at a room oblivious to her departure. That night, she'd sleep under indifferent stars, closer to home but adrift in certainty, carrying the weight of a thousand stones of untold responsibility, a Trojan's shroud for her people, a destiny unasked.

Part VIII: This is Elysium

Under a storm-heavy sky, Clara returned home. In her pocket was Elysium; in her mind, a plan that required Harold — an old friend and a knight by trade.

In the guild hall, Harold sat among knights and minstrels, a goblet in hand. "Look at this," Clara said, pushing the vial across the table without ceremony. Her words pierced the tavern's noise as she recounted her journey.

Harold looked at her, then at the vial. "You mean to say that one day, this will help us fight the spell?"

"No," said Clara, her voice deep with a new knowing. "It means one day, we won't have to."

"Heresy," Harold said. "You're risking death."

"So are we all," she answered.

"They'll burn you at the stake."

"If I'm right, they won't."

"A trial then, regardless," Harold said, his gaze dropping to the vial as the tavern's jovial banter became a distant echo for them both.

"So be it," Clara said, meeting his gaze. She leaned in, her fingers resting on his scarred knuckles. "The farms take our children. It's not right."

"It's how things are."

"It's how things *were*."

"A trial will not be lenient, Clara. I can't let you bring this to the king."

"Not the king. The people." She continued. "But don't trust me. See for yourself." Her eyes locked onto his. "Drink," she said, her words echoing Elric's.

Harold hesitated but finally drank. His eyes widened. He gripped the edge of the wooden table, his knuckles turning white. A sort of vacant gaze overcame him as if he'd journeyed to someplace far.

When the Elysium vision receded, he opened his eyes and looked at her anew, seeing the world for the first time again. He glanced around the hall as though it were a foreign land, his eyes lingering on the mundane — a crack in the table, the smudged goblet, a flickering torch on the wall—with awe and wonder. She knew then that they stood as one. Two visionaries shouldering the burden of transforming the world, ready to shepherd their people into a revolutionary dawn.

In the square, the stone eyes of old heroes watched. A crowd formed, silenced by expectation and unaccustomed to the art of public speaking. Autumn leaves swirled at their feet.

"A new dawn!" Harold broke the silence. "Generations sacrificed, giving years for meager sustenance. But the land wants not our years —

only our care and periodic reverence. The tales of a time without the toll of hunger, without a tax on life itself, from before the Great Famine, are not myths. They are forgotten chapters of our history, now on the verge of being rewritten."

He raised the vial. Sunlight mirrored in its gold. "This is Elysium."

Part IX: A Revolution Takes Shape

In the fading light of day, Harold and Clara stood by a murmuring brook, leaves rustling at their feet in quiet revolt. Faces young and old assembled around them, each one a silent rebellion against the servitude that taxed their years.

They drank, the chalice passing from hand to hand, a new ritual born. With each gathering, the numbers swelled; with each sip, more souls entwined. Slowly, yet with unyielding certainty, the kingdom shifted over the years. It changed not through a coup or uprising but through a still, relentless force, like water eroding stone. As the seasons passed and more villagers imbibed the Elysian brew, the weight of their invisible chains lessened, their atoms scattering into the evening air.

Shielded now, villagers sowed their own gardens and sanctuaries from the alchemist's dominion. Bountiful harvests followed, and hope supplanted despair. Word of the blooming private gardens spread like wildflowers, and fields once cursed by dark alchemy lay fallow and forgotten.

And there, by the unassuming brook, a revolution took shape. The soft sounds of the stream became an earthbound anchor for the myriad souls who opened the door to walk in the cosmic gardens of their minds. Each ritual added another stitch in the fabric of a new dawn; each sip, another brushstroke on the canvas of a world remade.

Part X: The Old Man

A decade drifted by. With each soul that tasted Elysium, the fetters of the old world loosened. The alchemist's spell, once a yoke around their necks, now waned like thick morning fog, giving way to the warmth of the day. Fields once cursed now bore food, not dread. Families gathered around bountiful tables, words flowing freely, unveiled.

Each year, townsfolk met by the sword in the square. Harold's blade, the first monument raised in ages, stood as freedom's spine, the axis of their new world. An old man approached, his eyes dimmed by memories of famine, leading a boy by the hand. Their eyes met, a chasm bridged: one soul untarnished by hunger, the other haunted by its ghost.

The old man stepped forward, his fingers quivering on the hilt of the sword. "Clara, what becomes of us if the land fails us again?" Years of hardship wavered in his voice, the ghosts of famine flickering in his eyes.

"It could," Clara said, her voice steady as bedrock. "But it's different now. Our fields are wider, our hands more skilled. We're not trying to trick the earth with alchemy anymore. We speak in simple terms it understands — soil, sun, water, time."

Above, the alchemist's fortress loomed, its towers now marred with cracks. Clara looked up. Empty windows stared back, like dead eyes on a fallen beast. Old times had ended; new ones had begun.

Part XI: The Note

Dawn broke, casting new light over worn cobblestones. Clara moved through the marketplace as if through a dream. The scent of cinnamon and rich coffee filled the air as she ran her fingers down silken tassels and through powdery barrels of golden saffron. Voices haggled; her feet felt the earth's warm embrace.

Traders argued leisurely, their time no longer taxed by the spell. Children laughed, unburdened by field and plow.

Fields that once caged both young and old now released thinkers, builders, and creators. The horizon changed form — bridges leaped over waterways, and roads bound the land. Each stone laid was more than a fixture; it was a vow, a pact between the present and the future. It was today's promise to a future yet unborn, anchored by the prosperity that now bloomed under Elysium's sky.

As evening descended, the grand hall filled with voices unburdened by yesterday's sorrow. In a secluded corner, Clara and Harold exchanged words about the loftier truths Elysium had laid bare.

A courier emerged from the crowd, extending a sealed parchment. "For you, *mademoiselle*."

With a nod, Clara exchanged a coin for the note. Her eyes brightened as she absorbed the message:

> *"Only a true renaissance resounds to the Whispering Pines. Continue, in health and strength."*
>
> *– Elric*

She passed it to Harold, their eyes locking in wordless affirmation.

"The Whispering Pines acknowledge us," he finally said.

"And so, we continue," Clara replied, her voice unwavering, guided by truth.

In the hall's enveloping warmth, laughter, toasts, and spirited debates blended into a harmonious score — a sound that would have been foreign to their ancestors, a sound that marked the close of an era and the dawn of something profoundly new.

13

Digital Gold

Luciano Rocha

A Dog Day

A dog day afternoon. Not the movie, obviously, but the day that Max was having. The siren rang in his ears, and the car rocked and juddered along at more than 80km per hour. *Damn idiots,* Max thought. They'd interrupted his shopping in the middle of this chaos. He kept his eyes on the bike and his mind on finding his groceries when he got back to the store.

His partner leaned his whole torso outside the window, his hands clutching a shotgun. Taking aim at the two guys ahead of him was easy, as Kevin was a police skeet champion. The problem was shooting, since the whole city decided to occupy that road precisely at the time of the chase. Kevin himself had to dodge another motorcycle that was coming in the opposite direction and nearly clipped his gun — and half of his arm.

"Come on, Max, speed that shit up! They're almost losing us!"

"This is a car, not a 1200. I can't go around cutting all these idiots up!" Max's head exploded with pain, and his eyes were dry from focusing so hard on the bike.

Right ahead, the bandits returned fire with a pistol. One of the shots hit the blue light of the car, and the other whistled past the windshield.

The shot nearly knocked an oncoming Ram out of control. Max clung to the wheel as the bullet punched into one of the crates in the bay.

"Those guys... they must have looted as far as Mom's house because of this mess," Max said, giving the Ram driver a middle finger.

Suddenly, the motorcycle turned into an alley and almost disappeared from view. Max jammed on the brakes and brought the car to a stop. The curve was too sharp for the car and the lane too narrow. They would never pass by, and the bike kept accelerating. Kevin cursed the names of all the gods his old *abuela* had taught him. Then, Max floored the car and accelerated forward, turning into the next corner. He took the street parallel to the rubbish-filled alley.

"Max, are you crazy?! They'll get away."

"Kevin, you want to drive this crap car?"

"No!"

"So shut up and keep your gun ready."

Despite Kevin's resistance, Max had nothing to worry about — after all, he knew these streets like the back of his hand. He had never lived here, but he grew up in this sector, playing basketball with his school friends on the old court. But that was before assholes like those on the motorbike spoiled the neighborhood with drugs, guns, and robberies. Driving with concentration, Max knew they only had one road to take, and he would be waiting on the other side.

Max calculated that he had time to close the entrance to the alley and make the motorcycle crash into the side of the police car. No sooner said than done. As Max reached the end of the alley, he slammed into the bike that was halfway out of the alley. The blow made the motorcycle hit the wall, knocking the thugs to the side. One of them went down, knocked out, while the other hit his face and fell to the ground, groggy but still alive.

They almost got away, thought Max. But the police's job is to improvise, and once again, it worked. Kevin tended to the groggy passenger, and Max lunged for the passed-out driver by climbing onto his chest. He was unconscious but breathing.

"Is he alive, Max?" Kevin asked, putting the handcuffs on the other.

"Yes, he is. He's just blacked out, but maybe my 'alarm clock' will work on him," Max said. Grabbing the collar of the guy's T-shirt, he began to slap his face.

"Come on, idiot, wake up soon, we don't have time to wait for the princess," he said in a commanding voice.

The motorcyclist on the ground woke up, and Max saw him looking at the fallen motorcycle beside him, along with two pools of blood. Then the guy looked to the other side, where Kevin had already immobilized his partner in crime. A bruise had formed during the fall. Before waking him up properly, Max handcuffed the guy, who still tried to struggle but was met with a nice punch in the face. Max knew that police rules didn't allow officers to hit defendants who had already surrendered, but he didn't care. It was riot time, and he just wanted to send those two to jail and get back to his shopping stash.

"You are under arrest for assault. You have a right to an attorney. You have the right to remain silent, and anything you say can be used against you in court,"

"What?! This is ridiculous! How did you get into this alley? There is no driveway here."

"There isn't but there is an exit, and we were waiting for you there," said the second officer with his shotgun pointed at the two of them.

"How did you know that?" asked the man in handcuffs.

"That's simple. I live here," said Max. "And now you're going to let me finish my grocery shopping."

"Kevin, will you take these two to the station?" he asked.

"Sure, leave it to me. But where are you going, Max?"

"I need to return to my shopping before I run out of stuff."

Kevin nodded, and the two of them got the thugs into the cruiser, making sure to fasten the handcuffs securely and close the window divider. Afterward, Max waved at Kevin and started to go, but his colleague yelled, “Hey, asshole.” Max turned and found Kevin passing him a gun. “Be careful. The streets are in chaos today, and we know it won’t get better.”

“Don’t worry, I’ll take my precautions,” Max said, heading toward the supermarket.

When approaching Martin’s supermarket, the closest one to his house, Max saw a scene that looked like a war zone. People running back and forth, many with carts full of groceries, others with their hands full rushing to fill the trunks of their cars with whatever they could carry.

From behind the counter, Martin came out with his rifle pointed at the mob, shouting, “Get out of here now, or the next person who picks up even a pack of cigarettes will eat lead!”

The threat took effect almost immediately, as luckily, no one else had a firearm. Shoppers ran outside, closely followed by the aim of the furious owner of the supermarket. Max went the opposite way to enter the market when he ran into the barrel of the shotgun.

“Didn’t you hear what I said? Get out if you don’t want a bullet!”

“I heard Martin, but relax, I’m not here to loot. I just want to do some shopping.”

The man looked at Max as if he didn’t quite recognize him. Then, Martin lowered his gun.

“Oh, Max, sorry. The adrenaline was too much. But I’m afraid you won’t find much here. Those marauding idiots took almost everything,”

In fact, other than a few cans of food and a few pieces of fruit, there wasn’t much of value that hadn’t been trampled by the maddened crowd.

“Why did they loot the place?” asked Max as he put what he could into a basket.

“Because of that damn control!” replied Martin, putting the shotgun on top of the counter. “As if confiscating our money wasn’t enough, the government’s now imposed card limits. They got mad, and before I could get the gun, they locked me inside and took everything they wanted. Then the gate opened, and everyone started to enjoy it. It’s a miracle I got out.”

"Damn," said Max. "I'm glad you weren't killed, Martin. I almost got hurt at Morrigan's two weeks ago."

"You were there. Wow, man, I read it in the papers. The massacre. The motherfuckers even killed a kid. Damn government! They opened Pandora's box, so everyone started acting like a herd of wild buffalo!"

The Morrigan's Massacre

When shit hit the fan, one of the first things the government did was to mandate strict financial controls. It did not go well. The withdrawal limit was set at $1,000 per month, a ridiculous amount, barely enough to pay for the month's bills. Cards were still allowed, but the government established a second control: purchase limits. Max still remembers the day he handled each of the two controls.

For the first, it was the trip to the bank that made him realize the seriousness of it all. Max needed three thousand bucks to buy a few things and change the car battery, but he couldn't withdraw more than $800 — he had already withdrawn $200 a week earlier. Angered, he went to the bank manager and demanded an explanation.

"Greg, good morning. Why the fuck can I only withdraw 800 bucks from my account? I have over 30,000 here, and I've been a bank customer for over seven years!"

Greg's face went pale. "I apologize, but unfortunately, these are orders from the board. Haven't you seen the new government decree?"

"What decree?"

"Withdrawal limit, my friend. No one can withdraw more than $1,000 a month. Went out last night, didn't you see?"

"No, I was out all day taking care of things. But I noticed the huge bank queue, obviously!"

"Yes, and unfortunately, it goes for everyone. Not even us bank unit managers can get more than this miserable amount. I don't— MAX, WATCH OUT!" Greg jumped on his client and pushed him down.

A stone hit the windowpane of the bank, which shattered into a thousand pieces. On the other side, Max saw a mob of people pouring into the agency almost as if it were a single entity. Enraged people, ignoring the warnings of the guards who were pointing their guns, began to loot the agency and assault staff, shouting the same desperate war cry:

"WE WANT OUR MONEY!"

These people weren't there to rob or loot the bank. They only wanted what was rightfully theirs — or it should have been before the government decreed otherwise and stole billions in one go. Unfortunately, the police decided to fight back and caused the Morrigan's Massacre: fifteen people died, including manager Greg, two bank employees, and a child. In response, all branches closed, and every bank installed sliding doors to protect the facades from glass.

Brave New World

It wasn't Max's turn to do the rounds, but who said being a cop is a 9-to-5 job? "This was not what he signed up for."

After the newspapers started reporting the event, simple journeys became epic ordeals. Max could have been at home stocking up instead of here, staring at window panes. But protecting the glazing was his job now, and the sheriff hadn't trained his men to question schedules or ask for time off, especially in times of crisis.

Facing the supermarket, the cop watched the crowds as they bubbled and boiled in tumultuous movement. Chaos everywhere. Earlier today, when passing in front of familiar houses, he found broken windows with boards filling the gaps, the vast majority abandoned because they no longer had value.

Queues began to form and fill the product boxes. Everyone was in a hurry to pay and, at the same time, keep an eye on the other customers. He didn't know if they were looking to steal the contents of their carts or to keep them from stealing theirs — maybe a little bit of both. No one was hurt (yet), but the alarming presence of aluminum baseball bats and shotguns on the carts, as well as a few pistols in their waistbands, spelled big trouble.

Max also had a gun, or rather two; both had the safety on at that moment. But something else was at the ready: his gaze, which now covered the entire place. He saw one of the customers remove a carton of canned food from the shelf, a favorite of those reality shows he watched — what was it, survivalists? That was right. The crazy ones have now become the smart ones. Now, they are safe in their basements without dealing with queues. He thought survivalists, in general, were a little strange, but he didn't criticize them either. After all, he kept a tool that could be considered extremely survivalist, which he never considered using in times of crisis, but today, it could save his life. He really needed to stock up. Resigned, he entered the supermarket and headed for the shelves.

The line at the supermarket gradually grew in the few minutes it took him to collect things. By the time he reached the checkout, there were already at least twenty people in line. The sign at the checkout said "maximum ten items," but that no longer mattered. Carts with bundles of canned food completely dominated the queue. Max himself took three of them and had a hard time keeping the most excited customers away from his cart.

They wanted what was already sold out in the only two grocery stores on the street. There remained only the great "predator," as the Carrefour grocery conglomerate was once called; today, however, it was a lifeline in the midst of turmoil and chaos that had lasted since *the Great Collapse*.

Little by little, even the Carrefour shelves, once full of products which reflected the golden times, gave way to emptiness — or rather, the flashy posters, which had replaced the equally flashy cereals and sweets. Now, the posters were merely bittersweet reminders that marked the height of decadence.

"We are out of stock"

"There will be no replacements"

"Last units of corned beef! Only two cans per family."

"We do not accept Reais, Euros, Dollars, or cards"

Cigarettes quickly disappeared, although the entire city had embraced the non-smoking *new normal*. Ironically, the lack of them was due to non-smokers and the owner of Carrefour himself. Non-smokers were *good citizens*, but these days, cigarettes were as good as money, both inside and outside prison.

Good Old Alfred

Mr. Alfred owned the only other establishment besides Carrefour that had resisted the looting and remained operational during the crisis. Refusing to accept what they called money just a few days ago, old Alfred summed up the situation well during Max's visit. "Those bastards caused this mess! Because of them, I have to barricade my shop with bars so vandals don't try to steal them."

"They don't want to buy anything?" Max asked, looking innocent.

He got a withering glare in return. "They want to pay in cash. With cash! If you want those paper notes, keep them and use them to wipe your asses." And with that polite and cheerful farewell, the man closed the shop and erected another sign to decorate the landscape: "Empty shelves. We are closed."

With the decisive slam of the shopkeeper's door, Max made his way out, his cart loaded with the final goods, the usual groceries, plus corned beef and a carton of Marlboro that could be bought in old Alfred's general store.

Right now, I'm probably the richest man with the most diversified block portfolio, Max thought. Then chills penetrated his spine, and his hands shot to the cart. The coat, protecting the groceries, was wide open, and any one of these freaks could have just whipped it away. The jacket was threadbare and worthless, but it had an internal tactical security pocket. And here was the true value of the play.

While his left hand gripped his coat, his right hand clutched the gun barrel. Max reached into his pocket with his left hand and held the small object. As he did so, he realized how skewed his list of priorities was: the items in the cart would be of little use if the item now in his coat pocket had been lost. This item contained treasure more relevant than any item it carried.

It was time to make the long journey to his vehicle. Long in theory — the distance itself was only twenty meters. However, the people streaming towards Max (running from who knows what), together with the cars abandoned in the middle of the street (some wrecked, others burned, most out of gas), made the trip even more difficult. And dragging a fairground cart didn't make him more agile.

Finally, Max spotted the 1989 Dodge Ram. A true war relic, and today, it is more current than ever. Inherited from his father, that car was a fortress alongside the *modern* cars that looked like they were made of plastic. The Ram's wide front end, capable of moving most obstacles with ease, had brought Max here. He hoped it would get him home safely.

Sammy

As he slid into the Dodge, he checked the gas gauge. "My second most valuable coin." This time, nothing had been stolen. The car was also in working order, which was a miracle considering the situation. Max emptied the cart and put the groceries in the truck. Although he had a big enough bay to carry everything, Max preferred to put things inside the truck. The bay had no roof, and he definitely didn't want to be mugged or have his precious food stolen. Beside him, *Sammy* was on the lookout in case any smart ones tried to act.

Max's friend and guardian was an AR-15 rifle, a gun that he bought for two reasons: first, to defend himself, and second, because it was the model he liked the most. But Max never imagined that he would need to use that weapon, much less in a situation like the one that was happening in the streets. There were no more guns for sale, as everyone emptied stocks from old Joe's store before the Great Collapse. Only Joe's guns are left in the shop, but no one in their right mind would start a gun shop riot.

It was 15,000 satoshis well spent. Although the law allowed easy access to guns, automatic weapons were virtually impossible to buy, mainly because of the stock issue. Max bought one only for its legal benefit; he was a federal employee and a member of the police, which gave him the authority to choose whatever gun he wanted. The purchase of Sammy, by the way, was the last *act of authority* that the position afforded him.

Until the first controls, Max didn't consider himself a man with an ideology. On the contrary, he showed contempt for what he called *doomsday theorists*. They were just obscure economists and analysts who had been predicting financial crises for years without ever getting it right. He believed, like the rest of the world, that governments would not let a crisis of great magnitude destroy the economy. He, of course, did not understand that the destruction would come precisely from the measures that the government would take to *protect* the economy.

Once the first indicators of the crisis began, the dreaded Withdrawal Control Event, the prevailing sentiment among Max's neighbors and a large part of the country's population was disbelief. This wasn't supposed to happen in the world's largest economy. Max could hear the neighbors talking at the top of their voices, with a mixture of disbelief and fear: "This is absurd. Withdrawal controls here in America? It must be fake news!"

Two days later, the Morrigan's Massacre happened. The government had regressed to barbarism. In a matter of days, millions of people, including Max himself, lost almost all their savings.

A New Hope

Max's only salvation was the book given to him by a friend who had lived in Lebanon for twelve years.

The work, written by an economist whose name Max did not remember, was treasured more than the Holy Bible. With the lessons in the book, Max could withdraw what little he had left before the second looting control, which gave rise to the riots seen now. He had also exchanged his remaining money for the satoshis he now carried in his pocket, the only thing the supermarket would accept.

"I can't believe I'm thinking about this," he said to himself while watching the bustling streets and carefully packing his things before some smart guy tried to attack him. I can't waste bullets here.

The irony is that until recently, Max would never think of spending his satoshis on basic grocery shopping — he would never take the money out of that little *pen drive*; it was his only store of value. Naturally, everyone wanted to get rid of their bad money, while some still accepted it. That's what bad money is all about. Suddenly, everyone only wanted satoshis and tangible goods, like guns and bullets.

Max had to trade most of his ammo for water with one of his neighbors, who hadn't been able to find enough bullets before they looted the gun stores. The water was almost gone, and the bullets Max had in his stash could no longer serve as a store of value.

Mine Your Own Business

The idea that real estate didn't lose value was another belief that Max had lost. Along with most of his money, its value was decimated by the crisis. Although he retained ownership of his home, he was one of the lucky few who did. Max was part of a privileged minority: he had no mortgage, his house was paid off, and he had no other loans.

His house contained the only possession he still saw as having any value. Max affectionately called it the *energy sink*, a nickname chosen by his ex-wife, who had left him months before. The equipment stored in his house was part of his obsession with getting hard currency, a mission he always performed every ten minutes. Most of the time, though, it was a pointless pursuit that required a lot of money, which caused his wife to leave him.

"Truth be told, I don't blame her," Max said, thinking of young Lily and how she would be in the middle of all this mess. When thinking about his wife, Max was surprised by the peace of mind that took over. His wife's abandonment occurred when Max was going through one of his worst phases. He was without money, having only his individual mining and hearing almost daily criticism from Lily. "Max, our energy bill is over $500 this month, and you won't turn those machines off. And what's that all about? Get some change with those game coins?!"

"It's not game currency, Lily. You can be sure this will be worth a lot of money in a few years," Max said. He repeated this phrase so often that it became a memorized mantra, his true conviction.

"Well, you aren't paying the bills, and I'm tired of waiting. I will spend a few days at my mother's house, and I ask you not to contact me. I need to be alone for a while, Max, and not stay by the side of someone I love less and less."

That same day, Lily packed her bags and left. Max's marriage ended, but the penny took at least a week to drop. After that, Max was unstable for a long time. He loved his wife, and, aside from financial problems, he wasn't a bad match for Lily. But less than two weeks after the end of the relationship, Max received a new blow when he saw Lily next to the drug dealer she presented as her new boyfriend on her social accounts.

For seven months, between that day and three months before the start of the riots, Max entered a deep depression and left his house only to go to the supermarket. Thanks to his skills as a military man, he landed a security post at Carrefour — yes, at the predator so feared by the city. But despite the locals' revulsion, Max enjoyed the job, which allowed him to resume mining. And he finally got it. Twice. In two successful mines, Max withdrew the equivalent of two years' worth of electricity. Even without a dollar in his pocket, he was already the richest guy on the street. After all, he was the only one with food and a car that still worked.

Citadel Danny

"Max. Hey Max!"

Max turned quickly. It was finally a recognizable voice among the screaming he left behind. More than that, it was a friendly voice. It belonged to Daniel, his neighbor, the man responsible for his good fortune. "Daniel!" Max saw the cart in the neighbor's hands. "I assume you were on time, too?"

"Yes. I was the last customer to leave before Miller closed Carrefour."

"So he's finally out of stock."

"So he is. He told me he had just enough on hand to keep his family alive. Closed the supermarket and left an entire crowd without food."

"What do you think they'll do? Do you really think they're gonna loot the supermarket?"

Daniel shook his head, pointing to the roof of the Carrefour. Even though it was far away, Max could see the generators his friend was pointing at. "Miller installed electric conduction in the gates. If someone outside tries to break in, they'll get shocked. That was 37,000 satoshis well invested."

Max nodded. "Smart." Miller had used his real money at the right time. Like Max, old Miller owed Daniel the credit for his ability to protect his supermarket right now. An old man with a millennial spirit, Daniel was part of a 21st-century hippie generation. He rarely ate meat. He considered himself a minimalist, but he had one of the biggest gun collections Max had ever seen. The guy didn't skimp — he even paid almost one bitcoin for a replica of the rifle used by Finnish Simo Häyhä in the war against the Russians. "A reminder that little men are the greatest defenders of freedom," he'd said when Max had asked him about the purchase. And at 1.69 meters, Daniel was more than adequate to live up to the saying.

Above all, Daniel's house was a real blueprint for how to create a modern fortress. The tiles, shaped into five columns of solar panels, provided a surplus of energy. The garage housed his car — a Tesla Model S bought just before the crisis — and also a generator, which helped the panels withstand power outages. Last but not least, the house's biggest consumer (and provider): the greenhouse.

Despite Daniel's fame as a 'prophet,' Max liked him. He had been accurate in his predictions about the crisis. Daniel carried a bundle of canned food in his arms and a newspaper under his left arm. Max put his groceries in his car — an armful of cans, probably the last ones in the supermarket.

Daniel walked unsteadily as if he were more tired than someone carrying only a few tins of sardines, tuna, and beans.

"It won't be long before these guys will start blowing up stores," Daniel said.

Max noticed that Daniel was sweating more than usual, but what startled him was the red stream from his neighbor's jacket sleeve. "What happened, Dan? Are you bleeding?"

"It's nothing. It's just a scratch."

"Well, anyway, let me at least help you carry this thing." Max took the bundle from Daniel's arms but soon saw that the bloodstain ran the length of the coat's sleeve. Without ceremony, Max tugged on his coat, ignoring his neighbor's protests.

A deep knife cut that ran the length of Daniel's arm. The wound was large but did not appear to be life-threatening, although it explained the fatigue. Max asked what had happened.

"When I walked into the supermarket, there was just this bundle of food on the shelf. It was just sitting there, almost like the Holy Grail in the middle of an empty shelf, so I grabbed it. Suddenly, there was this goon with a foul stench on top of me who tried to steal the food. I fought back. The fight was bad, and he had a knife. You know those hunting knives with serrations and everything? He pulled it out; he cut me good. I was lucky he didn't hit me squarely, or I'd be serving as worm food in the fucking supermarket. The idiot almost managed to kill me, but even with the blood, I managed to get in on the ground and stuck him in the chest. Right into his heart!"

Max looked at his neighbor in shock. He could barely breathe, and his face turned pale by degrees. Despite his military career, seeing someone so close to him talk about cold-blooded murder, even in the middle of all this mess, was not something he was used to. Daniel was always calm and attentive to his plants. Max never imagined this guy could kill someone. Would he? Of course, he did it. Any man can kill when faced with starvation. Max faced his new reality.

"So it's worse than the authorities make it out to be," Max said, mostly to himself.

"Oh, it's a lot worse," said Daniel grimly. "Besides, have you read today's headlines?"

Max raised his eyebrows. "Only the ones about the riots. I didn't even know the media and news were still in business, especially after all this trouble." He sighed. "I should have read them more carefully."

"Take a look here..."

Max took the copy of the Times from his neighbor. It was beat up, but it was the issue of the day. He read the headline written in bold letters:

"THE CRISIS HAS ARRIVED! EXPERT RECOMMENDS BITCOIN, GOLD, FOOD AND WATER FOR AT LEAST TWO WEEKS. DON'T LEAVE YOUR HOUSE AND DON'T WASTE FUEL. STAY SAFE AND PROTECT YOURSELF!"

Daniel broke into a wide smile as he looked at Max, who returned the gesture. "Lucky for us, we don't trust the newspapers," he thought. Max loaded Daniel's groceries into the car and then made his way to his own car. He nestled Sammy near him in the driver's seat and drove home. The Great Forfeiture took the world by surprise, but in his pocket was the hope of a better future that, even though he had rejected it in the beginning, brought a new future for himself.

"My miners are waiting," said Max, thinking of how many more satoshis he could collect while there were still power services available. At the same time, he hoped that there was still a world to return to when he had more of that prized possession — his digital gold.

14

Eye in the Sky

Eduardo Próspero

"We should have gone there instead," Simon Derwall complained.

His wife was furiously scrubbing a gigantic saucepan with a sponge, and the objection stopped her in her tracks. A deadly silence filled the air. She had explained this to him several times already.

"The king's visit brings eyes with it. Why are we compromising our OPSEC like this?" Simon continued.

Elena Negrón sighed and replied, "Father cannot travel, remember."

He opened the oven door, and the smell of well-seasoned meat filled the kitchen. "Oh, right," he said distractedly. "This is done."

Elena spent both the morning and the afternoon in the kitchen, one of her happy places. Despite this, and for no apparent reason, she was nervous. Of course, Eleazar and Nicolás, her two brothers whom she hadn't seen in eleven months, were on their way. That wasn't it. That excited her. The terror's origin was deeper. Elena stopped short, surprised that her inner voice admitted "terror."

From the garden, Simon shouted in surprise, "Why is the grill on? There's a whole barbecue here!"

Elena wondered if her husband was losing his memory or if he simply wasn't listening to her anymore. "That's the B meal," she said.

Simon couldn't make heads or tails of what she was saying.

"The B meal?"

Elena gave up. "For the driver and bodyguards."

A shiver went up Simon's spine. They were taking unnecessary risks. He restrained himself and calmly asked, "How many people are coming?"

"I don't know yet," Elena replied. "How does it look out there? Is it ready?"

Simon opened the grill. "Two or three more minutes. What do you mean you don't know?"

"You know how Eleazar is — always a mystery."

The Jungle

A stabbing pain hit patriarch Tomás Negrón's knees, but he needed to be there. He had not seen Eleazar since his last visit to The Citadel, some three years ago. Simon and his daughter used to go every six months to see their children and buy supplies. In the past, Tomás made a point of accompanying them. He began to stay behind because he was tired. Also, the solitude of an empty house was perfect for writing, and writing was the priority.

"They're two or three minutes away according to extitDeGoogled Maps," Simon informed him while keeping his eyes on the screen. From the sky, a series of lenses captured an overhead shot centered on two gray-haired humans in front of a 4x4 truck. They appeared to be in the middle of the jungle. Had they been younger, they might have detected the sound of the propellers up there. Playing dumb, Simon finally asked, "Did Eleazar tell you how many people he's coming with?"

The patriarch was puzzled. "I assumed he was only coming with Nicolás," he said, realizing he hadn't thought about the middle child until that moment.

"Sure, but I'm talking about bodyguards and his personal entourage."

Tomás had not considered that possibility. In doing so, he understood the veiled insult that came with his moronic son-in-law's question. He raised his guard and said, "However many they are, those are trained people. Serious people." His own lie surprised him. "Eleazar knows what he's doing. He wouldn't put us in danger."

With a superhuman effort, Simon managed to restrain himself and didn't utter his disapproval.

"What happened to the two or three minutes?" Tomás asked, trying to change the subject.

His interlocutor didn't answer.

The Surprise

Inside the kitchen, Elena identified the sound of her truck's engine and felt the curtain raising. And so it began. Encounters with her brothers were often theatrical, and this one would prove to be no exception. Only one vehicle arrived, which was a good sign. She calculated that the passengers would have time to park and stretch their legs, before flinging the doors open.

Elena saw only four silhouettes approaching and ran out toward them, "I can't believe it! Is it only the two of you? How is this possible?"

Eleazar ran to Elena, hugged her and said, "I drove all night just to see you, dear sister."

Incredulous, Nicolás froze still while looking straight at an imaginary camera. He drove, not Eleazar. And they made the whole trip during the day. There was no point in complaining, though. Those two were in their own little world already. He readjusted, shifted his focus to Simon, and asked him the question that was stuck in his throat. "So, can we visit the new facilities real quick?"

Grumpily, the brother-in-law replied, "No, it's time to eat."

"Show me the miners and the flowers quickly, and then we'll go upstairs. What's the rush? Are you *that* hungry?"

Nicolás sounded like a child, Simon thought. The middle brother had untapped potential but didn't know how to hold back. "Your sister slaved away all day cooking for us," he finally replied. "Act like you appreciate it, little shit."

The Dinner

Food and wine flowed like the river that powered the Negrón's complex. "Somebody pass me that little smokey sauce over there," Tomás requested.

"Enough with the chit-chat, Negrón family," Simon exclaimed, cutting off conversations. "Let's give the floor to our CEO, Eleazar Negrón, to present the quarterly report."

Eleazar caught and ignored the mocking tone. He immediately took control of the situation and the conversation. "Dear shareholders and board members, I am proud to announce that I met with the country's president. After talking to such a nice gentleman, I can assure you that The Citadel is in the right place. The government approves of our existence and understands what the project brings to the table. The Citadel is a business catalyst, the link to bitcoin-related companies. Venezuela isn't planning to adopt it as legal currency, so they need an autonomous zone for bitcoin companies to conduct business."

The information wasn't new to the people around the table, but the power of Eleazar's oratory captivated them. "Basically, as long as we pay the tributes we promised in the original negotiation, the president guarantees our independence," he said, expecting applause that did not come. In Eleazar's mind, he'd saved all of these people's life project, and they paid him with indifference.

Less than a year ago, a violent change in the Venezuelan government left The Citadel vulnerable. What once was a project supported at the highest levels, suddenly felt at risk. Negotiations with the newly installed government of General Tomás Máximo were Eleazar's first test. And as The Citadel's current regent, he felt that he had risen to the occasion and deserved applause from his inner circle.

The patriarch spoke first. "Phenomenal work, my son."

Relieved, Elena exclaimed, "So The Citadel lives! Who would have thought?"

Nicolás tried to hold back his laughter because he knew what was coming. Instead, he complimented the chef. "This roast meat is phenomenal, sister. Incredibly tender and tasty."

Simon sensed the perfect moment to strike and did not hesitate. "Good work Eleazar, but tell us, what did they say about The Citadel's proximity to the capital?"

This was a sensitive issue for all parties involved. Eleazar had picked the place; it was one of the few instances in which he disagreed with his father. Without success, Tomás, Simon, and Elena had exhausted all resources trying to convince him to change the location. And now, Venezuela's new government wasn't comfortable with the proximity between The Citadel and Caracas. They wanted all the benefits of having an independent zone under the bitcoin standard within their borders but without the risk of the population getting ideas.

"Excellent question, Simon," Eleazar replied, snapping them all out of their reverie. "Pay attention, this proposal will surely interest you all. And the Presidential House approved it."

The Laugh

Compliments aside, the clearest sign of the quality of Elena's cooking was how fast the food disappeared from the trays. "All of you were right. The location I chose for The Citadel was the wrong one," admitted the younger brother.

Surprised, Simon and Elena looked at each other and exchanged telepathic messages — what was going on? Eleazar never directly admitted his faults. Could the wonderboy have finally grown up? Did the version of Eleazar that the Negrón family was waiting for all these years to arrive at last? Or, on the contrary, was he setting them up?

More information interrupted their non-verbal communication. "The president himself proposed a deal on a large and privileged piece of land for us to build another citadel, this time away from the country's heartland. We will have full support from the government, and we have to continue operating as we have been, but far away. We'll perform certain services for them. I will take care of that, don't worry."

"Wait a minute, what kind of services?" Elena said.

"What's the catch, son?" Tomás asked simultaneously.

Amazed, the middle brother watched the situation unfold. This was going exactly as he imagined. He grabbed a bottle of wine from the center of the table, opened it, and methodically refilled all of the glasses. They were all going to need it.

Eleazar replied, "No catch, father. We just have to advise them and maybe help them buy and hold bitcoin for the nation's reserve. And I have a specialist who will handle it."

Elena stood up from her chair and was about to start pacing around the room, but she managed to stop herself. She couldn't show weakness. Instead, Elena picked up a few dirty dishes from the table and took them to the sink. In the kitchen, her instincts flickered, and she realized the whole thing sounded too convenient. Elena returned empty-handed, looked at her younger brother, and accused him. "There's something you're not telling us."

Nicolás let out a dry laugh. "Oh yes," he said right after.

Simon sensed a shift in the room's energy and braced for impact.

From a beaten black leather bag that barely kept its shape, Eleazar pulled out a small cardboard tube. "No need to put up a wall. This plan suits us all."

"Famous last words," Simon said instinctively.

"Are there any more of these potatoes anywhere?" the father asked.

Elena awoke from the spell Eleazar had her under, "Sure. Let me get them for you."

Eleazar caught her again. "Don't go, sister. Look at this." He pushed plates aside and unfolded a map. "The land where The New Citadel will be is marked in orange," he announced proudly.

"All of this is phenomenal, brother. You put in the effort and figured it all out beforehand. Being in charge suits you."

Her husband's heavy gaze called to her. It had a very clear message attached to it: something was wrong. She and Simon locked eyes.

Immediately, Elena knew she had to focus on the map and stop praising Eleazar. She also realized that Nicolás was trying his best not to laugh. The big sister looked down, and the pieces fell into place.

The Bigger Picture

In this particular situation, she was the eye in the sky. What did she see? Her house is also marked in orange. It was about ten kilometers from The New Citadel. "Is this some kind of sick joke, Eleazar?" she asked calmly. To add insult to injury, she realized that she was the last to notice.

"This location may work, actually," Tomás stated.

Eleazar tried his best to jumpstart the excitement. "Let's use this house as a home base and build that shit. A new and improved citadel. The citadel you guys always wanted."

Elena cut him off. "This isn't going to happen, brother. Do you remember the struggle it was to find an isolated area where one can live sovereignly in a country we don't know?"

"That is precisely why The New Citadel should be here — an area approved by you, the experts," Eleazar argued.

She swallowed thickly. "This location's whole point is to keep us away from prying eyes. We need privacy to keep the operation running. You know that, Eleazar. What the fuck is this?"

Eleazar smiled. "We need land with those exact characteristics. How hard is that to understand? Stop being so selfish. Look at the bigger picture."

From above, a spectator would've seen a round table full of dirty dishes and two basically empty metal trays. Among all that chaos, the map offered a contrasting perspective. Four of the five figures slouched over it, examining the terrain from different angles. The same spectator also would've picked up that the temperature inside that room was rising.

Elena considered burning the map right then and there but decided not to. She placed both of her hands firmly on the table and raised her voice for the first time that fateful evening. "This is ridiculous!

Unbelievable. This is your worst plan ever, brother. Are you going to leave your dad in the streets?"

Eleazar assured them that they could continue to live there. "Next to an entire citadel?! Are you stupid or what? We have a three-basement operation down here!" she replied.

Tomás and Nicolás were on the edge of their seats, watching different shows. The patriarch was worried but proud, analyzing the family's situation while, at the same time, uncertain about who was winning the argument. The middle child, on the other hand, remained uninterested in the end result and mocked everyone involved.

"The New Citadel is more important, sister. You know that."

Elena's face looked back in shock. This conniving bastard was using her undying loyalty to the bitcoin movement as a weapon against her. She would've respected the tactic if it weren't for the fact that Eleazar was stabbing her in the back and feeding her current life project to the wolves.

"This is a perfect plan, sis. Think about it. Sleep on it."

Elena had one more weapon under her belt: DRAMA! "How could you possibly consider relocating your own father? And all those cows, who are our family? Those crops out there, we feed them with our sweat."

Eleazar smiled. He had her. "It's the other way around, sister. Family and how we should stick together is all you talk about. Maybe I'd see Dad more often if I didn't have to drive five hours to do it."

Nicolás's chair screeched as he stood up abruptly. This, he could not allow. "Let the record show that I *drove* the whole way," he said.

The discussion progressed as if he had never spoken.

"You're willing to go that low, huh?" Elena asked before attacking. "You became a politician." She would later regret insulting her younger brother this way.

Eleazar answered with a politician's smile. "If we execute this operation accurately, you won't even have to move," he promised, not intending to deliver. Elena lost her decorum. "What the fuck are you talking about, little shit? We can't keep growing the flowers next to a city."

"It's just a citadel," he argued weakly.

"And the river, Eleazar?! Where are we going to find another river of that size?" Elena was already picturing the location change. It was over.

"The New Citadel needs the river," he replied.

Nicolás dissociated, pushed Elena's screams to the background, and congratulated himself. From the start, he had warned Eleazar that the family would hate his proposal. The stubborn younger brother assured him that both his father and sister would understand that it was the right plan. Otherwise, he would convince them.

His father's shouts brought Nicolás back. "...and don't use me as a pawn in your arguments! You know that I'll do what needs to be done. If moving is worth it, we'll move and set up the mine and flowers somewhere else. If the business isn't right, we'll stay. It's as simple as that."

Simon noticed the look on his wife's face. Elena had to tell him something.

"That's how it's done, father. That's wisdom," Eleazar proclaimed triumphantly.

Husband and wife's eyes locked, and Simon understood that he had to get Nicolás out of the room. Elena planned to reveal something that the middle brother had no business knowing. Without missing a beat, he said, "Well, this already seems settled, and your plates are empty. Come on Nicolás, let's go see the miners. I know that you miss them."

Nicolás came alive like a haunted doll. A fire ignited inside him when someone brought up a subject that interested him. The middle brother's aloof demeanor acquired subtlety and purpose. An outside observer would've suddenly realized that maybe Simon's theory about his potential was on point after all.

The Miners

From above, various lenses adjusted the focus to follow the movement of the two figures. In theory, Nicolás's acute hearing could've detected the sound of the propellers, but his surroundings monopolized his attention.

He could've been in a forest if not for the fact that all the plants were perfectly organized. Huge papaya and tamarind trees protected smaller orange trees, and perfectly cut grass covered the ground. It smelled like wet soil. Nicolás noticed track marks and realized that the road was wide enough for machinery to go through.

"The garden looks like paradise, Simon," he commented. His most interesting inlaw automatically replied, "One-hundred percent polycrop farming. Each plant is there for a reason." From some angles, the trees' many branches formed complex geometrical figures that weren't present in the natural world. Nicolás noticed the extreme order creeped him out.

"Here on the left, remember?" Simon said as he opened the discreet door that led to the mine. They crossed the threshold, and the panorama radically changed. The nauseating sound of hundreds of machines working overtime took over and muffled their conversation. The whole building was a Black Box that kept the maddening sound from the outside world, but they didn't use metal enclosures of any kind in there.

Artificial light fell on several immersion tanks housing dozens of miners that maintained the bitcoin network while competing for rewards and commissions. On top of other structures, hundreds of flowering plants grew. Fed by the heat that the machines emitted. Arranged by color — half of them red and the other half evenly distributed between white, yellow, and pink.

Nicolás skipped the natural beauty, accelerated toward the control panel and lost himself among screens, numbers, and wires. Simon was left pondering what the situation meant to him. The Citadel, bitcoin, the mines, and the flowers were the Negrón's business. His contribution was taking care of the animals and farming. And the possibility of creating a second quasi-sustainable agroforestry farm excited him, especially if someone took care of this one.

His brother-in-law's question brought him back to the material world. "So, the million-dollar flowers are downstairs?"

Simon looked at him, puzzled. "Sure, these are camouflage," he replied, then added, "Wait a minute, haven't you been to the other basements?" Nicolás explained that he installed the miners and left them running, but this was the first time he had returned. "Here are the keys if you want to go down. I ate too much. I want to sleep." Nicolás took the keys and walked away, rejoicing in the trust placed in him.

The Fall

Simon left the warehouse and took a deep breath. The hard part was almost over. One last glass of wine with the Negróns, and he was home free. Elena would surely stay late talking with her brothers, and he would have several hours to drink in solitude. It was going to be a great night after—

"Hands up, poet Simon Derwall," Nicolás interrupted.

His subconscious noticed a buzzing. Something approached.

"I thought about it, and you're right. It's family time," the middle brother explained. "I'll explore the gold mine calmly tomorrow."

A mechanical insect flew above them, undetected.

Simon surprised even himself. His instincts took over, and he drew from the holster under his left arm. The following scene defined Nicolás's life. Seeing the gun pointed at him, for the first time, he felt like the story's protagonist. And he liked it.

As Nicolás instinctively engaged in Matrix-like evasive maneuvers to avoid the upcoming bullet, adrenaline slowed the speed of time. It was obvious to him that Simon had military training because the man moved as gracefully as a panther, but he clearly wasn't in control of his body. Who was Simon before he met his sister? And what was this unidentified flying object that invaded the corner of his eye? Nicolás had a chance to consider the situation he was in as his body faced the sky and approached the ground.

A few minutes ago, Nicolás had sent a text with a photo of the underground mine attached. Was that small action the cause of his death? How did Simon find out? Was he on to him from the very beginning? A buzzing sound approached, and it suddenly felt like it was always there. Or were the Negróns' shady businesses to blame for this whole situation? Was Nicolás paying for his family's sins? The two shots reverberated in every corner of the property.

Nicolás's body hit the ground, and the impact let him know that he was alive. More alive than ever, in fact. He sat and double-checked that none of his body parts had a bullet hole. In front of him, Simon had more questions than answers. Nicolás slowly turned around and finally figured out what the object was.

About ten meters away lay a disabled military-grade drone with two holes through it. Simon was an extraordinary shooter. Nicolás knew his drones and was familiar with the brand and model, so he immediately realized that the Negróns' lives would radically change. The flying spy not only aimed multiple cameras at them, but it also had a high-range video transmitter. The receiver could be up to 100 kilometers away in any direction.

Simon passed him by, approached the drone, and examined it briefly. "This is not good," he mouthed.

EYE IN THE SKY

15

Who Let the Bitcoin Dogs Out?

Will Schoellkopf

The engine revs.

"I can't believe we were able to find an American Mustang in this French countryside." John celebrates by punching the air. "I am ripping down these narrow roads."

"Bloody hell. Slow down!" Lily begs as her oversized diamond dangle earrings sway side to side. "You've got nothing to prove, John. Big man in your Yankee ten-gallon hat. Let's just get there safely."

John slows to give her a smoldering look and charm her with his southern drawl, "Aww, my sweet British compatriot, you care about me."

"Bollocks," Lily retorts. "I care about not dying." She sighs and buries her face in her hands. Her mind is not just preoccupied with the speed of their automobile, but the fate of a hundred canine souls. English Border Collies, the dog breed she has loved since her childhood pet Baxter, are under threat from Frenchman 'Macaron.' Hiding her tears, she thinks, *Baxter, you were a good boy.* Macaron's plot to groom a boat full of beloved English dogs into Parisian poodles shook Lily to her core — so much so that it drove her to partner with a crass American to save them.

John, aware of the wrinkles on Lily's forehead, tries his best to assuage his new partner's concerns. Though the road ahead has twists and turns, their path is clear. As he adjusts his rearview mirror, he remembers he has all of U.S. history behind him. John's childhood was spent learning about America's might, including when his fellow countrymen saved the people of France by storming the beaches of Normandy on D-Day. With a self-confidence that's never been broken, he has been itching to be a hero in France, even if instead of liberating French people, he's saving English dogs. *She needs to know we'll win. After all, we're the good guys,* John thinks. He says aloud, "My sweet Lily flower, have no fear! My U.S. Hash Force will project power to coerce the French for the dogs' release."

Lily slaps the dash, "Yes, I've heard of your Hash Force, John. But may I remind you, dear arrogant wanker, my geographically challenged friend, MI6's intel says to steadily power on any miners as His Majesty's Hash Force may do. The Border Collies' barge will take about an hour to flee France, cross the English channel, and safely reach our shores, so we don't want to burst their souffle too quickly. Oh, and the barge is armed with explosives controlled by a remote detonator. When Macaron asks for his bitcoin ransom in exchange for the dogs' release. How do you cowboys plan to help from across the pond?"

John takes both hands off the wheel to flex his biceps, "Shock and awe, Lily. Full Throttle. We're not giving the French a single sat. Instead, we're diverting maximum energy to the U.S. Hash Force, of course."

Put off by John's arrogance, Lily drifts her gaze out the window. Rows and rows of vineyards she can't help but admire. *There is beauty in disciplined order.* As it gets later in the evening, she sees the shadows from the vines growing longer, crisscrossing, forming a grid. Lily guffaws, "And where is this sudden surge of readily available power supposed to come from undetected?"

"No need to worry, my English crumpet! Our back-of-the-napkin calculations suggest that, with a little help from the Texas of the North, there's enough flared natural gas in the U.S. to run the entire bitcoin network."

Lily's jaw drops, "So miners have already built out the infrastructure to capture wasted natural gas flares for the benefit of the U.S. government but are waiting to turn them on until commanded to by the U.S. Hash Force?"

"Yup. As soon as Macaron sees our hash power come online, we're going to try to start mining blocks on the bitcoin network to DOS attack any UTXOs with a known history of French transactions."

"A denial of service attack, for peace?" Lily asks skeptically.

"Peace through strength, baby. If you don't comply with America's dog rights standards, you get censored. America saves British dogs again and without a single shot fired." John steps on the gas, screaming in his head, *'Murica!*

"Not fair. It's only because our MI6 chain analysis intel knows which of Macaron's bitcoin addresses to censor that this plan even has a shot at succeeding. You're lucky Macaron is even more self-assured than you Americans. That's the only reason France doesn't have a Hash Force of its own to project power back."

John pulls the Mustang up to the front of the fancy French restaurant, *Chandelier*. Lily grabs her green purse that matches her elegant emerald ball gown. She checked its contents one more time to make sure her dog whistle to call for backup was still there. *In case I need it.* They head inside to meet Macaron.

***

John and Lily spot Macaron sitting alone at the white linen table closest to the dance floor. He's tapping his Louis Vuitton snakeskin shoes, checking his Chanel watch at the end of his silk gloves, and fluffing his floofy black French Hermès beret. The red French ascot spilling out of his black and white blouse looks ridiculous.

John lets out a big sigh, and Macaron stands with open arms, "Lily, John, welcome to France." Before John can flinch away, Macaron kisses him on both cheeks. He lifts up Lily's hand for a kiss. "*Mademoiselle*."

John raises his hand. "Waiter. I'll take a bourbon, neat. And make it a double!"

Slap!

"Hey, what was that for, Frenchie?" John asks as he rubs his face.

Macaron puts the silk glove he used to *Slap* John back on. "Rude American. Where are your manners?" He pulls out a hidden red detonator clipped in the folds of his ascot, a clear cover protecting the trigger. "Don't drive me to prematurely push this button and blow up the boat carrying your English doggies. First, send me my bitcoin. Then we can celebrate with drinks."

"In your dreams, Frenchie!" John presses his finger to his ear, "Uniform, Sierra, Alpha."

Macaron turns to Lily and scoffs, "What is this rude American man doing, Lily?"

Annoyed, Lily answers, "Check your bitcoin UTXOs. Notice anything?"

Macaron frantically queries his bitcoin node from his cellphone and sighs with relief, "*Phew*. No, I don't notice anything at all. All of my unspent bitcoin is still under the control of my government's private key."

"And it'll stay that way, too." John beats his chest. "You mess with the U.S., and you get the Hash Force! We just doubled the hash rate by turning on all of our miners — as many miners as the entire existing bitcoin network. Now you'll have to wait twice as long for your French bitcoin transactions to confirm! That is unless you release the barge of dogs right now."

Lily drops down to the table and buries her face in her palms to hide her embarrassment. As much as Lily would like to withdraw from the world at this time, the smell of delicious baked brie tickles her nose; her ears perk up to the sound of dinner guests breaking baguettes and her mind's eye sees the beautiful vineyards that she passed on the drive here. Her mouth waters. *Someone get me a drink*. The restaurant is at full capacity with every square table seated, either by romantic couples, just barely able to see each other's faces from dancing candlelit flames, or by tourists on a double date with their host. *Nobody better think we're dating.*

Flustered, Macaron furiously types a long text message with the order to release the barge of English Border Collies to cross the English channel. "There, I've let the dogs out! Will you two please excuse me for a moment? I have to call my government to confirm we haven't lost our property rights to spend our bitcoin in a timely manner."

Beaming with pride, John falls back into his chair at the table. "We did it, Lily. Quick, give the command for His Majesty's Hash Force to power on so we can 51% attack this guy."

Lily finally stops rubbing her eyes, "John, that isn't how any of this works."

"What do you mean?" he asks.

"Within a 2,016 block difficulty adjustment period, doubling the hash power means the global bitcoin network will mine new blocks twice as fast, not slower."

John's double bourbon finally arrives at the table. He doesn't bother to stop the waiter in case Lily wants to order a drink of her own and downs a big gulp. "But if you give the order for His Majesty's Hash Force to power on, won't we have over 51% of the hash power of the bitcoin network? We can write Macaron's bitcoin out of existence."

Lily crosses her arms, "Not exactly. It's not enough to simply surpass half the hash rate. We must also maintain a higher hash rate than the legacy chain to generate more chain weight and reorg the other chain. We would have to be mining this heavier chain secretly, but in one bombastic order, you just completely blew apart our whole plan. Now we'd need massive collusion between existing miners and secret stealth miners to have any power projection."

John mutters under his breath, "Frenchie's been gone a long time. Wonder what he's up to..."

Macaron returns, fluffs his white linen napkin, and sits at their table, "Thank you, John, for extending my French people such great mercy as to be allowed to transact freely on the blockchain." He extends his arm with a flourish toward a waiter, "Garçon? Champagne for the three of us." Macaron turns to John and Lily, "After my phone call, I am much better. Though I'm bitter you refused to pay our ransom, I'm grateful you're furthering the security of the bitcoin network." In his excitement, Macaron leans forward and claps his hands together. "You two are so lucky to be dining with me tonight. You won't have to drink that sparkling wine swill you have in your home country. Tonight, you'll get to have proper champagne from the Champagne region of France — my treat."

John grunts in disgust. "Macaron, you can order champagne, but I've got my bourbon."

Lily steps on John's foot.

"*Ow!* What was that for?" John shrieks.

"Aren't you going to ask me if I want anything?"

"Huh?"

Macaron takes Lily's hand, "*Mademoiselle,* in addition to champagne, can I get you anything else?"

Lily snatches her hand back, "Gin Martini. Shaken, not stirred."

"Lily, may I ask you another question?" Macaron asks sweetly.

She rolls her eyes. "Bloody hell, what is it, Macaron?"

"Why do I get the feeling that forgetting to ask you what you'd like to drink isn't the first time John has neglected to ask you what you wanted?"

Lily's eyes light up as she leans in closer to Macaron, "Why, yes. This isn't the first time John's disregarded my needs. You know, he's always only thinking about himself, his own ego, and he never misses a chance to interr—"

"—That's not true!" John huffs.

Lily kicks him under the table, "See what I mean?"

Cymbals crash as the drummer hits the sticks louder for the finale. The five-piece band on stage finishes their current rock song and begins shuffling sheet music to get ready for the next one. The local French band looks grateful to be playing at a fine dining establishment that doesn't insist on a stuffy grand piano. The audience can barely see the guitarist's and bassist's eyes behind their long hair, but the glint in the singer's eyes inspires hope. The singer adjusts his collar and clears his throat to get ready. The dance floor starts to clear, leaving the keyboardist motioning with his hands, eager to bring on the next song.

Macaron smooths Lily's hair behind her ear, "You have such beautiful earrings, Lily. Did John buy those for you?"

"No, John never buys me anything."

"What do you mean?" John protests.

Lily shrugs him off, and Macaron leans in closer to Lily to whisper just loud enough for John to hear, "You know, in my country, men like me know how to show a lady respect."

John stands up and extends out his hand, "C'mon, Lily. I think it's time I take you out onto the floor for a dance."

She shakes her head, so he stomps on her feet under the table.

"*Ow!*"

"I *insist*. They're playing my song: *Don't Stop Believin'*. C'mon."

"Just a small-town girl
Livin' in a lonely world
She took the midnight train going anywhere..."

On the dance floor, John pulls Lily close to whisper in her ear, "What are you doing? We've finished our mission. Let's ensure the dogs safely cross the English Channel and get out of here. The way you're flirting with him, we'll never leave!"

Lily blushes, "John, are you that blind? If Macaron is suddenly being sweet to us, then he must be scheming something."

"What's that supposed to mean?" John shakes his head. "Look, there's no time to argue. We can't risk him blowing up the barge as long as he's got that remote detonator clipped to his ascot. He's in a jubilant mood for now, but those French can be so melodramatic. We've got to get the detonator to ensure the dogs' safety until they reach safe harbor at your shores."

"Some'll win, some will lose
Some are born to sing the blues
Whoa, the movie never ends
It goes on and on and on and on..."

John's box-step dancing pace quickens as he looks over to check on Macaron. He spots him placing an order with the waiter and grits his teeth, "He's pure evil."

Lily breaks away from John to do a twirl on the dance floor; her elegant, flowy green dress tries to keep up. She flips her hair and winks at Macaron, "Maybe I should flirt with him some more? After all, he's so handsome, and he listens to me."

John stops dancing and stomps his feet.

"Aww, are you jealous, John?" Lily asks.

"Jealous?"

Lily floats back to John, digs her nails into the back of his neck, and nibbles on his ear as she whispers, "John, you better dip me on this dance floor. Otherwise, I'm going to ask him to draw me like one of his French girls. C'mon John, *Don't Stop Believin'*."

Ahem Macaron clears his throat, adjusts his detonator-pinned ascot, and taps Lily on the shoulder.

"*Mademoiselle*, may I have this dance?"

"Oh, certainly," she replies. "Better than this brute with two left feet."

John grunts in dissatisfaction and bolts back to the table as the singer belts out the final chorus:

"Don't stop believin'
Hold on to that feelin'
Streetlights, people..."

With Macaron dancing with Lily for what feels like an eternity, John defiantly presses his finger to his ear.

"MI6 — status report. What's taking so long?" he mutters under his breath. Gazing upon Lily and Macaron, John's eyes turn green with envy. Steam shoots out of his ears, his mind overheating.

"You just gotta distract him from detonation for ten more minutes," a British accent replies. "Intel shows the puppy barge armed with explosives has almost reached us across the channel. When it does, we can safely disarm it."

"USHF — come in," John queries.

"We've got trouble! The global energy grid has spiked along the Asian seaboard and among the French Alps. Looks like a secret French Hash Force we've never detected is colluding with the existing Chinese, Japanese, and Tibetan miners. They've stopped including American-linked bitcoin transactions in their blocks! Can you politely get him to back down? We've already played our power-projection show-of-force card."

"Ok, I'll do my best to play nice with Frenchie, but no promises!" John cautions. As he watches with disdain as Lily and Macaron dance, a waiter approaches him at the table.

"Here you are, *monsieur*. Your appetizer."

"Appetizer? I didn't order an appetizer! All I ordered was this bourbon."

"I'm sorry, monsieur, but the other gentleman of your party insists. He said he offers this delicacy as a gift. A token of appreciation for the mercy demonstrated today by you, the quote-unquote 'Big American Man.'"

The large 10m x 10m dance floor is pulsing to the beat of the dancers. Lined with well-dressed aristocracy, their smiles give away their relief to let loose. The guitarist has lost all restraint and has stolen the attention of the fine diners with an epic solo. The red and blue laser light show turns white to spotlight him as he shreds his axe. The bassist looks down at his feet, hair covering his eyes, strumming along. The singer shakes as he steals a sip from his water bottle before the next verse.

John searches the dance floor and sees Macaron give him a nod with a wiley grin. Lily gives him the "go-ahead" signal, so John pops one of the hot, slimy appetizer balls into his mouth.

"*Mhmm!* These are tastier than Ma's frito pie," he shouts as Macaron and Lily walk over to join him back at the table. John continues, "These remind me of the Rocky Mountain oysters we have back at home! Of course, I'm grateful they aren't if you know what I mean. What are they, anyways?"

"*Escargots,*" the Frenchman replies, "a local specialty."

"Es-car-what-now?" John asks.

"Snails!" Lily clarifies.

John gags and spits his half-eaten snail onto the floor. He stands up and slams his ten-gallon cowboy hat on the table. "Ok, that's it. I've had enough. Macaron, stop playing nice. We know you've activated some secret alliance with the miners on the other side of the globe. What're you up to?"

"John, don't upset him. Think about the puppies!" Lily pleads.

"To heck with the puppies. I'm not letting this man stand up a Hash Force to DOS attack us. You hear that, Macaron? You mess with the best, and we'll use kinetic force against your miners stashed in the caves of the French Alps."

Tsk, Tsk, Tsk. Macaron wags his finger and mockingly taps the clear trigger cover of the detonator switch clipped to his ascot. "Silly pompous American, did you forget I still have the detonator? Did you really think I would let you get away with rescuing your hideous English Border Collies? Life is one giant power projection game, and the way nation-states survive is by mutually assured preservation. In exchange for taming the unwieldy fur of Tibetan Mastiffs, Chinese Chow Chows, Japanese Shih-Tzu, and Shiba Inus, these countries pledged their miners to our stealthy French Hash Force when we're in need. Well, thanks to your little stunt, not only did I find the perfect opportunity to project power back at you arrogant Americans, but also dump these hideous dogs given to me onto your barge, so they're the British Isles' problem now."

"But we'll be overrun by doges!"

"Yes, Lily. That's what you get for partnering with John. What do Americans say?" Macaron asks rhetorically. "That's right, 'No dogs left behind!' But most of all, John, I just wanted one last dance with your girlfriend and to watch you eat snails!" Macaron tilts his head back to the ceiling to erupt in laughter, gasping two lungfuls of air, but as he exhales, it is not his vocal cords that tingle, but his nose that engorges. The most obnoxious, inhuman, Canadian-Goose-Honking sounds emit from his nostrils to fill the room, holding the dancers at a standstill.

Lily shouts back, "I'm not his girlfriend." She pulls the dog whistle out of her purse and blows it as hard as she can, but it doesn't make a sound. John looks at her, confused, and Macaron honks even harder.

At the entrance to the restaurant, an English Bulldog nuzzles open the door, races to pounce on Lily, and licks her face. As soon as Lily can recover, a second and third English Bulldog rush past her, almost knocking over Macaron. He stumbles but keeps his footing.

"What's this?!" Macaron shouts as the three dogs head towards the exit out the back of the restaurant. Gradually, the restaurant starts to rumble. Then suddenly, the chandeliers sway wildly as a stampede of bulldogs comes barreling through the dining room. Swells of dozens flip over tables, sending plates and glasses shattering onto the dance floor as the dancers scatter, looking for cover.

In the swirling chaos of stampeding dogs, one English Bulldog plants his paws and squares up with Macaron. Dangling from his collar is a tag that reads *Butch*. Macaron swivels his head and locks eyes with the beast. A chill shivers down his spine when he sees Butch lick his lips. Butch lunges forwards at the Frenchman. In his cowardice, he tries to turn away, but the Bulldog strikes him in the chest, sending the detonator clipped to his red ascot flying into the air. The cover of the switch is released, leaving the trigger exposed to the slightest of vibrations.

Lily gasps in horror. Her childhood dog Baxter lost his life too soon, so after all of this turmoil, she can't bear being responsible for one hundred

Border Collies, and now countless Shiba Inus, blowing up on a barge. *Not like this.* As the detonator tumbles back down to Earth, Lily leaps over Macaron and Butch to catch it, cradling it gingerly in her palms. She snaps the cover shut, safely securing the trigger switch to the detonator. *All dogs go to heaven, but not today. Keep chasing your tail, Baxter.*

John extends his hand to her, bewildered, and stammers, "You.... you let the bitcoin dogs out."

Lily gets to her feet, secures the detonator in her purse next to the whistle, and brushes off the dog hair. "You think you wankers got all the tricks? The English have a few surprises, too. Now, c'mon, let's follow those dogs out the back. My Mini Cooper is waiting, and this time, I'm driving!"

The Post Globe
OUR WORLD
Archaeologists Find Monument From 4000 B.C.
U.S. Dollar Strong Gold Standard Says

16

Shiro

Anonymous

The following article was found in The Post Globe newspaper dated Thursday, July 29, 1976

SANTIAGO, CHILE (AP) — An American military jet slips in from the sea, past the grim old monoliths that ring Rapa Sat Island, and roars to a short, dusty stop on the new airstrip.

Molish Moari dashes out of his pink stucco house and mounts his motorbike. "My butter is on that plane!" he yells. "Tonight, we'll have butter for the corn and lobster!" Excitement erupted throughout the village of Hangaroa, where nearly all of Easter Island's 1,500 mostly Polynesian inhabitants live.

The lobster feast celebrates a new discovery on Rapa Sat, a 48-foot-tall ancient monument has been discovered on the island, and the locals are brimming with questions.

Dr. Shiro Wakaranai of the Otis Institute of Archaeologists and his team have been excavating on Rapa Sat since January. While other symbolic structures have been discovered during that time, there has been nothing this grand in scale and character. "We discovered a rectangular granite post and assumed that digging deeper would uncover more of the same," said Dr. Wakaranai, "Imagine our surprise to discover the post floating above the soil, suspended in mid-air."

The team nicknamed the giant discovery simply "the Sat" in honor of the island. While the find is authentic, the reason for its construction remains a mystery. The team dates the Sat to around 4000 B.C.

FINAL Edition

The Post Globe

FINAL Edition

VOL. 135 NO. 211 THURSDAY, JULY 29, 1976 15 CENTS 56 PAGES

Rapa Sat Island —— Head archaeolo[illegible] Dr. [illegible]y (atop the monument) and his team measure the height of the recently disc[illegible] [illegible] when asked what keeps the horizontal sections suspended in mid-air Dr. [illegible]

OUR WORLD

Archaeologists Find Monument From 4000 B.C.

SANTIAGO, CHILE (AP) — An American military jet slipped in from the sea past the grim old monoliths that ring Rapa Sat Island and roared to a short and dusty stop on the new airstrip.

Molish Moari dashed out of his pink stucco house and mounted his motorbike. "My butter is on that plane!" he yelled. "Tonight we'll have butter for the corn and lobster!" Throughout the village of Hangaroa, where nearly all of Easter Island's 1,500 mostly Polynesian inhabitants live, there was excitement.

Not everyone was lucky enough to have an American friend bringing butter or soap or any of the many other things lacking on this island 2,350 miles west of Chile, which annexed it in 1888. But the twice-monthly visit of a United States Air Force transport has become nearly as great a thrill for most of the people as the occasional visits by the square-riggers of traders were to their ancestors.

The lobster feast is in celebration of a new discovery on Rapa Sat; a 48 foot tall ancient monument has been discover on the island and the island is brimming with questions.

Dr. Shiro Wakaranai of the Otis Institute of Archaeologists and his team has been escavating on Rapa Sat since March. While other symbolic structures have been discover during that time there has been nothing this grand in scale and character. "We discovered a rectangular granite post assuming that digging deeper would uncover more of the same," said Dr. Wakaranai, "Imagine our surprise to discover the post floating *above* the soil, suspended in mid-air."

The team nicknamed the giant discovery simply "the Sat." in honor of the island. While the find is authentic the reason for it's construction remains a mystery. The team dates the Sat around 4000 B.C.,

(continued on pg. 4)

U.S. Dollar Stronger Off Gold Standard Says Gov't

WASHINGTON (AP) — Financial security for American families are assured says the incoming Chairman of the Federal Reserve, Arthur F. Burns. "The burden of gold parity to U.S. bank notes has been lifted to allow an inflow of economic strategies that will allow your dollars to not only grow, but to grow mightily." said Mr. Burns.

For the end of time a single American worker will always have a living wage, an affordable home, and access to healthcare where a family will never have to struggle.

When asked about the dangers of printing money and removing the value of scarcity Mr. Burns laughed "Why would that be an issue? Endless at all." John Bishop of Evergreen, Illinois has his doubts. "I'm not an economist or anything but it seems to me that printing dollars that aren't fixed to anything defeats the purpose." Bishop said, "Isn't that a recipe for inflation?"

Of course time will tell if this great fiscal experiment will stand the test of time. Burns dismisses the doubt. "If it doesn't work, although we know it will, we'll revert to the gold standard again." he said, "Nixon and his advisors were smart enough to know that fail-safe measures must be put in place along with the full backing of the American banking system to make sure that citizens will not suffer financially. You'll see things getting better and better every year from now on."

What is particularly interesting about this story — besides the giant floating stones — is that it's not in any public record. In fact, this particular newspaper edition was never actually published. Why? And how does a regular guy who paints murals for a living know all this? Because I'm the one who found this newspaper.

I

In January 2176, I was hired to paint an animated mural at Álvarez Fusion HQ in Lincoln, Nebraska. I later discovered the building previously belonged to *The Post Globe* newspaper *c.1955 to 2004*. This job was already behind schedule. Once on-site, we discovered the size of the mural wouldn't fit on the lobby wall without hitting a 90-degree return. Animated murals tend to glitch at corners and get worse over time, so for this job, the client needed to tear out the corner and add two extra meters of straight wall to accommodate the mural. The BuildBots made a racket all around me as I worked.

One evening, after the bots powered down and I was packing up for the night, I saw a roll of paper peeking out of a destroyed wall. A newspaper! It must have been stuffed in the wall during the original building construction. I had never actually touched a newspaper before. They can be worth quite a bit, and this one wasn't in bad shape. On the front page was the article about "the Sat" discovery. Next to the article was an incredible picture of giant stone slabs weighing tons, seemingly floating in the air above an excavated hole in the ground. I had never heard of it. No one had ever heard of it. Lev tech was less than thirty years old, so nothing could have levitated 200 years ago. This must have been a gag, possibly a novelty newspaper printed one time as an inside joke between a group of pranksters.

I pressed the SeeRing on my finger and made a query: "Dr. Shiro Wakaranai, Otis Institute of Archaeologists." An image materialized of an affable-looking young man of Japanese descent, disheveled and in need of a proper haircut. He looked more like a ragged ditch digger than a scrupulously groomed man of science. To the right of his picture appeared his name "Dr. Shiro Wakaranai, MA, RPA, Assoc. Professor of Archeology, UNO. Born January 3, 1951, died August 11, 1976," followed by a brief but unremarkable record of his life and work. He died young. In fact, he died shortly after discovering the monument on Rapa Sat. What should have been a scientist's magnum opus was glaringly absent from his bio.

II

The University of Nebraska, Omaha, I thought, that's not too far from here. I pressed the ring again and said, "Dr. Shiro Wakaranai, present lineage starting 1976." An arrow materialized across my field of vision, drawn from left to right. More faces appeared, starting with his wife, Melissa Fields (née Wakaranai), a celebrated philanthropist. She lived well into her eighties. The next line revealed their only child, Dr. Michael Wakaranai, MD, PhD, Head of Pathology at Stature Health. He and his wife had three children. The line broke apart and became many lines; they blossomed into scores of fractal groupings. More lives, all connected to Dr. Shiro Wakaranai. More names followed by many professional credentials. Dr. Wakaranai would've been proud of his progeny. There were a lot of smarts in this family tree.

"Pause," I said around the fourth and fifth generations. Although my entire view was now filled with thousands of names and faces, one name stood out to me. I pointed my finger and gently spun my ring with my thumb to zoom in closer. "Deb Colleymore, Senior Scientist, Staheli Sciences. Born 2146." Hmm, we're almost the same age, I thought. *Staheli Sciences*. I've seen that somewhere before. I know that name from somewhere.

It didn't take long to figure out. 'STAHELI SCIENCES' were the giant words floating around a red tower adjacent to my hotel. The tower had been framed quite nicely by my west-facing window. Though clearly seen, it never piqued my interest until now. From then on, when I looked out the window, I saw nothing else.

Too many coincidences, I thought. Deb Colleymore, the great-great-great-great-great granddaughter of Dr. Shiro, works right *there*. The universe was screaming for me to take another step. I pressed my ring. "Is Deb Collymore listed?"

The SeeRing returned, "Deb Colleymore is not listed." I didn't sleep well that night.

The subterranean entrance to the Staheli building was directly across from the coffee shop where I was now sitting. I had been in this spot since 6:30 am, smelling cappuccinos and croissants while my line of sight was floating just above the sidewalk sign that read, *"Hey girl, how you bean?"* Every employee of Staheli Sciences had to pass directly by me before they reached the front doors leading to their workstations. It didn't take long before the morning rush moved past me like a flood. I stood to get a better view of each passing face, hoping I wouldn't miss her. What if she had cut her hair short? What if she dyed it from sandy blonde to some other color? What if she's on vacation? But then she made her appearance. She looked exactly like the picture I saw the day before. She stood out, walking tall with purpose while others around her were distracted, absently consuming the morning news or chatting away on their See.

I leaped forward into the crowd, making my way towards her but having no idea what I was going to say. "Excuse me. Deb?" I would try to sound like a colleague. I was too timid, and the noise of the crowd was not helping. There was a clearing in the flow of the crowd that would get me to within a meter of her, so I juked through it. *"Miss Colleymore!"* I said louder than I meant to.

She jumped and turned toward me wide-eyed, her hands raised in quasi-self-defense.

"I'm sorry," I said quickly. "I didn't mean to scare you."

She stayed rigid except for a subtle turn of her head, her eyes still on me.

I stumbled and stammered, trying to explain my existence. I was a muralist... the wall demolition... the newspaper... the name of her company. It all sounded so disjointed; she didn't wait for me to get to the point. "Oh, okay. Hmm, well, I must be going," she said as she turned her back on me and hurried towards the entrance, making a beeline to the uniformed security guard standing just inside the doors.

"Shiro Wakaranai is in that newspaper!" I yelled.

She stopped in an instant. All at once, the last of the commuters seemed to drain away, and the space around us suddenly became empty and quiet as a church. She turned around. "Say that again."

I held up the newspaper that was at my side, the picture of the Sat immediately grabbing her attention.

She walked slowly back towards me.

III

The people of Lincoln moved via underground tunnels in the deep winter. They were cozy but crowded tunnels. It was not an ideal place for private conversation without distraction, so we agreed to meet later that evening on Prairie Plains, an elevated park directly above my hotel. El-parks are spread out, warm, and shielded with enough protective energy that we could meet high above the city skyline even in the middle of the freezing Nebraska winter. It was public, but we could talk privately.

Deb was a pretty lady. She had green eyes and was professionally dressed. She wore a cream-colored business jacket along with a flowy orange scarf that swayed comfortably past her shoulders. I thought she looked more like a business executive than a scientist. She looked younger than me even though she was three years my senior. Working mainly on building sites like I do can age you prematurely. I could tell she wasn't a field scientist, unlike Dr. Shiro. As we sat on a secluded bench near the edge of the park, She held the newspaper gently with both hands, pouring over the article and the photo again and again, smiling all the while. Then she turned her eyes to meet mine, eager to listen to the details of my find.

When I asked if she had known about the Sat monument before her eyes no longer darted around playfully, she became present. She locked onto my eyes and stayed there for a while.

She said "Yes, I know all about this. My family holds Shiro in very high regard. He's left quite a legacy. How this article was printed and then successfully buried, however, is a complete mystery to me." Her expression softened as if a long-held breath was finally released from deep in her chest. She put her hand on my arm, "I'll share it with you. It's time, I think. You already know the beginning. You might as well know it all."

Rapa Sat, 1976. Dr. Shiro Wakaranai climbed up the ladder that was leaning on the lowest slab of the Sat and walked out of the excavation site. His small Datsun truck nearby had his water canteen on the front seat, and he was grateful to have a taste. He sat down in the driver's seat and pondered the stone slabs through the truck windshield with muddy wiper streaks, visualizing those streaks as a primitive measuring caliper to playfully gauge dimensions on the Sat.

Lately, he had preferred to work alone. He would rather discuss precise measurements and mass using state-of-the-art tools that he had ordered from the institute, but all his peers wanted to talk about was their imminent fame. The locals only wanted to talk about the riches tourist dollars would surely bring to the island. Shiro wanted none of it. His curiosity about anthropology and archeology had always been insatiable. He just loved digging. He imagined every handful of dirt brought him closer to mankind, and every significant find broadened his understanding of humanity. He had survived Vietnam only to return to violence here at home. Shiro thought of war as an absolute absurdity, and so did the voice.

Three weeks ago, Shiro heard a whisper in his ear — a murmur both old and kind coming from the ancient stones. The voice wasn't speaking a known language, but Shiro could understand it. It wasn't making a sound, but Shiro could hear it, sometimes in his ear, other times through his chest. He couldn't explain it, so, like any good scientist, he asked questions. The voice provided answers.

On August 11, 1976, the day he reportedly died, Melissa Wakaranai received a letter from her husband. On that day, the colossal Sat simply fell to the ground without warning. Shiro, who was working in the pit below, was killed instantly. No one else was injured, but the Sat was in ruins, broken apart, and returned to the Earth as a shattered rock. In the letter, Shiro spoke of *understanding* the Sat, explaining that it wasn't an inanimate object at all but more of a sentient force. He wrote about the voice. He could not say if it were theological, extraterrestrial, or even magical; all he knew was it was good. It spoke of old truths and universal knowledge that would benefit billions all over the world. He wrote about his own death, predicting the monument would fall back to the earth and be buried forever and him with it. Its purpose was done while his purpose was just beginning.

Deb Colleymore had a scan of that letter now floating between us.

"Only my body will be gone. I'm not useful to the world as Shiro Wakaranai, the archeologist. I'm too small, too human. I will share knowledge anonymously. I will speak as different people through time, planting world-changing ideas for the good of humanity. Ideas passed on from this wisdom of unknown origin.

I profess my eternal love to you, Melissa. Know that I will be with you and Mikey forever through time, watching lovingly. You will know when I am near, it will be impossible to miss. No matter what happens, I remain your devoted husband and Mikey's proud father."

When Deb saw that I was through reading the letter, she closed the See file and looked back down at the old newspaper between us, her eyes brimming with tears. We sat in silence for a few minutes while I digested everything.

"So," I finally said, "over the last 200 years, these anonymous discoveries... ?"

She nodded. "Jawahir Mirza?"[1] I asked.

She answered, "... Gave us cures for the world's most devastating diseases; nobody knows who they are, and they haven't been heard from since 2080."

"Guy Brisbois?", I questioned.

She replied, "The anonymous architect of a balanced justice system."

1 Jawahir — Gender: Female, Origin: Arabic, Meaning: Jewel
Mirza — Gender: Neutral, Origin: Arabic, Meaning: Prince

"Mateo Álvarez?"

"—Gave us a blueprint to harness the Sun… unlimited energy. He holds no patents. We don't know who he was."

"Mei Li!" I blurted out "revolutionized food distribution, then…"

"Poof," finished Deb.

Who else? I wondered.

"Satoshi Nakamoto," she said, "created the monetary system that freed us from financial subjugation. That was his first persona, back in 2009. Melissa and Michael had known it was Shiro because of the name: Satoshi… Sat. It had to be him. Each great contribution is given freely, and each great discovery or idea is passed through an anonymous figure. That's Shiro," she said proudly.

We sat in silence for a while. She fished in her purse for a tissue. I shifted in my seat to look at the clear night sky through the gently pulsing energy field, a technology made possible, coincidentally, by Mateo Álvarez.

"Now you know," she said, lightly touching the newspaper next to me. "Are you okay?"

I thought about it for a moment. "I think I am."

She nodded, then stood up. Three hours had passed. She put her hand on my shoulder and thanked me. Then she turned and began to walk away.

"Your newspaper," I said, lifting it toward her.

She smiled at me and said, "Finders keepers," then left me there. Alone with the stars. They were bright.

17

Panama One

Carl Andrews

Ricardo Castillo climbed the last few steps to the newly completed observation deck of Panama Four, careful not to betray his shortness of breath to his assistant. They had arrived at New Darién that morning from the mainland, part of an entourage ferried in on a small fleet of hydrocopters that skimmed over the Pacific waves. Disembarking, they gazed, wide-eyed like children, upon the colossal construction works. Ricardo had made the pilgrimage many times already, but for some moments he, too, could only stare in wonder at the scale of it all. New Darién, the vast artificial island fabricated several degrees south of Panama itself, was remarkable, but that was not the creation that drew their eyes to the heavens.

Long dreamed of and written about, Earth's first space elevator reared up endlessly into the sky before Ricardo's eyes, a gargantuan column that climbed and thrust out of the atmosphere to ascend thousands of kilometers above it. The support and observation towers, Panamas Two to Six, ringed the base of the elevator. Each of them was, by normal standards (pre-hyperbitcoinization standards), a mega-structure in itself, yet they were barely anthills next to the giant redwood of Panama One. Soon, a vast ring would connect its apex to the other towers that were under construction around the equator, a globe-girdling circlet that would open up the entire solar system for exploration. How strange to think that its progress could be disrupted or even brought to a halt if his opponents had their way.

"Rayo, it seems our guest will be a little late. Can I get you a coffee?"

"Late? I didn't think that was possible. Yes, thank you, Anna."

Ricardo turned back to the view. A little time, then, to further marshall his thoughts, if one could drag one's attention away from the sight before him. He smiled. Rayo. Only Anna called him that, though most everyone knew the childhood nickname his father had given him. My little Rayo, my lightning bolt! Dashing around here, there, and everywhere. He may have been naturally hyperactive, but as the first son of the president, 'the man who changed everything,' well, maybe the lifestyle had rubbed off on him too. Then he frowned, recalling his earlier exchange with the chairperson of the opposition alliance. The 'copter ride had thrilled everyone except for the corpulent, pasty-faced Carlsteen, who had nearly thrown up. He was still perspiring an hour later when he sidled up to Ricardo.

"Ah, Senator Carlsteen, I hope you've recovered. You looked a little unaccustomed to our mode of transport this morning, but then again, you so rarely leave the chambers."

"You've built yourself quite the holiday home here, Castillo." He fingered the moisture under his nose as he glanced at the party. "You may have fooled them, but we both know the Long Cycle plan is a fraud, a deliberate and grotesque waste of money. Or perhaps it's your secret retirement fund, eh? Time's up, Castillo. If your special friend fails to deliver today, we will move to dismiss you, your party, and your management of this scheme."

Carlsteen scuttled away at the approach of some of the delegates. He and his cronies had been against New Darién from the start. Even in these days of economic enlightenment, political hucksters like them could just about carve out a comfortable niche with their promises of free handouts. Though their numbers were dwindling, there were still snakes in paradise.

Far below, a sudden flare on the ground caught Rayo's eye. One of the geothermal tubes was venting. The island had been designed not only to sit on the equator, but also atop a high ridge on the ocean floor below, a finesse to better exploit the Earth's ceaseless, seething molten power. Of course, some of this energy would be tapped for bitcoin mining. No construction project of any significance nowadays was without some allocation of power to 'The Mining,' but chiefly, the energy was used to help send the island's architectural behemoth to the sky. Or its leviathan, seeing as it was on the ocean. Then again, wasn't there an analogous monster for the sky? Something like, Zeess... a Zisse.

"Your coffee, Rayo."

Ricardo pulled away from the glass. "Thank you, Anna."

"I'll leave it on the table. The administrator should be here in the next ten minutes or so."

With a smile, Anna left him alone on the observation deck. He had never doubted his friend before, but Carlsteen's snide insinuations had begun to make him wonder; the Long Cycle plan really didn't add up. How could that be? With the monolithic marvel of Panama One filling the vista before him, Ricardo's thoughts slipped back through the years to when all this had begun — The Day That Changed Everything.

***

"Rayo! Rayo, we did it. We did it!"

His father beamed, swinging them both around backstage, perspiration on his bearded face and dancing delight in his eyes. It was not often that the president of a small Central American country told the collected leaders of the First World how things were going to go, but today marked such an event. The culmination of several years of international planning, development, and diplomacy - with Ricardo at the heart of it — some ostentatious, some superficial, but most of it clandestine.

"We did, father, we *did*."

"Ah, Francisco. Bravo, my friend, a triumph!"

Manuel Ortega eased his way through the excited throng, his imposing height tempered by his suave manner. As the president of a neighbouring country, Ortega had been one of his father's earliest collaborators. "But I tell you, Frisco, they don't like it out there, not one bit."

"Well, let's give them some time to digest it. Eating your first bite of humble pie can't be easy."

Ortega laughed and moved past to buttonhole the Sub-Saharan delegation. Francisco put his arm around Ricardo. "Let us get a drink, Rayo, and sample the air?"

Francisco winked, and the two of them began to circulate in the lobby, testing the waters, taking readings amongst the assembled representatives.

Out on the floor of the assembly hall, the atmosphere was tense despite being less than a third full. The majority of the representatives exited following Castillo's announcement, having made their point. The remainder huddled around the front rows, mixing frantic whispers with raised voices, ties loosened beneath pale faces. Overall, it did indeed look like some of that humble pie had gone down the wrong way.

When Francisco, Ricardo, and their entourage had entered the United Nations Assembly Building that morning, rumours of a special announcement intensified. It was to be expected. For several years, the whole of Central America had developed at rates exceeding the likes of Singapore and China; the spectacular growth of these *jaguar economies* had propelled the emergence of a pan-regional infrastructure. Tourism had exploded, and citizenship applications had ballooned, up and up, year after year. It had all started with one country and its president, Ricardo's father, taking the leap and declaring bitcoin its official currency. Naturally, back then, bitcoin and his father became the target of all the dirty financial tricks and manipulations the IMF and its cronies could conjure. Now, after long preparation, Francisco was ready to play a trick of his own.

"To the members here today, my greetings; to the President of the assembly, my thanks for the invitation to speak about all we have been doing in our homeland." Francisco stood at the podium with its famous green marble backdrop, the delegates of the world before him. Rayo and Manuel were seated off to one side, taking in the mood of the hall. "It is true, my friends, that I could talk for many hours about what has been accomplished there and by our companions and neighbours throughout the region. The explosive growth of our economies, the feats of science and engineering, our cultural and artistic flowerings, and most importantly, the societal improvements that have made the everyday lives of our citizens worth living again. Yes, one could speak on these marvels for a long time, but word of our triumphs has already been carried far and wide across the globe. Instead, I shall talk about something far more interesting. What my colleagues and I now wish for most is for the world to follow in our footsteps, to do what we have done ourselves. Today, we are going to show you exactly how to do it."

It was funny, thought Francisco, that the Western delegates, clustered near the front as always, almost certainly presumed him to be addressing his fellow global Southerners. They would soon realise that the address was aimed squarely at them.

"The most incredible thing about our progress was what enabled it all in the first place — bitcoin. Well, now I can confirm the rumours. We intend to use bitcoin to take our development to the next level. We shall begin issuing our very own bitcoin Volcano Bonds. Yes, the perfect monetary asset, combined with the mining power of geothermal energy to guarantee its security. Legalised by our newly passed digital securities law and enabled by bitcoin's secondary and tertiary layers."

An excited murmur broke out. Francisco smiled in acknowledgment and continued. "Never again will our country or our neighbours need to beg at Wall Street's table to facilitate a fiat bond, nor will we need to go on bended knee to the IMF for an extortionate loan. By harnessing the power of our bonds, our markets, our money — bitcoin, we can break the chains of the fiat system that have held us all captive for so long."

Cheers spread from the back of the hall. At the front, quiet exchanges and notes passed. Ricardo and Ortega observed them; they did not seem particularly surprised by the announcement. They would have been briefed by their intelligence agencies, of course. Francisco's original experiment had drawn the full attention of the G20 countries' state apparatus, from central bank warnings to covert infiltration plots — all of them uncovered in the end. Talk of the Volcano Bond had been circulating for some time. It was prudent to assume they had already drawn their plans against the bond, knowing it would soon put their kind out of business. Yet, Ricardo sensed a puzzlement amongst them. Was that it? Was that all that Castillo had come with?

Francisco raised his arms to quieten the hall. "Yes, my friends, wonderful news. But perhaps, to some of you, old news?" He grinned at the front rows.

Ricardo could see uncertainty spreading among them.

"So let me tell you about the arrangement we have come to with our partnering nations. Tomorrow will see the launch, not just of our bond offering, but over one hundred other bitcoin bonds, in over one hundred countries, all at once. Trading will be available immediately, and like bitcoin itself, available every hour of every day, every day of the year. Most importantly, participation will be universally available, using Lightning micropayments, and there will be no minimum investment requirements—"

Cheering broke out again. Journalists typed frantically on their devices and various minions flitted between the front rows and an anxious press of bureaucratic types that had suddenly appeared at the entrance.

Francisco wasn't finished. "We call them, 'Tierra Bonds,' as they will unite the whole world by using the world's energy to power them. Volcano and geothermal, tidal and hydro, landfill and stranded gas, and naturally, fossil fuels and nuclear. Our engineers have been busy assisting the setup of these projects, and our diplomats too."

Very busy, thought Ricardo, watching the hubbub. The last several years had seen him live up to his nickname, zipping and zapping between the least-developed, under-developed, and developing world countries as one of his father's emissaries, laying the groundwork and smoothing the way. It had been surprisingly easy. Everyone had seen how successful his father's bitcoin experiment had been and were eager for a chance to slip their fiat chains and share in the prosperity.

"... with preferential priority going to that country's own citizens."

It was getting hard to hear. Delegates were on their feet, and an impromptu conga line was forming at the back. Ricardo tried not to smirk. This was the moment. A coordinated action to bypass the existing financial infrastructure — a preemptive strike calculated to send the price of bitcoin into orbit. They had been distracted by the possibility of a single bond, and this onslaught of overwhelming numbers would shake their system to the core.

"And finally, I would like to thank our partner nations, one by one. Honduras, The Democratic Republic of Congo, Indonesia..."

Ricardo, aware of how long the list was, tuned out and watched the standing throngs erupt with scattered cheering as each country was announced. The seated delegates were in disarray, the naming of each country like a bell tolling their expiration date. The speech was being televised internationally, and Ricardo was relishing the roll call's dramatic impact. Eventually, as pre-arranged, the bulk of the hall began to filter out into the lobby space just as Francisco was finishing.

"... Cameroon, Sri Lanka, and last but not least, Panama. *Vires in Numeris*, Strength in Numbers. Thank you all!"

Manuel Ortega turned and raised his eyes comically as he passed the marooned front row on his way to the lobby.

Ricardo laughed and ran to hug his father.

***

Everything had happened quickly after that night, thought Ricardo, still gazing through the observation window. Accomplishments, particularly in engineering, came in spate as civilisation moved up several gears. One of the earliest was the filling of the Darién Gap, the 100 kilometres of notoriously impenetrable rainforest and marsh that was the only break in the otherwise continuous 30,000km Pan-American Highway. Mired for decades in political and environmental wrangles, the road had been pushed through less than a year after Francisco's triumph, though few had anticipated the accompanying monorail. It had been a vital step for the construction of New Darién out in the ocean, and Panama One resting upon it — the tower that grew to the sky. The space elevator would always have been a theoretical plaything under the fiat system. Now, thanks to the advances in science that the Bitcoin Bond Era had enabled, along with a little outside help, Panama One was about to commence operations, ferrying cargo and passengers up along its length directly into space from the island below.

There was a shimmering in the air that Ricardo sensed rather than saw. He turned to the boardroom table behind him, but there was no sign of anything amiss.

At that moment, Anna came through the glass door with their visitor. He had to crouch under the doorway, then uncoiled himself to his full three-metre height. "Director Castillo. A pleasure to see you again."

"Likewise, Administrator, likewise."

Ricardo stretched to shake hands. Administrator Telluris glanced out at the tower he and his compatriots had helped build. The gamble that was the Interstellar Blockchain Broadcast Project had paid off far quicker and far beyond what anyone could have imagined when the first lunar arrays began signaling two decades ago. The day the Telluris and his people landed, Ricardo's father had been the first to greet them.

"A wondrous sight, this Ziz of ours? 'The giant creature of the air, whose feet only were covered by the ocean, and whose head pressed against the sky,'" quoted Telluris. "But *we* must press on. The time has arrived to finalise the unification of our economic systems."

This wasn't the first time the Administrator had hinted at some kind of psychical access to his thoughts, aside from his boundless knowledge of Earthly arcana, but Ricardo had never had any reason not to feel reassured by it. It spoke to insights beyond even the fantastic technology they had provided to the planet's inhabitants. As for signing bitcoin transactions with aliens, though...

"The Blockchain Broadcast Project," said Ricardo, "was a speculation and part insurance policy. But your Long Cycle Plan — you must know it can't work as it stands. They're calling it a fraud, and I can't prove it otherwise. I won't be able to stop them from taking control of Panama One and ruining it."

"Even though a demonstration of it would secure both the tower and your position? The benefits will be beyond question."

"We agree it would be wonderful for intergalactic harmony, but it can't get around the lightspeed problem, the distances. It needs to be instantaneous for it—"

"That was misdirection on our part," said Telluris. "The plan was a cover story. Please forgive us. We needed to know your intentions before we could show you."

"Show us?"

"Look on the table."

There was nothing on the table, except for the coffee cup. The whole complex had been swept for devices before the Administrator had arrived. Plus, the island was still in its construction phase and restricted to a vetted list of construction engineers. Ricardo moved the cup and was astonished to see a small and intricately carved golden cube nestling behind it.

"It's not magic, Rayo."

"Just sufficiently advanced technology," he said, completing the famous quotation.

"More than sufficient, I trust. We had to withhold some of our powers until you were ready. The cube itself is—"

“Teleportation. Instant communications. That means...”

“Bitcoin can be used in our world, or any other, in real-time. Everything will be synchronised. The Earth can enter into value exchange with the rest of the galaxy.”

The Administrator gave his analogy of a smile. “Certainly sufficient to secure your directorship and the future of the tower.”

The shimmer returned to Rayo’s eyes, but this time it wasn’t the teleportation field. Instead, images of immeasurable possibilities stretched out endlessly before him, further even than did Panama One.

EXTRAVGAN

18

Are We, or Are We Not?

Alex Gurevich

Rhonda sipped her tea and ran a hand through the mess of her uncombed curls. "I have to fly to Washington," she said.

"That's quite *extravagant,*" Emily replied on cue. "What gives?"

This was a gimme. Emily was lucky that "extravagant" had slipped right into the sentence. Rhonda pushed the reset button on her timer and glanced down at the crumpled piece of paper spread carefully on the tabletop. Her own next code word was *induction*. In fifty-seven seconds, she had to work the word "induction" into a sentence.

"Do you remember Anand Klein?"

"Of course, I remember him." Emily shrugged. Her image on the screen froze mid-shrug, but her voice was still coming through. "A complete nerd in school, but he made it big. I heard he was like a colonel in the Crypto Mining Force."

"He was in the CMF all right. But the rumor is that he's the president now. It kinda makes sense. If he kept getting promoted, then by *induction* he would rise to the very top." Rhonda took a deep breath. "What do you think?"

That was lame. Emily's face unfroze as another DOS attack ended.

Rhonda watched her friend's lips curve up as if to say, 'Is that all you got?'

When Emily spoke, she made no reference to the source of her amusement. "Can't help you there, babe. Here in Miami, the word is Abigail Lee is the president. But I don't think she is in D.C. In any case, I thought D.C. was no longer the capital. Isn't the kingpin in Austin now?" *Kingpin*. Another lucky break for Emily.

There was a genuine reason to work the code words in seamlessly. Malbots tended to detect extra security in conversations and increase the level of attack in the hope that there was a bitcoin transfer involved.

Trying to one-up each other at inserting the code words was also a game between them. There weren't many people around that Rhonda could actually have fun with.

"Well, here in San Francisco, they still call Washington the capital. I need to find out." "It's not safe to go there now. I don't know much about the government, but I know finance. I track the flows." Emily's smile faded away. "The Treasury has no currency. Its main store must be locked or hacked." She was clearly avoiding words like "crypto," "bitcoin," or "wallet" to escape attracting malware. "That would be the hack of the *era!*" Rhonda responded triumphantly. At last, she got a freebie.

"I don't know what it was, but something's up. If they have no reserves, they can't pay the Secret Service or any other security. There might be chaos around the White House, whether any government is there or not." Emily's eyes narrowed a bit. "But, really, why do you care if he is the president?"

Rhonda briefly considered telling Emily about the last time she had a link with Anand. If it had indeed been him.

Emily was the only bitcoinaire among Rhonda's friends, and she could help with her connections or advice. Rhonda hesitated and glanced at the paper again. The word she saw made her smile wickedly. She would wait for Emily to speak again first. Let her try to work the word *colander* into the conversation.

"Anyway," Emily continued, "If you do decide to travel, I have a website for you. Associated Airlines. For the next thirty minutes or so, you can reliably book plane tickets and transfer payment."

Rhonda's timer went off. She sighed, disconnected from the network, and entered the command to wipe her hard drive. She put the paper with her code words in the shredder and launched her profile on the spare laptop. What she had been talking to for the last few seconds of their conversation was no longer Emily.

While the start-up sequence spun on the new device, she got up and opened her safe. There were eleven sheets of paper in an old-fashioned plastic folder. The untitled green folder was for Emily. Eleven more secure conversations with the initial password and code words to last for thirty minutes. She wondered briefly if using *green* was in and of itself a security risk: somewhere on the net, there might be a record of green being Emily's favorite color.

There was no point in wasting another precious sheet to call Emily back. She was on the malware radar now.

Rhonda scooped a few gold and silver coins and a USB drive from the safe, leaving the green folder untouched.

Driving across the country was not an option — she'd never dare to plug in her car at an unknown charging station. Trying to search for airplane tickets on the Internet was useless as well. The malbots were now aware that she was in the market for air travel; she would just run into more scams like Fake Emily, leading her to the *Associated Airlines* website.

Rhonda had to go directly to the airport kiosk. There was nowhere safe to leave her car, so she asked her neighbor to give her a ride in exchange for permission to harvest produce from Rhonda's porch garden in her absence.

It took Rhonda hours to make it through the ticketing line at the airport. The clerk had a mass spectrometer to verify her metal coins, but still wouldn't accept them.

He sounded apologetic. "Sorry, I can't be sure of the price of gold now.

Normally, we're allowed to take some risk, but these days, everyone is talking about the government selling precious metals to make up for the lack of bitcoin reserves. All the quotes we get are like ten times apart."

Making a bitcoin transfer in public was dangerous. Taking a furtive look around, Rhonda tried to spot anyone who might intercept her transaction. Eventually, she dug into her pouch for her USB. Fortunately, the airport kiosks were still secure. She finally made it to the red-eye after spending the whole day in the airport.

The attendant on the plane did accept a silver coin in exchange for a stale bagel and an overcooked egg. Later, she wished she had skipped the meal.

The next morning, Rhonda awoke disheveled and exhausted. Fighting bouts of queasiness, she pushed through the throngs of Pennsylvania Avenue.

Entry to the White House was closed. Rhonda contemplated climbing the fence. However, despite what Emily had said, there were, in fact, a bunch of people on the White House Lawn. They wore uniform jackets with "Security" and "Secret Service" printed on their backs and sported fancy earpieces and shiny name tags.

Rhonda was reasonably certain these people had nothing to do with the government and would certainly not go anywhere near them with the USB in her belt pouch.

She wrapped her arms around herself as a shield against the jostling crowd and mumbled. "Anand, how do I get to you?"

"Rhonda? What are you doing here?"

She spun around to face his intense dark eyes and narrow nose. They were the exact same height, which was something she had always considered auspicious. His too-short khaki slacks showed old tennis shoes, and his sweater was too heavy for late spring in D.C. A sheen of sweat-covered his shaved face.

"Anand! What? Aren't you...?" She motioned at the White House.

He made a shushing motion. "Follow me. My digs are right here." He pointed at the Herbert Hoover Building. "I just stepped out for groceries."

"Oh, I am the president all right," he said once he locked and secured the door.

The Federal Building had long been a residential apartment complex, but Anand's place was separate, accessed only by a maintenance door left from when the National Aquarium was situated in the building.

The residence had no windows but was spacious and well-appointed. The large oval wooden table in the living room tickled Rhonda's memory as having something to do with movies she had watched as a kid.

"Not many people know my face," Anand continued. "So I can sneak around a bit."

"But the White House?"

"It's a decoy. Since the March Insurrection, it hasn't been safe for me to appear in public."

"So, there *was* an insurrection?" Rhonda blurted out. "I thought it was a media hoax."

"No, it was quite real. Guns and shit." Anand shook his head. "You look beat. Why don't you sit down?" He pointed to a plush armchair. "Tea, I assume. Or have you switched to coffee over the years?"

"Still tea." Rhonda nodded and slowly lowered herself onto the soft cushion and continued to study Anand as he bent over the kettle.

They hadn't spoken since the ceremony. It was conducted from the mining space station, which was his command, through a secure military link. Anand had stood with his back to the observation deck. She could see the enormous span of the solar panels powering the crypto mining facility, like wings above the insignia on his shoulders. It seemed too perfect to be real. In truth, it was even too perfect to be a fake.

Now Anand's shoulders were marked only by the fuzz from his sweater. He still projected authority.

"The insurrection," Rhonda said. "How did you survive?"

"Everything was compromised, everything was overrun. I thought I would be captured at gunpoint at any moment. Fortunately, the digital offensive before the physical attack attracted an army of random malbots. Their communication was scrambled, and they ended up fighting each other. All the Secret Service had to do was to clean up the mess afterward."

"And where is this Secret Service now?"

"Left for the private sector, I assume. The government's too broke to compete. And the job just got too dangerous." He poured the tea and stepped closer, gingerly placing the steaming mug on the polished wood. "Speaking of danger, I can't even imagine how hard it must have been for you to get to Washington."

Rhonda took a sip of hot liquid. It settled her stomach. She stood, gathering her courage, and fumbled for her pouch. She pulled out a glossy sheet of paper with multiple watermarks. "I came all the way here to ask one question, Anand." She held up the certificate. "Are we married or not?" Without a word, Anand walked to the wall and palmed an ordinary-looking panel. It swung open to reveal a safe. In continuing silence, he keyed in a password and let his retina be scanned. There was a stack of folders inside, but Anand reached for the yellow one without hesitation. He pulled out a sheet matching Rhonda's and placed it on the oval table. "When I thought all was lost, I encrypted access to the Treasury Bitcoin Wallet with our marriage certificate. Without you, I wouldn't be able to release the bitcoins, regardless of what they did to me. Later, I needed you to unlock the coins, but I had no way of approaching you securely. Thank heavens, you came on your own."

Rhonda lined up her certificate on the table next to Anand's and looked back toward the folder in the still-open safe. Yellow was her favorite color.

19
Diamond Hands

Mirio Mella

I woke suddenly, my phone vibrating angrily on the bedside table. As I gathered my senses, I was gripped by the ominous feeling that a call in the dead of night inevitably triggers. As I rubbed my eyes, that dread deepened. I saw 'Morticia,' the name my Uncle Mike and I used to jokingly refer to his humourless sister, flashing on my iPhone's caller ID. I hadn't spoken to her in over eighteen months, so a 2 AM call from the perennial fun-sponge could only mean bad news.

"Hi, Corinne. What's the emergency?" I mumbled, somewhere between still drunk and hungover.

Morticia replied in her familiar, economical tone. "You'd better come down to St. Thomas General. Mike's been in a serious car accident." Then she paused as if to compose herself, her voice quivering with an uncharacteristic show of emotion toward her younger brother. "They're not sure he'll make it through the night."

The words bounced around my head without really registering. I had no fucking clue how to feel.

"Alex, did you hear me?" Her insistence snapped me out of the fug.

"I'll come straight down. Just need to get dressed." I put the phone on speaker, stumbling comically around my room, trying to pull on track pants, hoodie, and trainers while mentally struggling to process my emotions and find a more meaningful response. "Is he conscious?" It was the best I could muster.

"He's drifting in and out. Seems aware of what's going on." Another pause.

"He's asking for you." Aunt Corinne seemed to struggle to let the words out of her mouth, but their impact on me was instant.

I felt a wave of emotion and a clearer sense of purpose. I had to see my uncle before it was too late. "I'll be thirty minutes max. Keep me updated." I hung up, grabbed my car keys, and headed out into a damp, gloomy, and eerily silent early autumn morning — the light from the LED street lamps reflected in the puddles with a surreal intensity.

As I slipped onto the motorway, I began thinking about how my relationship with Uncle Mike was so much more than an uncle/nephew bromance. He was a stand-in father figure, the only stable strand of a tangled web of family dysfunction spreading outwards from my estranged parents and rooted in money; what else? My parents had squandered their share of an inheritance on subprime, but Mike had zigged when they had zagged. He was a strange mix of free spirit and school librarian, tech-savvy, but far from your classic nerd. My uncle encouraged me to travel more and find my own path in life, but within a strict online security regime.

I pictured him peering over his reading glasses disapprovingly as I doom-scrolled on my iPhone. "You know the world is much more interesting first-hand, Alex." These exchanges were so familiar they became like a sitcom-style running gag; Mike would doggedly repeat his nuggets of wisdom, and I would roll my eyes. He had a real thing about password reuse, trying to convince me to use initialisms. "Just take the first letters from favourite song lyrics Alex, and you have a strong but memorable password"

"Really?" I would mock in a faux-English gentleman's voice. "How interesting" [cue canned applause]. I admired his determination, but the same dumb password still secured most of my worthless online life.

Just below online security on my to-do list was to read more books, or any books for that matter. *The Count of Monte Cristo* was Uncle Mike's favourite, but as much as the general blurb sounded interesting, I simply wasn't prepared to commit the time and effort to wade through the flowery language. I liked my gratification short, instant, and delivered via my mobile, but there was more to our relationship than tech-based nags and funky book recommendations.

The guy knew how to have fun. We laughed together and at each other, in equal measure. There were epic BBQs spent talking drunken shit around a fire pit. "Okay, Boomer, I'll up my online security game when you book yourself in for a hair transplant and veneers, then let me loose on your Tinder profile." That tickled him.

Those sessions often bizarrely ended with Mike bellowing some shonky 70s tune into my ear with a strange fervour that seemed to go beyond the effects of way too many brewskis and a long lost romance; but whatever that hidden message was, it was lost on me.

Now, speeding to the hospital, there was a sick feeling growing in my stomach that fate was about to break up this odd couple and those life hacks my uncle was desperate to share would remain on his bucket list, forever unchecked.

***

The nurse had tried to prepare me for the shock of how he looked. While his torso had taken the brunt of the impact and was hidden from view, his face still communicated the urgency of Morticia's phone call: his forehead and cheeks were badly bruised, his left eye swollen and closed, his right eye bloodshot, open and closing sporadically and lacking its familiar intensity.

I stood over him, trying to process what I saw, gently squeezing his hand. "Mike... Mike, it's Alex."

His right eye flashed with recognition, and his heart monitor spiked, catching the attention of the nurse sitting quietly but attentively in the corner. She motioned that I was okay to continue. He tried to respond, but his mouth was so dry that no words came out, just a strange rasp.

I saw a cup of water on the bedside cabinet and gently guided the straw into his mouth. It took a huge effort for him to draw a small slug, which lubricated his throat enough to speak. What came out made no sense and convinced me that the Uncle Mike I knew was already gone.

It sounded something like, "Diamond hands, Alex." He coughed and choked as he tried to repeat it, but this time, the nurse intervened, and I let go of his hand. Those three words would be the last I would ever hear from my Uncle Mike. He died soon after. He was 63.

***

His funeral was a simple humanist ceremony tarnished by the presence of Morticia and the rest of the Addams family feigning emotion. They were also in attendance when, several months after his death, the reading of his will took place at the offices of his lawyers. As much as I had seen this scene play out in countless movies, I had no idea what to expect in real life.

My Uncle had a quirky sense of humour, so part of me was expecting a beyond-the-grave video or *Brewster's Millions* type challenge, but the setting was drab and humourless, lightened only by the lawyer's likeness to Lionel Hutz from *The Simpsons*. Hutz kicked things off, opening a blue leather folio and reading aloud, with the familiar "sound body and mind" preamble, then getting to the nitty gritty.

"In the amount of $5 million in cash, the proceeds of my stock portfolio and sale of my condominium, I leave to the Electronic Freedom Foundation."

Morticia had been sitting nervously nursing her coffee and giving me the stink-eye as we built up to the main event, but now blurted out her frustration. "The Electronic what?"

"Mrs. Adams, you'll receive a full copy of the beneficiaries. Please allow me to continue without interruption."

I guessed there was no real need for this pantomime; from what I'd googled, this could have been executed by post, but I sensed that Mike saw symbolic importance in doing things this way, a kind of ritual public humiliation of his siblings.

"To Mr. Alex Miller, I leave the following package."

At this point, Lionel Hutz handed me an A4-sized padded envelope that had been sitting on the right side of his desk.

"Aren't you going to open it?" Morticia's abrasive tone barely concealed her resentment.

"I guess so," I stuttered with a mixture of apprehension and excitement. I slowly opened one end of the envelope, peeling back the seal, painfully aware of the eyes of Morticia, her husband (Fester), and several assorted cronies. I reached inside and pulled out a hardback book.

It was Mike's personal copy of *The Count of Monte Cristo* by Alexander Dumas. I opened the cover, and inside was a handwritten note, "Diamond Hands, Alex. Love, Uncle Mike."

As I grappled with the sudden realisation that my uncle hadn't been talking gibberish on his deathbed, I became aware that the eyes of the room were still on me, expecting some kind of comment.

"It's a book. Mike's favourite," I announced, waiving it above my head sheepishly for acknowledgement and doing my best impression of someone grateful for such a wonderful yet worthless memento.

"What's so special about *that* book?" Uncle Fester chimed in, with an approving nod from Morticia. "You're not one for reading, are you, Alex?" he added.

I began to feel a little awkward. Sure, it may have looked a little odd to an outsider but I didn't have to justify our relationship to these parasites. "Guess I'll find out," I responded, snapping the book shut. I looked pointedly back at Hutz, putting the spotlight back on him. He took the nudge and returned to his script.

"Thank you all. That concludes the execution of Mike Miller's will." He then directed his gaze at me. "Mr. Miller. If you could please remain behind, I just need you to sign a few documents." He began to push back on his chair, ready to stand and usher the others out.

"So that's it?" Morticia was visibly angry, her usually sallow face blushing red at being left empty-handed.

"Yes, Mrs. Adams. That's it." Hutz replied with confidence and disinterest that told me he'd met Morticia's type many times before.

Morticia rose abruptly, with Fester following in her wake. In my head, the Addams Family theme tune played, and I had to restrain myself from clicking my thumbs and fingers as they traipsed out of the office.

Once the family freaks had left the building, I was left facing Lionel at the end of the long glass-topped meeting table. He opened his binder at some coloured tabs and explained that various signatures were required, despite my inheritance amounting to a Penguin Classic. I signed without question, my mind more focused on figuring out what "Diamond Hands" meant, when Hutz broke my train of thought.

"There's one more thing, Mr. Mill—"

"Please, just Alex, is fine," I interrupted, feeling far too much like an adult with all this "Mr." bullshit. Anxiety rose up inside, sensing this wouldn't be about another book or request for a plaque on a park bench.

"Okay, Alex." He smiled. "The will requested that we notarise your uncle's death and send the proof to a specific service provider. I cannot tell you why, Alex. That kind of arrangement is relatively new and is normally to ensure privacy. The notification will trigger a smart contract to perform some specific action."

"A smart *what*?" This was completely baffling. Somehow, I felt that Mike was punishing my Luddite ways from beyond the grave.

"Think of it like a robot butler, waiting for instruction, like our notification of your uncle's death. That will trigger some other action, but it's designed specifically, so we don't know what that might be."

"And that butler robot thing has already received its instruction?" Fuck, I sounded *stoopid*.

"Yes, Alex. We fulfilled the instruction."

"So what do I do?" I looked pleadingly at him, like a child waiting for an adult to take control of a complex conversation.

"I'm afraid I can't help you, Alex, but your uncle was very particular with his instructions, so I can only assume you'll find out." He smiled, closed his binder, then glanced at his watch, the international sign for "off you fuck".

I took the cue, stuffing the package into my shoulder bag, thanking Hutz with a limp handshake, then gingerly left, feeling like I was on a hidden camera show.

***

That afternoon, sitting in my kitchen, I took another look at the contents of the package. A key fell with a *clank* onto the table. Was this connected to the robot butler conversation? Its bright rubber cap had a name and number, 021 - SafeStore, a locker service I vaguely recognised.

A quick google told me the storage facility was nearby, but to add to the growing sense that I was in a Dan Brown novel... it was about to close. If I was going to maintain the treasure hunt, I'd have to hurry. I smiled for the first time that day, imagining Mike nodding with approval as I followed his breadcrumb trail.

I parked my car haphazardly across numerous spaces in front of the non-descript SafeStore building, bolted to the door, pulled at a glass door that needed pushing, then finally burst into the reception.

"Hello Sir, how may I help you?" The desk assistant could easily have qualified as the robot butler that Lionel Hutz had described, the greeting delivered with a combination of machine-like insincerity and condescension.

I hesitated. "I'm not entirely sure. I have this key." Waiving it hopefully at her eye level, then I stopped, not knowing how to explain how I'd come into its possession.

"Did you find it? I can check if any have been reported missing." Her tone betrayed the frustration of ending her day with a crank customer.

"Sorry, no. It was the proceeds of a will." I replied with an unnecessarily apologetic tone.

"Ah. Okay." The desk assistant's demeanour changed. *How do you like them apples?* I thought to myself.

"Let me see the locker number, please."

I handed her the key, and she punched the ID from the rubber key cap into her computer, her glance back up at me, making it clear that she still thought I was a grifter.

"Do you have any ID, sir?" Her tone remained in the suspicious zone.

I handed over my driving license, sensing that she might be reaching for a button under her desk marked "release the hounds," but instead, her face broke into a more accommodating smile.

"Thank you, Alex. I can see you've been granted access." She printed something off her screen, which turned out to be a QR code that she folded into a plastic envelope attached to a lanyard and handed to me over the desk.

"The locker location is 021 D, which is on the fourth floor." The assistant pointed at the lift. "Use the QR for the security door. I'll be here for another fifteen minutes. There's floor-level intercom if you need assistance."

Mike's little game, whatever it was, now had my full attention, and I struggled to keep to a regular walking pace toward the lift.

Locker 021 D was easy to find. I slipped the key into the lock, and the door sprung open to reveal a small package the size of a cigar box. I grabbed it and stuffed it into my rucksack, for the first time feeling that the length Mike had gone to with this mission suggested the contents shouldn't be exposed to the watchful eye of the security camera peering from above the door.

***

In the privacy and clutter of my kitchen, I opened the second surprise package of the day to find a cellophane-wrapped box with a picture of some kind of USB stick and a description, "hardware wallet."

It may as well have been a flux capacitor for all that meant to me, but Alexa explained that it was a device for storing bitcoin, which set my heart racing.

Despite being clueless about new technology, I'd seen some Insta posts from teenage bitcoin traders flexing lambos, and there'd been a brief conversation at work after a request to list a property for sale in bitcoin. I'd ignored it, as it seemed like way too much effort.

In my ignorance, I assumed I would simply have to turn this USB thing on, and somehow extract this magical internet money to my Paypal or Venmo account, where I could convert it to USD and start planning a life of laziness — all thanks to my Uncle Mike.

But the USB stick had nothing stored on it. Reading the online instructions multiple times, slowly, and referencing multiple ELI5 forum posts, I realised the hardware wallet was just a gateway to a digital vault, protected by something called a *seed phrase* — a unique collection of 12-24 words.

So, the plan changed. I needed the seed to unlock the bitcoin, convert to USD, then I could start planning a life of laziness. But what the hell were those 24 words?

It was after midnight, and my head was hurting from the charade at the lawyer's, the strange treasure hunt, and the crash course in blockchain. But the bottom line was this: no seed, no bitcoin.

I'd checked all the emails Mike had sent, WhatsApp messages, and postcards (that's how old-school he was), but nothing seemed to fit the seed. My excitement had been short-lived, replaced by frustration and a sinking feeling that I was out of my depth, still captive to the world of real estate that would expect me to arrive bright and early the following morning.

Accepting defeat, I drained the dregs of my nth beer and, as I was going to switch off the kitchen light, glanced back at the table where *The Count of Monte Cristo* still sat ignored. At least I could belatedly fulfil one of my uncle's wishes and send myself to sleep.

Snuggled in bed, I started reading. My eyes were already drooping just a couple of pages in; who knew that 19th-century literature and beer didn't mix? But I stuck to a mental target of finishing the first chapter, a nod to more of Mike's fortune-cookie wisdom — always finish what you start. Reaching page 21, I noticed a word underlined in pencil. "Cupboard."

Half-asleep, it took a few seconds to realise its significance. Frantically flicking back and forth through the remaining 1,300 pages, I discovered another 23 unique words underlined in pencil. Mike's bucket list was now starting to make sense.

Suddenly alert, I jumped back out of bed and rushed down to the kitchen, reconnecting the hardware wallet to my laptop and walking slowly through the steps to unlock the vault with the seed, entering the 24 words in the order they appeared in the book, hoping and expecting to find the cheese at the end of this maze.

But though the seed was accepted, there was no gorgonzola; my security-conscious uncle had added an additional level of security, a final password. The boss man at the end of the video game was still wagging his finger.

I returned to the book, searching for more pencilled clues I'd somehow missed, but there was nothing. "You and your fucking passwords!" I dumped Dumas in the kitchen pedal bin in frustration, then trudged off to bed. Defeat snatched from the jaws of victory.

***

I remained defeated by that final password, trying combinations of names, dates, and places that meant something to my uncle, recording them systematically in a Google sheet. But as the days and weeks passed, my resolve to crack that final obstacle waned. I realised I was looking for a specific grain of sand on a beach. Bitcoin's security was designed to be impossible to crack, and my uncle wasn't keen on shortcuts. But my journey down the bitcoin rabbit hole hadn't been wasted. Having started my research wanting instant gratification, over time, my mindset changed. I started to understand and respect the technology and the idea behind bitcoin.

In the days after the bitcoin treasure hunt, I'd been mad at him for not filling me in while he was alive, but I came to appreciate his reasons for keeping a code of silence. Money had split our family apart once before. Nothing good could have come from it. Despite starting as a wild goose chase, the challenge he'd left had inspired the changes he'd tried, in his own way, to achieve when living.

With the emotional crutch my uncle had provided kicked away, I was forced to stand on my own feet. I began stacking sats (the equivalent of saving pennies), learned more about what diamond hands really meant — though not why it was my uncle's dying words — and through my own experience, was even able to help others grapple with seeds and hard wallets.

I began to think that maybe my uncle had never even intended for me to access his wallet. The journey itself was the reward.

***

Months later, I found myself in Guatemala, following another piece of my uncle's advice and expanding my horizons by travelling abroad. I'd sold my car and jacked in my job. Neither gave me any joy.

I was sitting in a quirky little bar on the shores of Lake Atitlán, drinking a beer, enjoying the view across one of the most beautiful lakes in the world and savouring the final chapters of *The Count of Monte Cristo*, when the song playing in the bar caught my attention. This was the tune my uncle used to screech into my ear when he'd had a few too many beers.

"Hey," I beckoned to the waiter. "This song?"

"You want me to turn it down, *Señor*?"

"No, no *amigo*." I laughed. "Who's singing it?"

"Neil Diamond. *Muy buena canción*."

Suddenly, a light bulb went off in my head, and as the chorus came around again, I wrote out on a napkin the verse my uncle loved to boom in my ear, emphasising the first letters, just as he'd tried to teach me.

"Money **t**alks, **b**ut **i**t **c**an't **s**ing **a**nd **d**ance **a**nd **i**t **c**an't **w**alk."

The final piece of the puzzle had been hiding in plain sight all along, I just couldn't see it. Maybe I was just too used to looking down and not up.

I glanced back to find the waiter laughing. He gave me the okay sign, then turned away to serve another table, and I laughed, too. "Diamond fucking hands, Alex."

20

The Journal's Alchemists

Gonzalo Coelho

In a dimly lit study adorned with ancient tomes and peculiar artifacts, a figure hunched over a weathered desk, immersed in the calculations that consumed his thoughts. Pierre de Fermat, a man of mathematical brilliance, was in a race against time, though he hardly recognized it as such. The room was permeated with the scent of aged parchment and the weight of centuries-old knowledge. The candlelight cast eerie shadows across Pierre's furrowed brow as he delved into a labyrinth of equations. He had always been driven by an insatiable curiosity, an unyielding desire to decipher the mysteries of numbers. Yet, as the years pressed on, an unsettling sensation gnawed at his mind. Time, it seemed, was slipping through his fingers.

Pierre's eyes darted across the pages, his fingers dancing nimbly over the paper. As he jotted down his latest insights, his thoughts veered into the realm of what lay beyond the numbers themselves. Outside the study's narrow windows, the moon hung like a guardian of secrets, casting a silvery glow upon his work. Hidden beneath his intellectual bravado was a sense of urgency — an unseen clock that ticked away the moments.

As Pierre wrestled with the symbols, the weight of unfinished business settled upon him. The hours seemed to slip past with the speed of sand through an hourglass. A manuscript lay open on the desk, its pages covered in his distinctive handwriting. The infamous margin, written long ago, had caused such a stir among mathematicians, and now it held his attention. Those cryptic words he had penned in the past seemed to beckon to him, a reminder of a challenge left unresolved. He traced his words, his musings on the problem that had tantalized him for years, and he allowed his thoughts to wander. Among those carefully inscribed lines, the declaration stood bold:

"I have discovered a truly marvelous proof of this, which this margin is too narrow to contain."

Pierre understood his initial proof, tucked from prying eyes, was flawed. Fueled by determination, he toiled tirelessly through countless nights to correct it. The margin's message was an inspiration, a journey extending beyond pages into the very fabric of his existence, and a reminder that his reputation was at stake.

What did it mean, he wondered, to leave a legacy? Was it merely about the theorems he penned, and the problems he posed? Or was there something more profound, something that transcended the boundaries of numbers and logic? Pierre's eyes lingered on his words, his contemplation delving into the depths of existence itself. Time was a cruel mistress, he mused, as he gazed at the candle's flickering flame. It burned steadily, yet its moments were fleeting.

And yet, amidst the shadows and the calculations, Pierre found solace. His pursuit of knowledge, his ceaseless quest to understand, gave him a sense of purpose that transcended the bounds of mortality. As the hours waned, his pen moved with renewed vigor, etching symbols onto the paper. He was running out of time, that much was certain. But in the quiet solitude of his study, Pierre found a semblance of eternity. The problem, like the mysteries of life, would continue to challenge those who came after him. And though the ink on the pages would fade, the echoes of his thoughts would persist, a testament to a mind that defied the constraints of time.

In the final moments before dawn, Pierre's weary hand paused. A sense of calm enveloped him as he gazed at the solution. It wasn't the answer he had relentlessly pursued, nor the conclusive resolution he had yearned to uncover. Yet, it was an answer, a fragment of the enigma that would one day intertwine with the whole. A knowing smile, one born of contemplation, tugged at the corners of Pierre's lips as he studied his creation. The gentle flicker of the candle's flame cast a soft glow upon the parchment. And in that serene moment, he yielded to the elegance of the unresolved.

Pierre rose from his desk, his steps deliberate and heavy with a lifetime of purpose. He approached an old bookshelf that held volumes of knowledge collected over the years. With a careful hand, he selected a timeworn tome, its leather cover bearing the scars of age. Inside, amidst the pages filled with wisdom, he found the passage he sought. He retrieved a quill and inkwell and, with a solemn determination, scratched his name atop his theorem postulate in the book, signaling to any future alchemist interested in the topic to continue the pursuit.

As he placed the altered page on the desk alongside his unfinished work, Pierre de Fermat, the brilliant mathematician, accepted defeat with grace. And in that serene moment, he yielded to the elegance of the unresolved. It was a journey he had embarked upon with the understanding that the destination might elude him. He had often wondered if these last couple of years were an earnest struggle or mere motions through time. Perhaps, in the depths of his subconscious, a plan had always existed to entrust the pursuit to those who would follow. An unspoken understanding that the legacy was greater than any individual revelation.

With a satisfied sigh, Pierre closed his eyes. The weight of time seemed to lift, replaced by a sense of contentment. As the first rays of dawn broke through the window, illuminating the study, he leaned back in his chair. The journey was not over, but he had traveled far enough. And so, Pierre de Fermat, found a quiet resolution. He had not conquered the problem that bore his name, but he had embraced the journey that the problem had set him upon. The candle burned low, its feeble flame a symbol of his relentless pursuit of knowledge, flickering against the ever-present current of time.

The Path Carved

Santiago's eleventh birthday party was not as disappointing as he expected. He and his buddies played in their unkempt backyard for a few of those endless summer hours only pre-teen boys are privy to. They started playing catch, but it grew into something more complex involving made-up powers and detailed descriptions, rules, and modifications that would make any Dungeons & Dragons game master proud. The elaborate specifications tended to last longer than the actual play time. Santiago and his buddies would grab withered planks and wield them as the mythical weapons they envisioned.

While enjoying fun activities, Santiago looked out the vinyl double-hung window and saw his parents playfully arguing as they made the sliders. He realized he was thirsty, momentarily abandoning his adventuring party that had been assembled in his backyard and entered the house. Upon entering the kitchen, he heard his mom joking about those leftover planks' broken dreams of becoming a humble shed, the one long since forgotten by "the man of the house." She remarked that the man left them to rot and be battered by children's play, as if his dad were just a mere spectator.

In fact, Santiago's father had spent months building a huge bookshelf (for a basement he would not set foot in) to hold random books that, judging by his reading pace, he would never finish. Books about math, history, chemistry, music, and such, rested immaculate and untarnished, waiting for someone to thumb the pages so that they would not stack so neatly when closed. Maybe now Santiago was eleven, he'd be able to understand *Introduction to Electrodynamics* by David J. Griffiths, justifying its place on the enormous bookshelf.

"Isn't it nice you and your buddies finally got some use from those forsaken planks?"

The question that made Santiago cringe from within. He replied with bare minimum politeness. "Yes, mom." Santiago's father replied with a silent hug as usual. That was good enough. He was not there in the kitchen with his wife. He was preoccupied with matters of greater worth.

The Surrogate Mentor

Serge met his wife around the same age as Santiago was now. Mom knew being chatty was never a quality of her partner. He fancied spending hours building anything (except for her shed). He was a good man; she wondered about having a second child — a child of their own.

It's not that they didn't love Santiago like he was their own. If anything, they wanted to introduce a balancing force to his life.

It was not so much that Santiago disliked other kids; he enjoyed playing with them, but he couldn't care less about what they had to say or what was on their minds. Ever since he was a toddler, Santiago displayed exceptional command of logic compared to his peers. Not only was he smarter, but he emphasized how much of their focus was devoted to topics he deemed meaningless. They talked about other people talking about video games, how much money they spent on a GPU, and argued about which character from the Marvel movies could actually lift Thor's hammer. They were kids, just like him. But he rarely found common ground in their interests. There was one time when he brought his brand new Rubik's cube to school to see if the other kids could figure out a way to decipher it. They were thrilled at first, but by the second school break, some kid was able to solve it by memorizing an algorithm he found on the internet. Soon, everyone lost interest in the puzzle. In Santiago's eyes, they had all missed the point.

Santiago was cunning, but he aspired to be even more so. He wanted to be as intelligent as his father and felt troubled by the idea of a "normal" life. What would happen when he died? What would he leave behind?

Was it his life's purpose to leave a legacy? Maybe not something most eleven-year-olds were concerned with.

Putting The Pieces Together

The role-play in the backyard came to a close, and all guests gathered for a feast. Santiago pretended to listen to his friends' conversation, but just like his father, he was somewhere else. He speculated about his father and their next project together. It was likely that was his surprise after all. They would always start something ambitious after his birthday. Last year, they spent the entirety of the summer programming a MIPS computer processor that had no chance of competing with its modern contemporaries, but Santiago could proudly say it was his effort. Whenever his father committed to something, he did not give up. When they stumbled upon a problem, he would find a way to make things work. And Santiago was starting to learn his ways. It didn't matter if his father liked the activity much. He was trying to teach Santiago, and Santiago had an appetite for knowledge.

Santiago peeked through the kitchen door, trying to steal a glimpse of his father in search of some clue as to what was coming after all the guests left. He saw him eating cake. When Serge noticed his son looking at him, he silently lifted the piece of cake he was holding barehanded as though that were good enough for a toast and saluted him. There was something in the way he looked at Santiago. Something Santiago had not seen before. He recognized that he was not being looked at by a fatherly figure; he was being looked at by a long-lost old friend. Santiago replied with a military salute in conjunction with a poker face. He thought that was funny, and his dad agreed with a slight grin without forgetting that his mouth was still full.

The last guest had left, and his mother already had dinner ready. She was an early bird and had trouble sleeping, so they would often race to dine as early as possible whenever they could. Birthdays, gatherings, and similar events disrupted their regular schedule, so she made sure to have everything almost ready before Santiago's friends left. Not-so-warm steak, with vegetables as ornaments. The once-steaming dishes now sat as lifeless remnants of a meal, their vibrant colors fading to a muted, unappetizing hue. Condensation had formed on the edges of the plates, like teardrops frozen in time. The gravy had congealed, now resembling a thick glaze that clung stubbornly to its surface. The vegetables surrendered their vitality to the cold air.

His mother would actually eat the green decorative plants for some reason that Santiago and his father did not really understand, but they paid no heed and let her be. She was secretly waging war against her husband by trying to make her son eat some vegetables, but she was losing on all fronts. Breakfast, lunch, and now dinner. She accepted defeat silently and tended to the wounded vegetables by storing them for the next day.

Santiago was underwhelmed by how hushed his father was. After all that cake, he still silently ate his way through dinner. Much of the talking was done by his mother, and it involved topics like which distant relatives called to say happy birthday while he was outside. Though he didn't remember these people all that well, he was happy they cared.

Dinner was over, and Santiago wondered if his father had forgotten about the surprise. He excused himself for not eating his vegetables and went to his room, disappointed by his apathetic father. Perhaps tomorrow.

Santiago ended the day with a WWI book he found in the basement library. He used to have a thing for fantasy and science fiction, but recently, learning about past events excited him more than any epic novel. It made him feel more mature.

There was a knock at the door.

"Come in."

"Hey there."

"Hey."

"You thought I had forgotten, right?"

Santiago's eyes filled with joy. "Yeah, I did."

His father had something behind his back.

Santiago didn't have much time to speculate as his father brandished an old book. Well, old was an understatement. The leather cover had deep cracks that were older than Santiago, and centuries of exposure to dampness had all but ruined the leather. When water dried and evaporated, it drew out the leather's oils with it. The book had suffered this process countless times since the day it had been bound.

"This is for you," his father declared as if he were an old king passing the crown to his heir, along with all the lands and power attached to his name.

Santiago received the huge tome with his hands facing upwards to gently assess the strength of the binding before opening it. He traced the heavily abraded engraving on the now obvious front cover. What he could not recognize was the archaic language it was written in. The barely visible markings on the cover resembled the Egyptian pictographic characters that he had seen in an anthropology book he found in the basement library, but there was something off about it. These seemed much simpler in their traces. The structure of the first twenty or so pages was suggestive of a thorough procedure with unknown goals. No pictures or drawings were provided. The rest of the pages looked like entries in a journal to Santiago. These were written in different languages that seemed more accessible to him.

"What exactly is this?"

His father paused. "A legacy."

"I don't understand."

"This book is special, even magical, you could say."

Revelations

As Santiago's father stood in front of his son, his demeanor held a quiet resolve that might have appeared rehearsed to someone who knew Serge well. It was as if every step he took toward this moment had been measured, each word carefully chosen over the years. Deep within him, he carried a burden — an unspoken weight that had lingered in his thoughts for far too long.

"Santi, it's time you knew the truth. I am not your biological father."

Santiago's world came to a screeching halt. He stared at his father, his eyes widening like the ground beneath him had just given way. Could this be a joke, a prank, or a lie? But deep down, he knew his father well enough to sense the sincerity in his voice. A whirlwind of emotions churned — confusion, disbelief, and a profound sense of uncertainty.

For a moment, silence enveloped them, broken only by the distant hum of the evening crickets outside. Santiago's mind raced, grappling with the enormity of what he had just heard. His father watched him with a blend of worry and sympathy, waiting for his response.

It took Santiago a few moments to find his voice. When he did, it was a fragile whisper. "What do you mean, Dad?"

It's not like I simply adopted a random child. I made a pledge to a dear friend of mine to see to your good health and prepare you for the mission. You see, I am not sure how it works, but I like to believe that *you* have lived many lives before this one. You wrote an entry every time, and by some mystical process that only the first alchemist could understand, you are here. You can dump the book, but the cycle will go on regardless. There is nothing we can read about how it started and how to stop it. I think you should keep it and try to make the most out of it."

This was not an elaborate trick. Santiago's dad seemed quite nervous and took his time to find the right words. He pointed at symbols on the cover of the book. "See this? Thanks to more recent entries, we know this stands for 'The Journal's Alchemists.' My best friend was the last one, and he trusted me with the book before... before he became you. Check these out."

Santiago renounced the book timidly, and his father took it and turned the pages to show him specific sections of the journal. Each journal entry followed the same pattern, but this one shook Santiago.

Charles Darwin
1859
On the Origins of Species

WHEN ON BOARD H.M.S. 'BEAGLE,' as *naturalist, I was much struck with certain facts in the distribution of the inhabitants of South America, and in the geological relations of the present to the past inhabitants of that continent...*

It went on for a couple of pages, but only included the introduction as a mere reference to his work. When Santiago had had enough time to examine the entry, his dad showed him another one, several pages back:

~~*Pierre de Fermat*~~ ~~Andrew Wiles~~ ANDREW WILES
~~*1637*~~ ~~1993~~ 1995

Cubum autem in duos cubos, aut quadrato-quadratum in duos quadrato-quadratos, et generaliter nullam in infinitum ultra quadratum potestatem in duos eiusdem nominis
Pierre de Fermat
1660
De linearum curvarum cum lineis rectis comparatione dissertation geometrica

***

From then on, it was Latin, and just like Darwin's section, it spanned a couple of pages.

"What does it all mean?" Santiago muttered.

"You are all of them. You share the same traits and interests. You want to know everything. You want to build great things. You aspire for meaning above pleasure and even happiness." The last word broke under the weight of helplessness only a father can feel for his son departing on a voyage never to be seen again.

The awkward silence between the two reluctant men offered an opportunity for Santiago to ponder what he had just heard. His father had never let him down. The timing for an intricate joke was totally off.

"Wh-What should I do now? They were all geniuses; I am not a genius at anything."

"You are only eleven. I am certain they all felt the same way when they were your age. You will have to work hard, but every entry in that journal has had an impact on humankind, and I know that you are capable of that. You want to leave your mark here. He was just like you when I first met him."

"You mean, the previous 'alchemist?'"

"Yes. Every time I look into your eyes, I see him, albeit you do not share the same physical appearance. He only told me about this when he was about to die, but he had the same doubts as you do now."

Santiago gestured with his hands, indicating his intention of grabbing the journal, and looked for the latest page that was not blank. There. He got it three-quarters of the way to the back cover. There was a decent chunk of vacant space left. The last entry was quite short and read:

SATOSHI NAKAMOTO

2009

BITCOIN: A PEER-TO-PEER ELECTRONIC CASH SYSTEM

Santiago was speechless. He realized the implications of this and asked the most intriguing question in his mind.

"Are we secretly rich? Was I rich?"

"If we ever find your private keys, yes, but I wouldn't worry all that much about that. He never told me anything about his bitcoins before dying, so I suspect he might have lost them on purpose."

They kept talking for an hour or so. By the end, the idea had started to grow in Santiago. He did not know it, but after that day, he would start living his life to the fullest, knowing that his destiny was to maintain this legacy of brilliance. He would not let it go to waste by being lazy or avoiding struggle. Nonetheless, he also followed his father's teachings by staying humble throughout.

As Santiago's father was making his way out, Santiago asked him, "Can I still call you Dad?"

"Of course, Santi." He said, looking straight into his eyes with a nostalgic gaze of someone who is reliving past memories of past memories.

21
The Galactic Playbook

Reed

External Memo #263 from the Emerging Civilizations Council (ECC)

This memo intends to brief the federated societies of the galaxy on the status of one specific emerging civilization that has increasingly been of interest to our members and, further, to recommend caution when traveling unannounced nearby their planet.

As you are all aware, it is the intention of our federated societies to isolate any emerging civilization in order to allow them the freedom to evolve and innovate independent of any external knowledge or technology. The benefits of this are twofold. Firstly, if, during their scientific exploration and development, they are able to reach the same conclusions as us about the fundamentals of the universe, then we receive additional independent confirmation of our existing knowledge base. Secondly, and of much greater interest, is that all of our most advanced zero-to-one technological innovations have originated from these isolated civilizations because they are permitted to solve problems without bias from more advanced societies.

In earlier times, some of our members practiced strategic infusions of knowledge into emerging civilizations that would be disguised as native discoveries in order to accelerate their advancement secretly. While this was effective in developing advanced and peaceful civilizations more quickly, it was observed that those societies rarely developed any meaningful new technologies. As we have since learned, once a bias is introduced into an emerging civilization, it is typically destined to only innovate around our existing knowledge base.

More dangerously, societies that become aware of more advanced galactic civilizations almost always become focused on extrasolar power projection. This is an extension of the local evolutionary pressures that led to their domination as the apex predator on their planet. Only after they access the virtually unlimited resources of the galaxy and they have resolved their internal struggle over the distribution of those resources will they be granted full federation status, and interspecies technology transfer can be permitted. Prior to this stage, technology transfer from advanced societies must be avoided, as it can destabilize their development and often lead to the destruction of our most precious galactic resource: independent, decentralized technological innovation.

The dominant intelligent species of the specific civilization that is the focus of this memo identify as "Humans" and collectively inhabit a planet they call "Earth." The Humans of Earth have yet to discover any advanced technology that would be useful to our members at this time; however, based on a key recent milestone in their development, their status has been upgraded to that of "pre-federation," making them the leading candidate for our next admission into the galactic federation. As such, it has been estimated that first contact with the Humans of Earth may be possible within the next 1-2 GmRs.[1]

This recent promotion to pre-federation status is based on their discovery of inviolable absolute scarcity — a key event that was independently reached among all federation members and typically triggers exponential advancement within two to four local generations.

1 One Galactic micro-Rotation (GmR) equals approximately 200 Earth solar orbits and spans approximately ten human generations.

As is the case on Earth, inviolable absolute scarcity is virtually always used to develop undiluted intraspecies communication of value (the so-called perfect money). This has shown to be critical for cooperation and advancement among planetary apex predators throughout our galaxy.

The Earth-based discovery centers around a simple massless ledger system that is secured by electric power projection and is rapidly being adopted among the Humans of Earth. As with most apex predators, human trust is extremely difficult to scale across their entire population. However, the new Earth-based monetary system, which they have named "bitcoin," is quickly gaining the trust of humans as it continues to prove inviolable. As has been the case among all emerging civilizations since the formation of the ECC, scarcity alone, even absolute scarcity, has never been enough to trigger exponential technological growth. The source of absolute scarcity must also be inviolable. Otherwise, it will never be sufficiently trusted among a population.

The new currency of Earth is in the process of proving its inviolability by surviving numerous attacks with no meaningful disruption. Notably, even those closest to its discovery attempted to violate the properties of Earth's initial implementation of absolute scarcity but were unsuccessful. Today, it continues to withstand external attacks by those who have the most to lose, as the adoption of true and fair economic communication threatens to expose the opposition's less productive, less efficient ideas. This, of course, is the specific class that must be disintegrated in order to allow the Humans of Earth to innovate freely and unlock exponential advancement. This same scenario has played out in all of our ancient histories following the discovery of inviolable absolute scarcity.

Because bitcoin has only existed for approximately one-half of one human generation, proofs of inviolability have only been apparent to those who are closely examining the implications of the new discovery. Unsurprisingly, the humans who are the most inadequately compensated by the previous monetary systems are the first to find the benefits of inviolable absolute scarcity.

The highly anticipated exponential advancement from the now pre-federation Humans of Earth has attracted the interest of many of our members. Note that at this juncture, the galactic playbook permits members to approach a pre-federation civilization undetected in order to fairly attain small quantities of their local implementation of inviolable absolute scarcity. The purpose of this practice is to allow our members to obtain a compatible and trusted source of compensation to be used in exchange for the first valuable innovations of a pre-federation society in a way that avoids unnecessary exposure to our technology prior to its full federation status.

Fortunately, all members who have taken part in this practice have fairly participated in the securitization of the bitcoin network, contributing small amounts of energy to organize and record transactions onto its independent time-based ledger system called the "Timechain." Fair participation is critical to establish trust upon first contact.

Further, our members have, thus far, successfully minimized their impact on the new monetary system of Earth. It is important to disguise our existence, but it will also help gain trust in the future as no member will be seen as having abused its privileged access to overwhelming amounts of energy and computational power. It is, thus, believed that none of our members have collected more than a single payment for their energy contributions, meaning that no member society has more than 50 out of the full supply of 21,000,000 bitcoins (the smallest attainable payment for this form of fair participation, originally).

The ECC asks that you please continue exercising caution, keeping your contributions to the bitcoin network to an absolute minimum. As a reminder, even a single service payment (currently 6.25 out of the full supply of 21,000,000 bitcoins) will likely be sufficient compensation for any of their innovations following first contact. Once awarded full federation status, Humans of Earth will be permitted to act as a full trading partner and will be eligible for other means of value for value payment.

However, the purpose of this message is not simply to commend our members for following those aspects of the galactic playbook. All federated societies of the galaxy should also be aware that there have recently been an increasing number of atmospheric anomalies detected by the Humans of Earth. Many believe that these anomalies are primarily caused by the influx of near-earth TDEs[2] following their upgrade to pre-federation status. We are, therefore, requesting that all members voluntarily announce their travel coordinates to help ensure that any TDEs in the future are adequately dispersed in space-time to avoid detectable events on Earth.

Although it has been almost 50 GmRs since the last emerging civilization was upgraded to pre-federation status, it is imperative that we maintain the complete isolation of the Humans of Earth at this critical juncture. As stated, if the Humans of Earth begin to suspect the presence of an overwhelmingly advanced species, they are highly likely to skew their innovations toward violent technologies that could destabilize their society and disrupt their potential for future contributions.

Thank you for maintaining our core principles as we begin to prepare for the next member to be admitted into our peaceful, decentralized federation.

End wideband galactic transmission...

2 Temporary Distortion Events are a byproduct of most means of galactic travel

About the Authors

John Champaign — The Last Mugging | johnchampaign.com

John Champaign grew up in Northern Ontario, Canada. He's worked as a software developer and computer science professor and lives with his beloved wife, frequently moving. Information about his books and writing is available at.

Decent Money — Hello World | @decentmoney2009

Decent Money is a husband, father, computational biologist, data analyst, and a bitcoin maxi who came for the profits but stayed for the revolution to separate money from the state... one story at a time.

SF — Behemoth | @LePlebRoyale

SF is a self-proclaimed pseudo-intellectual. A hedonist cum laude, looking to improve life for each and every one of us. As a professional dabbler, he has had his hand in a lot of various escapades, doing odd jobs around the bitcoin verse. If he's not busy creating or animating logos and illustrations, or — quite literally — pushing Bitcoin (confectionery) Orange Pills, he's collaborating with other bitcoiners to further our shared bitcoin future. His free time is spent submerged in music, art, bitcoin, and now, writing too. Who knows what this creative madman will bring us next?

Niko Laamanen — The Noderoid Saga: Dreamers | @OmniFinn

Niko left a career as a construction engineer to go all-in bitcoin education. Publisher by day, minced meat maximalist by dinner. Sauna puritanist forever. Ice baths before they were cool. Traveled in 40 countries, now more intrigued by trips and tricks of the mind.

Watched Kill Bill on VHS before it was in theaters.

KT Morley — Lowery Station Terminal | facebook.com/AuthorKTMorley

KT Morley is an Eastern Pennsylvanian author. He spent twenty years conspiring to teach the youth of America about algebra and the plight of a hopelessly lost X before advancing to manage his school's humanities department. He has published in several anthologies, Rogue Blades Entertainment's *Crossbones and* Crosses and *Death's Sting*, the Dragon Soul Press Anthology *Coffins and Dragons*, *Glass and Ashes* by OWS Ink, and *Weirdbook Annual: Zombies!*, edited by Doug Draa. He occasionally posts on his author page, where he has a series of videos titled *Storytime with an Algebra Teacher*.

Knut Svanholm — The Construct | @knutsvanholm | knutsvanholm.com

Knut Svanholm is an international village idiot whose biggest claim to fame is the infamous bitcoin meme "Everything divided by 21 million," which is also the title of his best-selling book. Currently, he spends his days hosting the Freedom Footprint Show and advising a handful of bitcoin companies and non-profit organizations. His writings are (generally) revered in the bitcoin space. Recently, he wrote a book about the science of human action, *Praxeology*. Occasionally, you'll find him entertaining people at conferences by speaking, playing guitar, moderating panels, or reciting inappropriate dad jokes to the wrong people. You can count on Knut to deliver a healthy dose of real stupidity amidst the A.I. revolution.

Fanis Michalakis — Bitter Fly | @FanisMichalakis

Fanis is a developer and a Bitcoin and Lightning Network educator, as well as a huge science-fiction lover. He's currently working at LN Markets, a bitcoin derivatives platform built on the Lightning Network, and enjoys writing stories in his spare time.

Daniel Crow — Jo Buys a Planet

Daniel Crow is a PR professional, publicist, and former journalist based in Germany. Having grown up on Tolkien and Stephen King, he has long been in love with writing, drawing inspiration from myths and folk tales of the past. His other passions include high-tech, history, and old comedy movies. His works appeared in Metastellar, Arterial Bloom, and other anthologies and publications.

Philip Charter — Legacy | philipcharter.com

Philip Charter is a writing coach who swapped the UK for Spain. He is the author of two collections of short fiction and Fifteen Brief Moments in Time, a novella-in-flash. He likes crisps.

Angelique Fawns — The Baked Goods and Bitcoin of Skirophoria | fawns.ca/

Angelique Fawns is a Canadian journalist and speculative fiction writer. She began her career writing articles about naked cave dwellers in Tenerife, Canary Islands. When she returned to civilization, she worked at Global TV in Toronto and has been cutting primetime promos for the last three decades. She lives on a farm north of the city with her husband, daughter, and far too many horses. After selling her first story to EQMM, she fell in love with weird fiction, which is ACTUALLY stranger than non-fiction. You can find more of her work in DreamForge, The School Magazine, and various anthologies and podcasts.

Satillionaire — The Bitcoin Overlay | @Satillionaire21

Satillionaire is an Oscar-winning producer and a refugee from the entertainment industry. His body of work includes producing TV shows for multiple networks and selling films to various streaming platforms. A transformative moment came in 2017 when he discovered bitcoin and its potential to reshape society. Now, he focuses on merging his storytelling talents with the revolutionary possibilities of bitcoin. His goal is to inspire a future where entertainment and hard money harmonize to unlock untapped human potential.

TechnologieKultur — Transit | @technologiekult

TechnologieKultur is a German native speaker and linguist by training. He has always been into science fiction because it explores the human condition in light of the mutual push and pull that happens between – you guessed it – technology and culture. In the bitcoin protocol and its network participants, he found the perfect blend of hard and social science fiction that can even be explored interactively while it plays out in reality. He considers himself a meshtadel pleb with sovereignty deficits and great learning opportunities in his many spheres of interest. These include the cultivation of really hot chilies.

Ioni Appelberg — The Fable of the Tyrant Alchemist | @IoniAppelberg

Ioni Appelberg (pronounced Yo-Ni Apple-Burg) is a bitcoin philosopher, futurist, author, and content creator. His content centers around science fiction, human history and it often takes the form of swashbuckling journeys to the frontiers of technology, space, and the human mind. His love of sci-fi, psychedelics, and futurism may take his stories (and unsuspecting readers) to strange but exciting places. He is also an avid reader, a medical doctor, a freedom fighter, an MMA fighter, a psychonaut, and a terrible chess player.

Luciano Rocha — Digital Gold | @lucianorocha89

Luciano Rocha is a writer and content editor with training in content production and digital marketing. He currently writes for the news portal CriptoFácil, one of the largest cryptocurrency portals in Portuguese, and is the author of the books *Bitcoin, Criptoativos e Blockchain: um Guia para a Nova Economia* and *Do Zero ao Cem Mil com Bitcoin*.

Eduardo Próspero — Eye in the Sky | samplesandexamples.wordpress.com

Eduardo Próspero is a pseudonym, but rest assured, he's a bitcoiner through and through. Sure, as a journalist, he wrote for some questionable publications. If you ask Próspero, however, he'll tell you that he infiltrated crypto news sites to spread the bitcoin ethos. If you don't believe him, the articles are out there.

Without blowing his spot, he informs the reader that he's Venezuelan and is currently a digital nomad. He enjoys meditation, old-school hip-hop, and "Kill Tony" on YouTube.

Read his work blog to rehash his transformation into a bitcoin maximalist.

Will Schoellkopf — Who Let the Bitcoin Dogs Out? | @realBitcoinDog

Will Schoellkopf is the author of the narrative nonfiction book *The Bitcoin Dog: Following the Scent to The Bitcoin C++ Source Code*, and the fiction novel *Bitcoin Girl: Save the World*. He is published in print at Bitcoin Magazine and Citadel21 and online at Satoshi's Journal. Follow him on X, or email will@realbitcoindog.com. Subscribe to his free weekly newsletter to receive a high-resolution PDF of his print Bitcoin Magazine article *The Prisoner's Keys* at realbitcoindog.com.

Anonymous — Shiro | satsymbol.com

This anonymous author is one half of the design team that created the sat symbol used in this story. They are forever grateful to Satoshi Nakamoto for freely giving bitcoin to the world and for his brilliant ability to "move on to other things" without the need to be known personally — a discipline this author hopes to duplicate.

Carl Andrews — Panama One

Carl Andrews has previously worked in various clerical, admin, and IT roles. Presently, he is delivering chess coaching in schools for a national charity. His rekindled interest in writing has coincided with his recent personal 'discovery' of bitcoin. He is currently writing an introductory guide to bitcoin that he hopes will turn out to be not too eccentric.

Alex Gurevich — Are We, or Are We Not? | @agurevich23

Alex Gurevich is the Founder of HonTe Investments. He previously ran Global Macro Portfolio at J.P. Morgan Chase. Alex is an author of investment books and articles, as well as speculative fiction stories. He frequently appears in financial media, discussing global asset classes, including digital assets.

Mirio Mella — Diamond Hands | nofreelunch.co.uk/blog

Mirio Mella has been writing bitcoin explainers for several years, but his contribution to *21 Futures* is his first experiment using fiction and a bit of humour to demystify and explore concepts like custody and privacy. His journey down the Bitcoin rabbit hole has inspired a broader interest in monetary history, and he now writes about all the fascinating ways humans try to create, exchange, and store value in his blog.

Gonzalo Coelho — The Journal's Alchemists | @coelhogonza

Gonzalo Coelho, a software engineer living in Argentina, has witnessed socialism and inflation firsthand. With a deep appreciation for freedom and a penchant for the Austrian School of Economics, he now spends his free time educating others about bitcoin. His contributions include translating *The Fiat Standard* by Saifedean Ammous and *The Blocksize War* by Jonathan Bier into Spanish, helping to make the history of money and bitcoin widely accessible.

Reed — The Galactic Playbook | @FreedomMoney21 | nostrplebs.com/s/reed

Reed is a Christian, father of three, husband, bitcoiner, mechanical engineer in the nuclear power industry, science nerd, and passionate about the pursuit of truth. Reed also organized the Western Mass Bitcoin Meetup and is active on bitcoin X and Nostr.

Learn more about the project

21futures.com

Printed in Great Britain
by Amazon

44407772R00148